The Unquiet Spirit

Penny Hampson

DARK
STROKE

www.darkstroke.com

Discover us online:
www.darkstroke.com

Find us on instagram:
www.instagram.com/darkstrokebooks

Include **#darkstroke** in a photo of yourself
holding this book on Instagram and
something nice will happen.

For Mike, who came up with the idea in the first place, and Darcy, my little ray of sunshine in a challenging year.

Acknowledgements

My grateful thanks go to all the people who have helped, supported, and inspired me during the course of writing this book. They include my anonymous reader from the RNA New Writers' Scheme, whose encouragement spurred me on; Sue Fellows, a friend whose close reading of all my tales has helped immeasurably in getting them right; Falmouth and its friendly people – the many great holidays I've enjoyed there have been the inspiration for this story; and Laurence and Stephanie of Darkstroke Books for their confidence in me as a writer.

Most of all, thanks to my family for putting up with me when I've been engrossed in writing, especially my husband, who first suggested that I write a contemporary novel.

About the Author

Penny Hampson writes mysteries, and because she has a passion for history, you'll find her stories also reflect that. *A Gentleman's Promise,* a traditional Regency romance, was Penny's debut novel, which was shortly followed by more in the same genre. With *The Unquiet Spirit,* Penny is now exploring the paranormal, because where do ghosts come from, but the past?

Penny lives with her family in Oxfordshire, and when she is not writing, she enjoys reading, walking, swimming, and the odd gin and tonic (not all at the same time).

Follow Penny on **Twitter - twitter.com/penny_hampson, Facebook - www.facebook.com/pennyhampsonauthor**, or to discover more about her writing, **visit her blog**: **pennyhampson.co.uk/blog/**

The Unquiet Spirit

Chapter One

Eyes squeezed shut, Kate held her breath and strained her ears for the sound of pursuit. The thud of footsteps had stopped – only the drum-like pounding of her heart discernible above the distant hum of traffic. Seconds passed. Her lungs were about to explode. She took a breath. Nothing. No hand reached in to grab her. She counted to sixty before risking a peek over the rim of the skip. At the end of the alley a figure paced to and fro. Kate's grip on the cold metal rim tightened. It was definitely the guy from the bar, his leather jacket and distinctive shoulder-length hair illuminated by the sodium streetlight. Kate ducked back down and considered her next move.

He can't stay there all night. Give it a bit longer.

She counted another two minutes before raising her head again…and froze. He was still there, peering up the street and scratching his head. Thank God he had his back to her hiding place. Who'd expect a woman to duck into a dark alley, after all? As she watched, he pulled out his phone and made a call. She was too far away to hear what he said, but he seemed agitated – angry even – waving his hand to make a point. At last, he shoved the phone into his pocket, turned, and stalked from view.

Kate's muscles lost all tension, and like a deflated balloon, she slumped down in a heap. Her heart was still hammering, but at least she had time to get control of her nerves. How she'd made it over the rim of the skip, she'd no idea – through sheer panic or her gym sessions were paying off at last. She silently thanked the person who'd dumped the mattress covering the shards of glass and builders' rubble. Things could have been very nasty.

The evening had started so well. She'd been out for a final drink with the girls. Her official leaving party had been held a few days before and had been a much more sedate affair. Well, one couldn't invigilate a reading room in the Bodleian Library when three sheets to the wind. This time, sore heads were definitely on the cards for several of her girlfriends tomorrow morning, though Kate herself had kept to sparkling water after her first two glasses of Pinot Grigio. She wanted to keep a clear head for the weekend. There was a lot of packing to do before Monday.

Initially, she'd thought the guy was one of the usual after-work crowd, but he'd remained apart, not speaking to any of the others lounging and joking at the bar. He leaned with one elbow on the counter, one foot hooked negligently on a bar stool, and took an occasional swig from his beer. He never took his eyes off her. Every time she looked over, he was watching... Not smiling, just staring. At first, she was flattered; he was not bad looking with his floppy long hair, chiselled features, expensive leather jacket, and close-fitting jeans. But she'd grown more uncomfortable as the evening wore on, and he made no move to engage her in conversation. Just watching. Emily had noticed too.

"You've got a fan," she'd giggled, nudging Kate in the ribs and indicating with her eyes to where he stood. "He's been staring for ages. Wonder why he doesn't come over?"

"Me too. Probably shy. Anyway, I'm not interested. I'm off men, as you well know." Kate pulled a face. Yes, definitely off men. Robin had seen to that, the deceitful bastard.

She'd avoided looking over at the bar for the next thirty minutes, and it was only when she stood up to leave that she realised he'd gone. It took a while to say her goodbyes. There were tearful hugs, slurred demands to stay in touch, and much giggling when Emily fell over a bar stool, laddering her tights and upsetting somebody's pint.

After making sure her friend was all right, Kate finally made it outside and breathed a sigh of relief. It was good to be in the cool evening air. Her relief didn't last long. By the

4

time she'd walked up the High and onto Cornmarket, prickles up her neck told her something was wrong. Pushing aside her uneasy feeling as just her imagination, she paused outside Gap, drawn by the window display. She glanced sideways and spotted his distinctive leather jacket and long hair hovering in a nearby shop doorway. Even though he was partly obscured by the milling passers-by crowding the pavement, she knew it was him. That's when she'd legged it, hoping to shake him off amongst the gaggles of students heading back to halls, and the throngs of patrons pouring out of the New Theatre. Darting into the alley, knowing it was a shortcut, had been a good decision. Spotting the skip and leaping in had been inspired.

She waited another fifteen minutes for her pulse rate to settle before hauling herself back onto the cobbled pavement. Rapidly brushing the worst of the brick dust from her jeans, she set off on ungainly legs, wincing as her foot hit something slimy and she nearly toppled over. There was a taxi rank at Gloucester Green. Blow the expense, she'd get a ride home. Besides, she could afford it now, thanks to Win.

Brushing her teeth in the tiny bathroom of her Summertown flat, she squinted at her reflection in the partially steamed-up mirror over the basin. Divested of makeup, the face that gazed back was remarkably calm. Inside, she was seething. Spitting out the toothpaste and rinsing her mouth, Kate paused to think. She hated being made to feel fearful. That was why she'd taken that self-defence course. Her eyes suddenly glared back at her from the mirror, reflecting her angry thoughts. Kate gave an involuntary giggle. Perhaps she should have pulled a face like that in the bar. That would have put him off. Her mouth twisted in annoyance. There was no point in replaying things in her mind. She was off to Falmouth in two days and it was unlikely they'd cross paths a second time. It would be pointless to report it to the police...but if she saw him again she knew exactly what she would do.

Kate put her toothbrush away and headed to the bedroom,

flicking the bathroom light off as she went. Her stomach gave a lurch of excitement at the sight of her half-packed suitcase, open at the foot of the bed. The move on Monday would be the start of a new life. And after this evening's unsettling episode, there was even more reason to be grateful for this new start.

Win's bequest had been a massive surprise. Not only the house but also a sizeable amount of money.

"You'll need most of it for the upkeep," her father had joked, breaking the shocked silence induced by the solicitor's words. Funnily enough, her parents hadn't been surprised at all by the generous bequest to their daughter.

"Well, Win always said you were the daughter she never had," were her mum's words. "And you are her goddaughter. She was over the moon when you decided to do history. Win always regretted not going to university, so I suppose you were living her dream."

Still, Kate found it puzzling. Had Win lost it, in her final months? Though to be fair, the will had been signed and dated some two years before Win's death, and she'd seemed fine the last time Kate had seen her at Christmas. Apart, that was, from the weird conversation she'd had with Win on Christmas Eve. Well, she'd soon find out. That was just one of the puzzles to be solved when she got there.

Nestled under the duvet she knew she was too wired for sleep. Frowning, she scanned the sparsely furnished bedroom. Devoid of her personal belongings, which were now piled up in the living room ready for packing, it felt bleak. She spotted what she was looking for on the bedside table and smiled. She picked the book up and ran her fingers reverentially over the embossed spine, enjoying the feel and its faintly musty smell. Bought in a newly discovered shop on the Cowley Road, it was a first edition of Egan's *Walks through Bath.* She'd been lucky to find it, on a crowded shelf almost hidden from view. It still had all its plates – that was the first thing she'd checked – stamped with a library stamp so that no-one would be inclined to remove them, but they were there all the same... making it affordable. She hadn't

6

been able to resist. Books were her passion, the older the better.

She settled back into the pillows and started to read. It would be great to visit Bath and see for herself how much things had changed from Egan's descriptions. But that wasn't looking likely in the near future. There were far too many things to be sorted before she could do anything so self-indulgent. Kate sighed. She knew she shouldn't complain – she was a very lucky girl.

Chapter Two

It was good to be finally on the move, but Monday morning was definitely not the best time to travel. Kate's knuckles clenched round the steering wheel. Whose idea was it for so many roadworks to take place at the start of the holiday season? she asked herself. She should've waited until rush hour was over, but impatience had triumphed over common sense. The miles crawled by. Two hours later, and not a minute too soon, the sign for the exit she needed came into view. Kate exhaled a breath of relief. At last she could leave the motorway behind, taking the A30 and skirting the top of Dartmoor. Crossing the Tamar before Launceston, her shoulders relaxed. She was home.

Cornish by birth, Kate and her family had moved to Oxfordshire when she was still a baby. Her parents had brought her back each year to visit grandparents and of course, Mum's dearest friend, Auntie Win, Kate's godmother. Win wasn't really her aunt, but Kate had always called her that. She'd always felt close to the diminutive, intelligent woman who'd spoiled her rotten whenever she'd stayed with her. It was Win who'd encouraged Kate to follow her dream of studying history, when her parents – both scientists – had wanted her to have a more 'useful' degree.

Kate had last spoken to her godmother at Christmas, when Win had come to stay with Kate's parents at their home in Burford. Her mum and dad had gone to bed, leaving Kate and Win alone in the living room. It was past midnight, and the sound of late-night revellers singing tuneless carols as they returned from the pub could be heard in the distance. The twinkling of the Christmas tree lights gave the room a magical glow.

"No young man to celebrate Christmas with, then?" asked Win, a wicked gleam in her eye.

Kate chuckled. "'Fraid not… Not that I'd neglect family at Christmas. Men are too much trouble anyway." She sipped her gin and tonic, enjoying the tang and feeling of warmth as it went down her throat. It soothed the lingering bitterness of her last break-up. Robin had certainly been too much trouble. She silently wished him a miserable Christmas, hoping his wife was giving him a hell of a time. He deserved it. She would never have got involved if she'd known he was married – his divorce just another of his fabrications. She wondered how long it would be before she could trust someone again.

Win sipped her whisky and gave Kate a speculative look.

"You should come down to Falmouth. Help me with a bit of research if you're at a loose end. I think it would be just up your street."

"Oh? What's that then?" Kate's interest was piqued, despite her inner gloom.

Win's mouth pursed. "I'm not going gaga, but I'm sure… well, I'm almost sure that The Beeches is haunted."

"You're having me on?" Kate got the impression that Win wasn't joking.

"No, I'm not. But…perhaps I am imagining some things." A thoughtful expression crossed Win's face. "No, I didn't." She shook her head. "I definitely heard noises last week and…I've seen things, Kate."

Kate scrutinised Win's anxious face; a frown creased her brow and her lips were thinned in a tense line – an unusual expression for the normally upbeat and smiling older woman. Kate knew she was not being wound up. Suppressing growing feelings of alarm, Kate moved to the sofa where Win was perched at one end, and settled cross-legged at the other, cupping her glass in her hand.

"Go on, tell me all about it."

Win's hand jerked as she brought her glass to her lips to take a quick slug. "You know I don't believe in ghosts, don't you? Or rather, I didn't up to a few weeks ago." Win shifted

9

against the cushions. "I'd been up in the attic, going through some boxes of family papers, looking for my grandfather's army records. I was going to sort them out, and pass them on to the museum."

Kate nodded and took another mouthful of her gin and tonic. This was all getting a bit… she wasn't sure what.

Win continued. "Then I remembered there were a few things kept in the cupboard in the spare bedroom. You know, the one next to yours?"

Kate nodded again. Every time she'd visited Win, she'd stayed in one of the front bedrooms. The other room, although it contained a bed, was rarely used.

"Well," Win went on, her voice more animated, "I found the folder I was looking for, and I was about to go downstairs, when I noticed one of the floor boards near the cupboard was a bit loose. When I looked closer, I could see something underneath. I rushed downstairs to get a knife, and used it to prise the floor board up." Win paused dramatically. "And guess what?"

Kate arched her eyebrows, hoping Win would not expect her to actually try and guess. "I can't. Go on, tell me."

"A small package wrapped up in oilcloth."

"Gosh." Kate wondered where this was going.

"Indeed," said Win, pausing to take a swig from her glass. "Kate, as soon as I touched the package, the room went cold. And I do mean absolutely freezing. It was so weird."

Kate blinked. It wasn't like Win to be fanciful, and she didn't seem inebriated. By the wide-eyed expression on her face, the memory of the event was obviously still vivid in her mind.

She leaned across and took Win's hand. "Go on, what happened next?"

"You do believe me, don't you? You know I'm not one given to fancies." Win drained her glass. "Good grief, I've lived in that house forever and never experienced anything like that before. And there were never any family stories about ghosts."

"You used to tell me there was a witch in the woods."

"Ah, yes." Win flushed. "That was to keep you out of them. My mother told me the same thing. I learnt years later that there was a rumour about a building of some sort in them... It must have been an ice house, I think. But the woods were so overgrown and my parents never had the money, so I suppose they thought it best to leave well alone and scare me off from exploring."

"So you tried the same trick on me?"

"Mmmm..." Win shook her head. "Where was I? Ah yes, I took the package downstairs to open it and have a proper look. It was a diary. Pretty sure it was written by a woman, going by the handwriting, and when I opened it I found a desiccated sprig of rosemary in between the front leaves. Don't think a man would do that." She sighed. "Anyway, I couldn't read much. The handwriting was too difficult. I've left it with Ruth to have a look."

Kate knew who Win meant, even though she'd never met her. Ruth Morris was a librarian at Falmouth Library and had become a close friend of Kate's godmother since the death of Win's husband. They were both widows.

"Has Ruth got back to you about it?"

"No. She's too busy at the moment, what with Christmas and everything. I told her not to worry. There was no rush. I expect I'll hear from her soon enough." Win's hand trembled as she lifted the glass to her mouth to take another sip. She swallowed, then added, "But that's not all. Ever since I found the journal, weird things have been happening."

"What sort of things?" Kate's concern grew and she sat up. She'd never seen Win in this sort of state before.

"Things being moved...and I keep smelling rosemary, especially in the dining room. I can't understand that at all. There are a couple of rosemary shrubs in the garden, but not near enough for them to be smelt in the house. In all my years living there, it's never happened before. I think somehow these things are connected – the journal, items being moved, and the scent." Win turned worried eyes to Kate. "You don't think I'm mad, do you?"

Kate hastily reassured her. "No, of course not. But have

you been under stress recently? Is there anything worrying you? The mind can play tricks, you know, especially if you're under the weather. There's probably a rational explanation for everything you think has happened."

She was pretty certain Win was suffering from stress. There were no such things as ghosts or the supernatural.

"No, I'm not under stress. Well, not now... But maybe I was a little bit," Win conceded, looking sheepish. "I don't know if you remember that little portrait that used to be in the study?"

Kate wondered why Win was going off the point. "No, 'fraid not."

"It came with a job-lot of old bits and pieces that Frank bought at an auction in Exeter." Win paused to chuckle, the way she often did when recalling her husband. To anyone who knew her, it was obvious her marriage had been a happy one, based on deep affection, respect, and salted with mutual teasing. "Oh, I did tell him off for bringing more junk into the house. But anyway...when we went through it, there was this portrait of a gentleman. It looked quite old, wasn't too big, and I have to say, he looked rather nice." She smiled. "Lovely eyes and a bit...mmm...wistful, I think you'd say. Quite sweet. Anyway, last year I decided to get it valued." Win's smile disappeared, and she rolled her eyes. "What a mistake that was. They kept badgering me to sell it. Kept sending me letters and emails. It was so annoying, and they wouldn't take *no* for an answer."

Kate bristled. What sort of louse would bully an elderly woman living on her own? "Give me their contact details. I'll deal with it."

"Oh, it's all sorted now, Kate. I haven't heard anything from them since I threatened taking legal action." The corners of Win's mouth quirked up in a smile. "I suppose it was all quite stressful, but nothing bad enough to make me imagine things. I got a bit upset after that break-in, but nothing was taken, and I had the locks changed, so I'm over that."

Kate remembered her Mum mentioning Win's house had

been targeted by burglars a couple of months previously. Fortunately, they had apparently been disturbed, and escaped empty-handed.

"No, I've not been imagining things…and no, I was not inebriated, before you ask." Win's tone held a tinge of belligerence. "I might enjoy a tipple now and again, but it's not a solitary pastime I indulge in, I can assure you."

Kate patted her godmother's hand. "I know." Inside, she was not altogether convinced that Win's experiences were based in reality. Nevertheless, she promised that, next time she visited, they would get to the bottom of things. Win made Kate swear not to say anything about it to her parents. Because they were scientists, Win was certain they would not understand, and think she was off her trolley.

Kate was inclined to agree.

The subject had been dropped and forgotten, and it was only when news reached her of Win's untimely death, that Kate's faint suspicion that Win had been heading towards some sort of mental breakdown hardened. What else would cause her to leave a warm house and go wandering in the middle of a freezing March night? Kate wondered guiltily if she could have done something to prevent it. Her only consolation was that, in all other respects Win had been her normal chirpy self, and she'd forbidden Kate to discuss the matter with anyone else.

Kate pulled into a parking space on the pier. She'd planned on staying at her parents' holiday flat for a couple of days, until the paperwork for The Beeches had been sorted. The solicitors had taken a while to get back to her, and she didn't have a key yet to the old house.

She lugged her suitcase up the clanking metal staircase to the neat row of apartments on the first floor. Fear of being trapped stopped her from using the lift – the memory of being locked in a wardrobe for several hours as a child, when playing hide and seek with her cousins, had seen to that. Lifts were not an option as far as she was concerned, certainly not when she was on her own, and only *in extremis* if she was accompanied by someone she trusted.

She opened the front door and her nose was assailed by the pungent artificial smell of lavender. She grinned. Her mum hated air fresheners, but even she'd given up trying to convince Betty that they were evil. Betty was the sprightly widow who cleaned the flat every week, and it was evident she'd been in that morning. In addition to the overpowering smell, everything was spotless. Kate plonked the suitcase down on the polished parquet floor and went round opening all the windows. Despite Betty's penchant for air freshener, Kate was hoping the widow would agree to clean The Beeches once she'd settled in. Kate knew she would never be able to keep on top of all the extra work a larger property would require, especially if she was going to be away for substantial periods, if her upcoming commissions were anything like the previous ones. Besides, she owed it to Win to keep her treasured home cared for. She would just have to lie to Betty and say she was allergic to air freshener.

It was too late to visit the solicitors' office, so Kate decided to have a quick shower and then go for a walk instead. Thanks to the stiff breeze now rattling the blinds, the sickly aroma of lavender was rapidly dissipating – replaced by ozone-filled air and a faint smell of cooking fat from the café below.

Kate towelled her short and still-damp chestnut hair then slung on a clean pair of jeans and a hooded top. It would be chilly out by the water. She set off up Market Street towards Custom House Quay, glad to be stretching her legs at last. The crowds had dispersed, the shops were closing, and the restaurants were preparing for their evening trade. It was the quiet lull between the noise of the day and the buzz of the evening crowds. At the end of the quay, Kate paused to admire the yachts bobbing in the marina; she'd never been sailing, but had always wanted to give it a go. The sleek lines and varnished woodwork of some craft contrasted sharply with the workmanlike and battered dinghies and rowing boats also moored up. Nets and wicker lobster pots lay in piles, ready for the next morning's fishing trips, and seagulls squawked and swooped in the rapidly cooling evening air. She ignored their cacophony and concentrated on the rhythmic slapping of the water against the walls of the quay. She inhaled, filling her lungs with the smell of the sea. She'd really missed not being by the coast. Oxford, lovely as it was, smelt of diesel most of the time... That, and books and beer, not to mention bad memories. Not that there was anything wrong with books and beer, she thought, grinning.

She gave herself a mental shake and sobered. No point in dwelling on what was a finished episode in her life.

I really need to get my act together. Be more assertive and not take people at face value.

She'd made that mistake with Robin, and look where it had got her! He'd turned her into the other woman without her knowing it. Thank goodness she hadn't moved in with him, despite his pleadings about being lonely. *Lonely, my foot!* He'd just wanted a fall-back for when his wife discovered what a lying cheat he really was.

Kate grinned again and realised that she'd moved on to being able to see the funny side. The world hadn't ended and she would get on with her life; perhaps a little more cautiously, but she would move forward. There were plenty more fish in the sea. And she needed to do a bit of digging about Win – see if she had been having a breakdown of sorts. Maybe Win's friend Ruth could shed some light.

A sudden loud barking disrupted her thoughts. A black and tan canine, straining on its lead, was pulling its distracted owner in her direction. Kate stiffened. The dog wasn't that big. *But it does have teeth.* An unfortunate incident with a neighbour's territorial Jack Russel, who'd refused Kate access up the shared drive to her flat, had made Kate very wary. The teeth marks in her ankle had taken a while to disappear. Dogs had now been added to confined spaces as things that shook her nerves.

"Heel, Sal!"

The dog, of course, ignored the growled command from its owner and kept straining on its lead, moving ever nearer. Kate looked at the guy at the other end of the lead. He was tall, athletically built, with glossy thick dark hair and saturnine features. She would have described him as handsome, if it hadn't been for the scowl on his face, making him look quite intimidating. He was evidently in the middle of a phone conversation, and oblivious to Kate's presence.

"Sorry, have to go. Sal's playing up. Call you back later." He shoved the phone back in his pocket.

The dog by now was too close for Kate's comfort. Kate's scant knowledge of breeds told her it was a King Charles spaniel. *The fact that it has royal connections doesn't mean it won't bite.* Perhaps it wouldn't sense her fear. She stood stock-still against the steel railings separating her from the drop into the brine below. There was no escape without getting closer to the dog. Her skin went clammy with fear-induced sweat. She bit her lip and held her breath, folding her arms across her chest.

"For goodness sake, Sal!" The guy swept the dog into his arms, barely glancing at Kate, the scowl still on his face. She got the impression he couldn't get away fast enough. He stalked back up the quay, turning once to glare in her direction, as if daring her to follow him. As if, she thought.

Kate slumped against the railings and recommenced breathing. Her recent fear of dogs was irrational, but she couldn't help it. Nips on the ankle were painful. The dog's owner was another matter. What was his problem? No apology, not even an acknowledgement, just a scowl. *Arrogant prick.*

The light was beginning to fade. It was getting late. Kate shivered, it had turned cold, too. Time to get something to eat, then head back to the apartment. She was going to be first in the queue at the solicitors' in the morning.

Chapter Three

"Here you are. The full English and a latte, right?" The waitress plonked the laden plate and brimming cup on the table.

"This looks great. Thanks." Kate wasn't exaggerating. It was just what she needed to keep her going. She intended spending the day at The Beeches once she got the key, and she didn't plan on traipsing backwards and forwards to get lunch. Her next meal might not be until evening. Well, that was her guilty justification for the indulgent full English breakfast sitting in front of her, a more than adequate substitute for the croissant she'd intended ordering. She settled down to devour it.

As she ate, Kate mused on the events that had brought her back to Falmouth. Last month, her contract at the Bodleian Library had nearly expired, and she'd been on the point of deciding which private research commission to take up next, when the solicitor's letter informing her of Win's bequest had arrived. Win had died some four months earlier, in circumstances that had both shocked and saddened Kate and her family. Win's body had been found in woodland near The Beeches. What she'd been doing outside on that freezing March night was a mystery. The police had found no evidence of foul play.

Kate had put all other considerations aside. She would move to Falmouth and get to the bottom of Win's strange death.

Plate cleared, she sipped her coffee and scrolled through her emails – it would be another fifteen minutes until the solicitors' office opened – when she became aware of a warm, hairy presence under the table pressing against her bare leg. She looked down to see a pair of chocolate brown eyes gazing back up at her. She froze. It looked alarmingly like the dog she'd encountered the previous evening. She comforted herself with the thought that it wasn't barking. A pink tongue poked out and gently licked her leg. Kate's eyes darted round for its owner. Was that horrible guy somewhere near? She really wasn't feeling up to a confrontation. A commotion at the door caught her attention.

"Where is she? Oh bugger! Jenny, did you see anyone untying Sal's lead?"

Kate's heart sank. Framed in the open doorway, head turning this way and that, was the impressive form of the guy from the previous evening. She watched apprehensively as he spun round and stalked to the counter, his face like thunder. He'd be drop-dead gorgeous if only he'd lose that frown, she thought, and wondered fleetingly what might induce him to smile. Dismissing these frivolous thoughts, she steeled herself. Setting her cup down, she cleared her throat – despite the liquid, her mouth had dried.

"Excuse me. Hello?" She tried to make herself heard over the hissing of the espresso machine and the loud, agitated conversation taking place at the counter. It didn't work. The dog was now running a damp nose over her calf.

Kate tried again, louder. "Excuse me? Are you looking for a dog?"

This time the guy's head swivelled round in her direction. "You again?" So he had remembered her, but his frown indicated that he wasn't filled with delight. "Yes. Have you seen her?" His voice was deep and not unpleasant, even though his words were terse. He scrutinised her through narrowed eyes... Eyes that were dark and filled with suspicion.

Kate squirmed involuntarily. Did he think she went round deliberately luring dogs? She gestured to the mutt at her feet. "Is this who you're looking for?"

The transformation was instantaneous. He was indeed handsome when he smiled, though he was smiling at his dog, not her. Never mind.

"Sal! You naughty girl. What have I told you about scrounging for scraps?" His voice had lost the growl. Kate, despite her inclination to dislike him, felt herself soften. Anybody who spoke so warmly to their dog couldn't be all bad. The dog's tail began to swish backwards and forwards across the floor, but she didn't budge from Kate's feet.

The guy came towards her. "Seems like Sal's taken a shine to you…or more likely, your breakfast." His voice had a gruff edge, as if he was reluctant to come across as too friendly. "She knows she's not allowed in here." Thudding down in the seat opposite, he scrabbled under the table to find the dog's lead, giving the strong impression that he did not wish to linger.

"Not a problem," said Kate. "I'm quite nervous around dogs and she gave me quite a fright last night." Might as well let him know how upset she'd been. Not that she expected him to apologise. "But she's quite sweet really, isn't she? Sal, did you say? That's a nice name." Kate cautiously patted Sal's head and was rewarded with another wet lick. "I'm Kate, by the way." There was no harm in giving him her first name, and she might even discover his. Not that she wanted to get to know him better – unless he lost the scowl and smiled at her instead of his dog.

His head jerked up, and she felt herself being scrutinised again. Disappointingly, his frown reappeared. "Do I know you?"

"I don't think so," she replied. "I've only just moved here."

"Hmmm…" He was still frowning, but it was a frown of puzzlement, as if he was trying to figure something out, rather than an angry frown. "I'll buy you a coffee as an apology for last night," he said at last.

"Oh there's no need, honestly."

"I insist." He turned towards the counter and signed to the barista that another coffee was required. Then – abandoning his attempts to persuade Sal to move – he leaned down and scooped the reluctant dog into his arms. "Bye." He'd turned on his heels, picked up his own coffee from the counter, and headed out the door, before Kate had time to thank him for the drink. Slightly dazed by the encounter, she watched as the door of the shop closed behind him.

"Think you made a bit of an impression there." Kate jumped at the waitress's voice. The woman placed a fresh cup of coffee on the table.

"Sorry?" Kate guessed she meant the dog. The guy had wanted nothing to do with her. Hadn't even given his name.

"On Tom…and Sal, of course. Lovely dog, but very shy; doesn't like strangers. Bit like Tom, really. Sal usually sits good as gold outside the door while he gets his coffee. It's his parents' dog, but he brings it for a walk first thing. Nice bloke." The woman started to clear the table of Kate's now empty plate and used mug.

"Really?" Kate was unconvinced. He was brusque and overbearing in her opinion.

The woman nodded and put the dishes back down. She was in no hurry to work. "Yeah. Known Tom for years. We were at primary school together. He went on to the grammar and then university. He was working in London, then out the blue he came back." The waitress gave a sigh. "S'spect he'd made enough money. Keeps himself to himself. No girlfriend as far as I know – and that's not for want of trying by some of the local girls." She giggled and leaned forward conspiratorially. "Most he does is one date and that's it." She smirked. "Yeah, there's a few disappointed ladies in Falmouth, I can tell you."

"Hmm?" was Kate's response to this flood of unwanted information. Why would anyone think a guy so rude was a catch? Though she had to admit, he was easy on the eye when he wasn't scowling.

The waitress leaned her hip against the table. It seemed she had time on her hands and wasn't ready to finish the conversation. "You on holiday then?"

"No, I'm here for a while. It might be permanent, not sure yet."

"Oh yeah? What do you do?" She eyed Kate suspiciously. "Not setting up another coffee shop, are you?"

Kate couldn't help laughing. The idea of her running her own shop, especially one with a steaming, hissing, and amazingly complicated piece of machinery behind the counter, was ludicrous. She was a complete technophobe when it came to mechanical devices.

"Goodness, no. I wouldn't have a clue. I'm sorting things out for a relative, and might stay on if things work out. I'm a writer, so I'm able to work from home." She didn't want to give too many details.

The waitress's expression relaxed. "Oh, a writer, eh? Thought you might be checking us out. So many coffee shops have opened this season, and most of them won't last the year. Not enough business in winter, you see?" She nudged Kate's shoulder and smiled. "We've been here five years now. My Dave knows all about coffee. We've won awards, see." She pointed to the framed certificates on the wall behind the counter. They proclaimed the Ubiquitous Bean to be the West Country's favourite coffee shop.

"That's great. Well done! You should have an award for your breakfast too. I really enjoyed it." Kate wasn't fibbing. Her cleaned plate was testament to that.

The woman beamed at her. "Thank you. We're trying hard. Put everything we've got into it. Neither of us wants to work for someone else."

"Know what you mean." Kate grinned and started to gather her things. "Anyway, I'd better get going, but I will call in again. Keep up the good work."

Kate stepped out into the sunshine and headed toward the solicitors'.

Kate turned off the main road and drove up the driveway to The Beeches, a lump forming in her throat as she at last caught sight of the old house. It was perfect. She'd often imagined living here, but had never dreamt that her godmother would leave it to her. Win had surprised everyone by remaining at The Beeches after Uncle Frank died. But stayed there she had, insisting that it had been in her family for generations, and she wasn't going to be the one to sell it.

The gravel crunched beneath the car's tyres as Kate pulled up on the drive near the steps leading to the kitchen door. It was a substantial stone-built dwelling, double fronted and two-storeyed, set at the end of a long, curved drive, amidst tangled woodland just off the coast road, and only two miles outside Falmouth. Secluded, but not too far from neighbours. There was a cared-for cottage on the coast road just before the turn-off for The Beeches. Win had never spoken of her neighbours, and Kate assumed the cottage was an upmarket holiday let.

The key turned easily in the front door lock, and Kate stepped into the familiar, flagged hallway. She cast her eyes around. Dust lay on every surface, from the picture frames on the walls to the antique hall table. The bowl containing the potpourri gave off only the faintest scent of cinnamon and dried pine.

No pain no gain. She smiled ruefully and headed back to the car to haul out her bag containing paint-stained jeans and an old tee shirt. Her decorating clothes, saved from the time she'd helped paint her parent's living room. Next came a large box with cleaning materials, though she was fairly certain that there would be a stock of these already in the house. Win had always liked things spick and span.

Kate arched her back and rolled her shoulders. She was exhausted. Muscles ached in places she didn't know she had muscles, and a persistent pain hovered over her eyes. She'd started in the kitchen, throwing away out-of-date items from the cupboards and cleaning the musty fridge. Then she'd tackled the bathrooms, the main one upstairs, the smaller ensuite one to the bedroom she intended as hers, and the ground floor cloakroom. Finally, she'd dusted and hoovered all the ground floor rooms.

She put the vacuum cleaner away and decided a coffee was in order. Five minutes later, Kate slumped into a chair at the kitchen table to wait for the kettle to boil. She must have nodded off, because the next thing she was aware of were the clouds of steam and water running down the windows. Blast!

She leapt up and got to the kettle just in time. The last thing she needed was a hunt round Falmouth for a new one. She slugged back two paracetamol with her coffee – her head was banging now – and considered what else needed doing. Tomorrow, she'd bring a scarf for her hair and possibly a mask. She'd been sneezing all day. Who knew dusting would be so...dusty? And she'd get food. No point in making herself ill. She looked out the window to the darkening sky. It was getting late. Just one final check round before leaving for the night.

The stairs creaked as she went up to what had been Win's bedroom, part of a large eighteenth century addition to the eastern front of the house. Both its windows overlooked the main drive, and a swift glance told her that they were secured. The bathroom windows, which were at the back, were also locked. Now for the first of the two small bedrooms at the centre front of the house. The door handle wouldn't budge, even though she'd already been in the room. She grimaced as she struggled, mentally adding a can of WD40 to her shopping list. The handle suddenly gave way and she almost tumbled into the room.

Her eyes widened at the sight of the sash window. It was open at the bottom, and the curtains were flapping about in the breeze. Kate was pretty sure it had been closed earlier. She went over and pushed down hard, but it wouldn't budge. Scratching her head, wondering what to do, she jumped when the sash moved on its own, slamming shut with a crash.

"What the...?"

Behind her, the door closed with a loud click. She spun round.

"Bloody hell!"

Frowning, and trying to keep her rising panic under control, she stalked over to the door. Again, the handle wouldn't budge. A spike of fear went down her spine. Her stomach churned. *Stay calm. Deep breaths.* Goosebumps rose on her bare arms. She shivered.

The temperature had dropped several degrees, in fact, it now felt positively Arctic. She sniffed. Was that rosemary she could smell? Imagination, she told herself. She gave the handle another try. It turned easily.

I'm going round the bend, she scolded herself... She shouldn't have taken those tablets on an empty stomach. Still shaking, she took the stairs two at a time, grabbed her bag, and headed for the car.

Convincing herself that the unsetting events of the day were the result of an overactive imagination, Kate put them out of her mind once she arrived back at the flat. She'd come to the conclusion that low blood sugar must have been the reason for her stupid delusions about windows and doors opening and closing on their own, and smelling something that wasn't there. Yes, they were delusions. Nothing to worry about.

Chapter Four

Two days later, Kate threw the last of her things from the flat into the car and drove to the large supermarket at Ponsharden. Stocking up with food, some booze, and a box of chocolates, Kate had decided that a little celebration was in order, even if it was only for herself.

She opened the front door into the stone flagged hallway, set her shopping bags down, and cocked her ears. Silence, apart from the faint sound of birdsong wafting through the open doorway from the woods. Her lips curled into a smile. No noisy neighbours, or insistent hum of traffic to disturb her peace. No car alarms to wake her up at night, no drunken passers-by tipping the remains of their takeaways across the front steps. The smile turned to a wide grin. If anybody saw her they'd wonder about her sanity, she told herself. But she couldn't help it. Her very own house! *Thank you, Win.*

The bedroom Kate had chosen for herself was in the original seventeenth century part of the house. Facing west, its windows overlooked the path to the kitchen door below. It wasn't the largest bedroom, but it was more than adequate, with its own bathroom, and a charming compact sitting room overlooking the rear garden. Win had reserved it for visitors, usually Kate's parents on their annual trips south, until they'd bought their own apartment in Falmouth. Kate herself had always been put in one of the front bedrooms.

She looked round at the furnishings. A bow-fronted set of drawers stood under the window, the rich warm shade of the mahogany giving the room an air of elegance. From its spare lines and lack of ornamentation, Kate guessed it was Regency. Win and her husband had been avid collectors of antique furniture and didn't mind which period an item dated from as long as it was beautiful. This was definitely beautiful. The drawers all had keyholes, but the keys themselves were long gone. Win had shown Kate the secret of the hidden drawer on one of her numerous visits as a child. Kate smiled at the memory and couldn't stop herself from turning the hidden catch. The drawer slid open. It was empty.

By contrast, the large bed was modern. True, it was in an antique bateau style, but the mattress was definitely the latest in mattress technology.

"I don't hold with antique beds," Win had once said. "Bloody uncomfortable they are, give me a decent mattress any day."

Satisfied that her bedroom was ready, the bathroom stocked with fresh towels from the linen cupboard, and soap that she'd bought that day, Kate returned downstairs. In the snug, the room that Win had used as her study, Win's computer sat on the desk, its screen and keyboard now cleared of the dust that had accumulated over the months since her death. Kate switched it on, and watched as the screen flickered into life.

No great fan of technology, Win had conveniently left her password on a post-it note attached to the monitor. Kate rolled her eyes as she tapped in *PassWord58*. Thankfully, Win had not done her banking online. There were email files, some Word files, and a financial spreadsheet containing simple accounts of Win's monthly income and outgoings.

The inbox of her email account was full of the expected newsletters and updates from blogs, shops, and businesses that Win had subscribed to. Kate chuckled when she saw the ones from a Singles agency.

Never had an inkling you had such a hectic social life, Win. You kept that quiet.

Kate scrolled back to before the date of Win's death, finding similar messages. It was then she spotted a few different ones.

From art dealers in Truro called Smith and Jevson, the firm that Win had told her about. Kate frowned. These messages were larded with phrases like '*Don't miss this*

26

opportunity to sell' and *'Theft of valuable works of art is a growing crime'*.

Emotional blackmail. Kate swore under her breath. This was not looking good.

Kate brought up all the messages from Smith and Jevson. The first, sent in March the previous year, offered a valuation of some paintings that Win was thinking of selling. Win's reply agreed to a home visit, which was carried out in June. Kate vaguely recalled Win mentioning a de-clutter, and telling her she'd sold some old watercolours.

"Nothing special," Win had said at the time. "Just a few amateur daubings by an aunt."

Win's subsequent messages to Smith and Jevson had an annoyed tone about them. No, she was sure she did not wish to sell the small pastel portrait of the young man. It had been a gift from her husband and she wanted to keep it.

Kate grinned. *Good for you, Win.*

Kate googled 'Smith and Jevson'. The results showed that they had branches in Falmouth and Truro. The home page revealed that the business was run by two cousins, and included a photograph of two oily-looking characters in their fifties, wearing cravats and broad smiles. Kate decided she wouldn't trust either of them as far as she could throw them.

She scratched her head and looked round the cluttered snug. Where had Win put the portrait? Most of the wall space was taken up with book shelves. Only a small pencil portrait of Uncle Frank, done when Win and her husband were on holiday in St Malo, hung on the wall near the desk. The artist had caught his character well, intelligent eyes and a mouth that Kate remembered as being always curved in a cheerful smile. Win had placed the drawing there shortly after his death some ten years previously, saying it was how she wanted to remember him.

Her curiosity piqued, and determined to locate the missing portrait, Kate moved on to the dining room. There were a couple of landscape paintings, but no portrait. In the drawing room it was pretty much the same story, with the addition of some framed photos of Kate as a child, her graduation in

York, and, in pride of place on the sideboard, one taken when she'd been awarded her doctorate in Oxford. Kate smiled. It seemed so long ago.

She climbed the stairs to investigate the bedrooms, though she couldn't recall seeing anything matching the description when she'd been cleaning. She hesitated for a fraction before going in the bedroom she'd panicked in the other day. To her relief, the door opened smoothly, and a quick glance round told her that the portrait was not there. It wasn't in her own bedroom or sitting room either. That left Win's bedroom.

Kate shivered – it was definitely chillier in this wing of the house. She stood in the open doorway, gazing round the shadow-filled room, and flicked on the light. The bold floral-patterned bedspread and matching curtains almost hurt her eyes. Win had been very fond of Laura Ashley prints. Here there was an abundance of them, all vying for attention. Matching cushions were scattered across the bed and on the flounced armchair under the window. Kate shook her head. Definitely overkill.

She spotted a photo of herself as a child by Win's bedside table; it had been hidden by the bedside lamp. She couldn't recall seeing it there before, but then, she'd rarely entered Win's bedroom when she'd been alive. Curiously, as she moved closer she saw that the photo wasn't actually in the frame, it was covering something else. She picked it up, and as she did so the photo slipped, disclosing what was concealed underneath. Kate let out a breath. It was a pastel portrait of a dark-eyed handsome man, his lips curving in an enigmatic and inviting smile. From the hairstyle and neckcloth she guessed it had been painted in the early nineteenth century. This must be it. But why had Win hidden it up here, and behind an old photo? Had she thought someone might steal it?

Kate sat down on the bed and reached for the switch of the bedside lamp to examine the portrait more closely. The bulb flickered then died. Then the main light went out. *Damn*. Two bulbs going at the same time? A noise at the window startled her. The curtains were flapping about. Telling herself

28

it was just a draught, she went over to check, the portrait still clutched in her hand. The window was closed.

Imagining things again. Nothing to eat, and too much time on the computer.

With a thudding heart, and shaking steps, Kate headed for the door. She wasn't going to run, and allow her growing unease to turn into full blown panic. It was Win's own room after all, and Win would never harm her. Not that she believed in ghosts...although Win had begun to believe, hadn't she? She swallowed. *Nonsense.* Her mind was playing tricks on her.

Back on the landing, the contrast in temperature hit her. Win's bedroom had been like a fridge. Here, it was pleasantly warm. The bedroom door closed with a click behind her. Without looking back, Kate scuttled down the stairs to the dining room.

Her legs were still shaking when she reached the kitchen. Leaving the portrait on the kitchen table, she filled the kettle for tea, and made herself a sandwich. She needed to eat, she told herself. Hunger and thirst were making her imagine things again, that's all.

Half an hour, one crusty cheese baguette and several mugs of tea later, she was feeling much better. She cleared the dirty dishes away from the table, and told herself there were no such things as ghosts. Propping the portrait up, she examined it under the bright kitchen lights. It was an accomplished work, done by a craftsman, she was sure, but no matter how much she screwed up her eyes, the signature at the bottom remained indecipherable. The sitter's face, vibrant and curious, with alluring, come-to-bed eyes, peered out of the frame at her. Whoever the artist was, he had captured his subject's intelligence and zest for life. Kate instinctively knew this gentleman would have been good company.

Convinced that this was the painting mentioned by the art dealers, Kate wondered if it was also the reason for the break-in that Win had mentioned. Perhaps that was why Win had moved it out of sight. Her stomach lurched. If someone was trying to steal it, were they the source of the ghostly happenings that Win had been convinced had occurred, and not the supernatural? It made sense. The solicitor had told Kate there'd been a second break-in shortly after Win's death. Nothing appeared to have been taken, and the door that had been the entry point had been quickly repaired by the insurers.

Kate's lips pursed. For some reason, the thought of someone real breaking into the house was far more alarming than ghostly apparitions.

Chapter Five

Kate was mulling over the unsettling thought of attempted burglary, when a knock on the kitchen door made her jump. A dog barked outside, sending the hairs at the back of her neck to stand on end. No burglar comes with a dog, and I won't let it in, she reasoned, so she got up from where she'd been slouched at the kitchen table, and cracked open the top half of the kitchen door. There was a sharp intake of breath from the figure standing on the doorstep. It was the guy from the coffee shop. His initial smiling expression transformed into a glare. Kate's own expression was one of shock.

"Bloody hell. Not you again!" His growl was loud enough to be heard over the dog's barks.

Goaded into anger, she blurted out, "Yes. I do it on purpose, you know." He stepped back, and she was pleased to see she'd taken the wind out of his sails. He was far too overbearing and sure of himself. "Anyway, who did you expect? And what do you want?" She'd show him he wasn't the only one who could growl and scowl.

His face flushed as he attempted to grab the collar of a very excited Sal, who was still jumping and scratching at the door. "Sorry." His voice lost its aggression. "I saw the light… I thought I'd check. I knew the house was empty after the lady who lived here died. Didn't know it had been sold." Kate had the satisfaction of seeing a sheepish expression appear on his face. "Sorry for disturbing you. And I'm Tom, by the way." He started to pull Sal away.

Kate immediately relented her sharp words – he was only checking to make sure everything was ok, so she ought to be polite. "I know who you are. The waitress in the coffee shop told me. And the house hasn't…been sold, I mean. Win was my godmother. She left the house to me. I moved in this morning." She swallowed. "Thanks for checking."

She jerked back as Sal made a sudden bid for freedom, jumping up at the door in an attempt to lick her hand.

"Don't worry, she won't bite. She's just a bit over-enthusiastic, I'm afraid. Get down, Sal! Don't be a pest." He grabbed the dog's collar with one hand but Sal didn't take a blind bit of notice.

Kate had never been the object of a dog's affection before. As a child, she'd never had a pet. The violent tail wagging made her smile. She glanced up to see Tom's features soften as he spoke to his dog. It occurred to her that maybe he wasn't always a bad-tempered grouch. Perhaps it was just women he didn't have much time for.

Kate risked moving her hand out to pat Sal on the nose. "She's very affectionate, isn't she?"

"I think you mean boisterous, don't you?" His tone was decidedly friendlier now. His lips curled into what Kate thought might be described as a smile, and there was a definite twinkle in his hazel eyes. "Anyway, I live in the cottage down there." He pointed down the drive to the main road. "I met your godmother a couple of times. Nice lady." So it wasn't a holiday cottage after all, and she did have a neighbour... Pity it was Mr Grumpy. "I saw your lights through the trees when I was letting Sal out for her constitutional. She legged it over here. Couldn't stop her. Not sure what I would have done if it'd been burglars. Run the other way, I expect." He chuckled, a warm sound that sent Kate's pulse unexpectedly racing.

An attempt at humour. Kate had an inkling why he was a big hit with the ladies. He knew how to turn the charm on. But she wasn't going to fall into that trap. Oh no.

"Well, would you like to come in for tea or coffee now you're here?" The words were out of her mouth before she could stop them. What on earth was she doing inviting him in? She was done with men, wasn't she? For the time being anyway. And he'd shown her how grumpy he could be. But she'd invited him now. She could only blame his twinkling eyes and boyish smile. He was very attractive when he smiled. A shame he didn't seem to do it very often, and when he did it was mostly directed at his dog.

"Cheers. That'd be lovely." He gave her another knee-trembling smile. "I've just got back. That's why Sal's so frisky. She's been in the house for hours, poor love, haven't you?" He leaned down and patted Sal's head. Kate opened the lower part of the door, and was nearly knocked over as Sal hurtled past. Tom followed, rather more slowly, taking in Kate's questioning look. "My mother was going to take Sal for a long walk, but something came up, and she could only get over for five minutes this afternoon. Good job she managed that, though, or there'd have been a mess to clear up. Sal's my parents' dog, but I've been looking after her for a while. They've got a lot on at the moment."

By now, Sal was sniffing at cupboard doors, tail wagging, and generally making herself at home.

"Why don't you sit down and I'll put the kettle on? Tea or coffee?"

"Tea please, milk and no sugar."

She heard the chair scrape across the floor as she busied herself finding two mugs and the teabags. At least he was doing as she asked, unlike his dog who was still exploring. Kate was grateful for the fact that she'd remembered the biscuits. Now she wouldn't be tempted to eat them all herself. She opened the larder and got them off the shelf, feeling Tom's eyes on her as she moved about. He hadn't said a word since telling her how he wanted his tea. His silence was becoming uncomfortable. She decided it was up to her.

"So, how long have you lived in the cottage?" She handed him his mug and put the plate of biscuits on the table.

"About twelve months now." He picked up a biscuit and bit into it with even white teeth and began to chew.

Kate tried again. "The girl in the coffee shop said you'd moved back from London. Didn't you like it there?"

He frowned and bit down hard on his biscuit.

It seemed she'd touched on a nerve with her question. She waited while he chewed and swallowed, determined that he should be the first to break the silence – she'd seen enough cop shows to know that was the technique to get people to talk. It worked.

"London was fine. I decided to come back home, that's all." He shrugged. "My family live down here."

Kate guessed that there was far more to it than that, but decided to let it go. She nodded. "This is a bit of a homecoming for me too." He raised his eyebrows in a question. "I was born near here. We moved away when I was a child."

He was looking at her now, but she had no idea what was going through his mind. The intensity of his gaze made her skin prickle.

He blinked and looked away, his eyes alighting on the portrait which she'd forgotten was still lying on the table. "This looks interesting. Who is he?" There was animation and genuine interest in his voice.

So, he's averse to anything perceived as personal probing, but otherwise he's happy to discuss neutral subjects.

"I've no idea. It was Win's." She decided to play his game.

"Looks quite old… What on earth?"

An eerie howl cut through the house, making the hairs on the back of Kate's neck leap to attention again. Tom pushed his chair back with a squeal on the flagstone floor and charged out of the kitchen towards the noise. Kate stumbled after him, nerves on edge and heart pounding. Her mind somehow registered that the sound was being made by Sal. Nothing supernatural, but that did not make it any the less unnerving. Kate halted at the door to the dining room and took in the sight of Sal crouched at the bottom of the separate staircase leading up to the east wing, ears flattened against her head, and a low rumbling coming from her throat.

"What's the matter, girl? There's nothing there, you daft dog," Tom got a grip on Sal's collar and pulled her away. "Never known her do that before. Is there someone else in the house?" He tugged the now quiet Sal back into the kitchen, brusquely brushing past Kate.

"No." *Not as far as I know.* Kate bit her lip, and followed them back into the kitchen. She propped herself against the counter top, certain that she would slide on to the floor without support, her legs were shaking so much.

Tom must have noticed her ashen face.

"Would you like me to check? Can't understand why Sal carried on like that." His voice had lost its brusqueness.

"No, it's OK. I'm sure it's nothing… Probably a mouse or something," Yes, that's all it was, she told herself, not quite believing it. Tom's expression told her she hadn't convinced him either. She glanced at Sal, now curled up in the corner as if nothing had happened. Well, she wasn't bothered. It can't have been anything.

"You're sure you're all right?"

Kate nodded and forced a smile. "Of course. Just not used to dogs, that's all."

He shrugged, drained his mug, and took one more biscuit. The pile on the plate had diminished considerably. "I'll be off then." But instead of moving, he cleared his throat. "Look… Here's my number." He thrust a business card into her hand. "Give me a call if anything bothers you." He gave a tight smile. "You're right, it was probably a mouse. Sal should have been a cat."

Kate watched as he wiped the crumbs from his lips. He did have nice lips. Lips that were very inviting, especially when he smiled. She jerked her gaze from his mouth to his eyes and saw the hint of concern there. She looked at the card in her hand. *Tom Carbis, Web Designer.* There was an email address and a phone number.

"Thanks for this, though I'm sure I won't need to bother you."

"Well, just in case, eh?" He smiled again, his eyes crinkling. "Now, are you sure you're all right? You still look a bit pale to me." He took a step nearer and she caught the tang of his aftershave.

"I'm fine, honestly," she lied. "Just overtired. I haven't stopped all day." She didn't want to give the impression that she was some weak, ditsy female bowled over by a few odd noises and an overpowering male presence.

After one final searching look, and a reassuring pat on her arm, he moved towards the door. "OK, I'll see you around then." He loped off into the darkness after Sal who, once she'd seen her master rise, had bounded out of the open door.

Kate flopped down into a chair. The room seemed even more empty and quiet after he'd gone. It was funny; she'd not felt lonely before. It had been good to have someone else in the house, even if that someone was a bit prickly. Despite his abrupt manner, there was something about him that attracted her. He was handsome in a rugged way, with his dark hair and strong sculpted features, and when he smiled... Well. Kate sighed. Her first impressions of him now seemed to be way off-beam. The evening's encounter had taught her there was sensitivity beneath his hard shell. The way he spoke and cared for his dog – and his insistence that Kate should call him if she was worried – that didn't denote an insensitive man.

She remembered the waitress's words. He was considered a catch, but he avoided long-term relationships. Why would a guy that attractive, and seemingly successful, by the expensive cut of his casual clothes, not have a girl hanging off his arm every night? He was a bit of a mystery, in fact. Enigmatic. What was he hiding beneath that intimidating facade?

Come on, Kate. Pull yourself together. Don't fall for the first man you meet. She'd been down that route before. No. She didn't need a man around, and she would need to know this one a whole lot better before becoming involved.

She took in the state of the kitchen and grimaced. The mugs needed washing and she needed to tidy up. She hauled herself up and made a start, grateful that her legs had stopped trembling.

Later, after a quick check of the dining room, she stood at the bottom of the stairs, her ears straining to catch any sound. All was quiet. She returned to the kitchen, checked that the door was locked, switched off the light, and climbed the main staircase to her bedroom.

It had been a long day.

Chapter Six

Kate stood on tip-toe and stared bleary-eyed at her reflection in the bathroom mirror. When she was more organised she would get someone in to set it at a more convenient height for her. It was one of the many disadvantages of being only five feet two. She'd had another awful night, and the shadows under her eyes were proof. Since Tom's visit she'd been unable to sleep; every night she'd lain in bed, alert to every creak – and the old house certainly had its share of those. But she'd never felt anxious enough to justify telephoning him. An old house was bound to creak and groan, she told herself. She didn't believe in ghosts, and the lock on her bedroom door would give her time to call the police in the event of hearing someone break-in downstairs.

But last night had been peculiar, she had to admit. After managing to drift off for a few hours, she'd suddenly woken up. At first she'd not moved, trying to work out what had roused her. Through the open window an owl hooted somewhere in the woods, and a vixen called her mate, but the house itself was quiet. She came to the conclusion that a car backfiring on the road had woken her. Sounds carried at night and that explanation seemed logical. Certainly nothing else was stirring or making a noise. Perhaps a mug of hot chocolate would send her back to sleep. It was worth a try.

The stairs creaked as she padded down. There was no way to get up or down them unheard. Any lurking burglar would surely have fled by now, she told herself. She hesitated in the hallway. All was silent apart from the ticking of the hall clock. Better check the dining room, she told herself. She opened the door. A shaft of moonlight through the half-closed curtains gave the room an eerie glow. Kate's nose twitched. A heady perfume, unusual but somehow familiar, enveloped her. Her sleep-fuddled mind struggled to identify it, then it came to her: it was the pungent aroma of rosemary.

What on earth? She flicked the light on and spun around. She hadn't bought any flowers, or anything that might have contained rosemary, and she certainly didn't use air freshener. She remembered the conversation with Win – she'd mentioned something about smelling rosemary. There must be a rational explanation, she thought, something Win had left somewhere and forgotten about. She'd have a good scout round in the morning. Her sleepy eyes settled on the portrait on the dining table; she'd need to find a safe place to put that too. But that was also something for tomorrow. She went back across the hallway to the kitchen, where the only aroma to assail her nose came from the Brie de Meaux as she opened the fridge door.

It was only as she remembered the night before that it hit her – the portrait. She paused, toothbrush halfway to her mouth. It shouldn't have been on the dining room table. Yesterday, she'd put it in the study, locked inside the desk drawer. In her confused state last night it hadn't occurred to her.

She sucked in her cheeks, trying to think. Was she going mad? She checked again in the mirror. Sleep deprived certainly, but not mad. She finished her teeth, returned to her bedroom. and sat down with a bump on the edge of her bed, and tried to figure it out. There was only one rational conclusion. She must have moved it herself without thinking. No other explanation, or none that she dared to admit to.

Kate flexed her shoulders. What she needed was a brief change of scenery. She'd been on her own in the house for a few days, and a stroll round Falmouth would blow the cobwebs away. She'd call into the library to see if Win's friend Ruth was on duty. It'd be good to chat to someone who'd known Win. Apart from Tom, and he didn't count, she told herself, she hadn't really spoken to anyone since leaving Oxford. And she must remember to ask Ruth if she'd finished deciphering the diary.

Feeling energised now that she had a plan, Kate ensured the portrait was safely locked in her desk drawer before slinging on a clean pair of jeans and a tee shirt. She swiped a lipstick on her lips, and without stopping to make herself breakfast, jumped into the car. Soon after, she parked at the apartment, knowing the space would be empty. Her parents were abroad for the summer – a conference in the States, followed by the road trip of a lifetime. They weren't expected back for several months, and she wasn't going to contact them to share her stupid worries.

The streets were still quiet, just the odd local fetching milk for the first cuppa of the day and a newspaper. Kate made a beeline for the Ubiquitous Bean and took a seat at the table she'd used the other day. If it was going to be her regular hangout she might as well have her regular spot. She draped her jacket on the seat and placed her order with the sleepy-eyed teenager behind the counter. The woman who'd been so chatty on her previous visit was nowhere to be seen.

Kate was wiping the last crumbs from the corner of her mouth when she heard a familiar voice and looked up from her phone. 'Dave's wife', as Kate had mentally tagged her, had reappeared, and Tom was standing at the counter chatting to her.

He must have seen her when he came in, Kate reckoned, but he'd made no attempt to say hello. What was it with the guy? She decided to take the initiative.

"Good morning."

His head whipped round. "Aah, good morning…er, Kate. Didn't see you there." He had the grace to look embarrassed.

"Nice day, isn't it?" Devilment made her want to prod him into some sort of conversation.

"Mmm, yes it is." He turned his back on her.

She gave up.

Two seconds later, his phone rang and he pulled it out of his pocket. In the mirror behind the counter Kate saw him frown. "I'll be right over, don't worry." He switched the phone off and jammed it back in his pocket. "Sorry, got to dash." There was a clatter of coins on the counter and he sprinted out of the door without his drink.

"Blimey. Tom's in a hurry today." Dave's wife pulled a face and shrugged at her teenage assistant. So it wasn't just her he was abrupt with, thought Kate. It wasn't much consolation.

Feeling a bit more human after her coffee and a bacon sandwich, Kate strolled to the library. Fingers crossed, Ruth would be there, and be able to shed light on Win's state of mind before she died. Kate needed someone to confirm that Win had been suffering delusions, as awful as that might be. There were no such things as ghosts.

Disappointment, however, awaited. It was Ruth's Saturday off.

"Would it be possible for you to give her a call and let her know Kate Wilson, Win Saunton's goddaughter, is trying to contact her? I can give you my phone number to pass on to her. I'd really appreciate it." Kate gave a friendly smile to the young librarian who, beneath her heavy Goth makeup and piercings, looked uncertain.

"Mmm... I'm not sure." The young woman chewed her black-painted lip, glanced round the almost empty reading room and then looked at Kate. Kate continued to smile. "Don't suppose it will do any harm to give her a quick bell," the Goth said at last. "Give me your number."

Kate took the piece of paper the girl shoved across the counter and scribbled down her details.

"I'll just be a minute." The Goth disappeared into the office. Five minutes passed before she re-emerged, a grin on her face. "That was lucky; caught Ruth as she was going out. Said she'll call you later today. She'd love to see you."

Feeling pleased with this result, Kate left the library and ambled down the High Street towards the Maritime Museum. Squinting in the bright sunlight, she remembered her hat, and pulled it out of her backpack. It would give some protection from the glare until she got home. In her rush to get out that morning, she'd forgotten her suncream and dark glasses.

The town centre was busier now, frustratingly so. Kate skirted the huddles of tourists gawking at souvenir shop windows and manoeuvred past parents pushing tank-like buggies, their occupants wailing and squalling. It wasn't quite the relaxing outing she'd planned.

Something caught her eye. A brightly-coloured work, depicting bobbing yachts on a sun-kissed sea, stood on an easel in a shop window. The colours were vibrant – the artist had captured not only the light as it bounced off the waves, but also the sense of movement. It would make a great present for her parents' anniversary – if she could afford it. Mum had mentioned she was looking for something to hang in the dining room, and the colours were just perfect.

Kate stepped inside and soon lost herself gazing at seascapes and landscapes of Cornwall and the Cornish coast, many by the same artist whose work in the window had tempted her in. She was examining a watercolour of vivid poppies in a sun-washed green field when a voice interrupted her thoughts.

"Can I help you?"

Startled, she spun round to see who had spoken, and her ready smile froze on her lips. The person who addressed her was horribly familiar. She'd seen him recently, his features were engraved on her memory. The shoulder-length hair and slender physique. It was the guy who'd followed her in Oxford.

Immobilised by shock, it was a few seconds before it dawned that he hadn't recognised her, thanks to the hat obscuring the top half of her face. He was not really paying attention, but distractedly shuffling papers into a folder on the counter. His question had been one of polite inquiry, not really expecting to make sale.

"No, just looking, thanks." Kate inched towards the doorway and once there, plunged into the crowd. Heart thudding in her chest, she didn't stop, or turn around to check if she was being followed, but forced her way up the busy street, in an effort to get as far away as possible. The churchyard was up ahead and she veered off into it, spotted a vacant bench, and slumped down. She needed her legs to stop shaking and to get her breathing under control.

Grimacing, she swiped a hand across her sweaty face. This wasn't like her, she wasn't one to panic. But so many weird things had happened in the last few days…and a lack of sleep could account for her frayed nerves. That's why she'd run instead of tackling him, she told herself. Wrapping her arms around herself, she rocked back and forth and tried to think.

"Are you all right, dear?" An elderly lady was peering at her with some concern. Dressed in a black coat, shiny with wear, she cocked her head and gave Kate a sympathetic smile as she put her supermarket carrier bag of chrysanthemums and shabby, over-stuffed handbag down on the gravel path.

Kate unlocked her arms and wiped the frown from her face. "I'm fine, honestly. Just had a bit of a shock, that's all. Be all right in a minute."

The old lady nodded. "Well, if you're sure. Our vicar will be along shortly. A nice man if you need to talk to someone." The parishioner turned to go. "I'll get on with my flowers. If you change your mind, just pop in, and knock on the vestry door." She hobbled slowly up the path and disappeared into the darkness of the church doorway.

Kate gave herself a good telling-off. What was she doing, cringing pathetically on bench and looking so fragile that a little old lady was taking pity on her? Her pent-up anger helped her to find her nerve. She'd face him, report him to the police, do…something. But first of all, she needed to double check she hadn't got it wrong, to confirm it was him before making accusations.

With growing confidence, she got up and marched back the way she'd come. Stationing herself in a baker's shop doorway on the opposite side of the road, she pretended to examine the cakes on display, trying not to reveal her distaste at the unlikely, and quite frankly unappetising, colours they were iced in. A quick glance over to the art shop told her he was now involved with a couple of genuine customers. Standing near the door in full view, there was no mistake – it was definitely the Oxford guy.

His smile was smarmy as he nodded in an obsequious manner to the couple who stood with him. Kate's lips curled in disgust. His customers appeared wealthy, the woman sporting lots of jewellery and, like her partner, a mahogany tan. Kate guessed they were off the large cruise ship berthed in the harbour. They were pointing at the painting in the window and after a few minutes discussion, all three trooped back into the shop. It seemed like a sale had been agreed.

Her eyes crept up to the sign above the shop – Jevson. Her heart stopped. Smith and Jevson were the art dealers desperate to buy Win's portrait. Kate belatedly recalled that their website said they had a branch in Falmouth. She frowned. It was all too much of a coincidence. Maybe she should call it a day and return home to think things through.

Kate's phone rang as she was about to drive off. She didn't recognise the number.

"Hello. Is that Kate Wilson?" It was a woman's voice.

"Who's calling, please?" Kate's answer was evasive – some illogical part of her brain thought the caller might be the art dealers.

"This is Ruth Morris, Kate. We need to have a chat."

Kate breathed a sigh of relief. At last she might start getting somewhere. After a brief conversation she arranged to meet Ruth on the following Monday.

"I've got that day off, I'm having a long weekend," said Ruth. "We can have a picnic in the garden if the weather stays as fine as it is today." She sounded friendly. "I've missed my chats with Win about history and books, so it will be nice to meet you at last. She thought very highly of you. And I must tell you what I've discovered about the diary. I guarantee you'll be fascinated."

Intrigued and excited about what she might learn, Kate's mood lightened. She put all thoughts of the guy from Jevson's out of her mind, and set off for The Beeches.

As she drove past Tom's cottage, she checked it out. Built of local granite, it was set back off the road, with a small walled garden at the front. There was no sign of a car. She shook her head. Why was she thinking about him? She didn't need another man to disturb her thoughts, although, to give him his due, he was more aggravating than sinister. He'd annoyed her this morning in the coffee shop, for sure.

Men – would she ever understand them?

Chapter Seven

That night followed the pattern of previous nights, with little sleep and restless dreams. A vivid nightmare of being trapped in the dark somewhere underground made Kate toss and turn. When she woke up, the bedsheet was wrapped round her legs, which she put down as the cause of her nightmare.

She kept herself busy that day, determined to tire herself out so she would sleep. After spending some time updating notes for her book, she went out for a long swim at one of the nearby beaches. Passing Tom's cottage twice, there was still no sign of life. That evening she decided to make a pizza – kneading the dough was therapeutic, especially when she pretended it was Robin's head she was pounding. It didn't take long to prepare, and soon she was settled down to eat it in front of the TV, where a cold glass of wine also contributed to her now mellow mood. She had high hopes of a good night's sleep, but when she went to bed, sleep was as elusive as ever.

On Monday morning, feeling pretty pissed off, Kate attempted to work on her book before setting off for Ruth's, but after half an hour gave up and settled for reading the latest Rebus novel on her Kindle. She smiled wryly at how the detective managed to solve the most complicated of cases on very little sleep and a diet of alcohol, cigarettes, and junk food. She was a wreck after just a few bad nights.

On the way to Ruth's, not wanting to turn up for lunch empty-handed, Kate bought some flowers and a cake from Marks and Spencer. Ruth's house turned out to be a pleasant Regency terrace not far from the centre of Falmouth. A petite lady with spiky, cropped hair, dyed an unlikely shade of red, and wearing a brightly-coloured tunic paired with black leggings, opened the door to her knock. She looked to be in her fifties.

"You must be Kate. Come in, come in. It's lovely to meet you at last." Ruth's face beamed as she ushered Kate into the narrow hallway.

"These are for you." Kate handed over the flowers. "Oh, and I thought I'd bring this. I hope you like chocolate cake."

"Goodness me, you shouldn't have, dear. How thoughtful. I'll put it in the kitchen for now. Don't want it melting in this sun. Come through, do." Ruth led her down the hallway into a cramped but sun-filled kitchen, and through patio doors into a small paved courtyard garden. Pots of lush plants and flowers stood in groups around the courtyard. It was delightful, a little oasis in the middle of town. A wooden table dressed with a bright red tablecloth and laid with plates and cutlery stood in a shady corner. "Do sit down, dear. Would you prefer tea, coffee, or a cold drink? Once I've sorted those out we can sit and chat."

Before long they were both seated at the table, a pot of earl grey and a plateful of sandwiches between them. They chatted as they ate, exchanging memories of Win and laughing about some of her idiosyncrasies.

"She definitely went for it, once she got the bit between her teeth. Determined she was," said Ruth. "I do miss her; she was a good friend. Kept me going after Ted died."

"The feeling was mutual," said Kate. "Win always claimed that it was you who dragged her out of the doldrums when Uncle Frank died."

"Yes, we were quite a lively team. We scared the life out of some of the more sedate members of our local social club." Ruth chuckled.

Looking at the elfin-featured lady sitting cross-legged in her trendy leggings, Kate thought she was probably correct.

"Well, now we've eaten, let's get down to this diary," said Ruth at last. "Come inside and I'll show you my notes."

They cleared the table of the remnants of their feast, and Ruth took Kate into her small dining room, where piles of paper and notebooks covered the table. Ruth opened a drawer in the sideboard and pulled out a small grey conservation box.

"My friend at Truro archives gave me this to keep it in." She opened the box and lifted out the leather bound volume. "Well, this is it. I removed the dried plant stuff that came with it… I put that in a separate freezer bag. Win and I came to the conclusion that it was rosemary."

A prickle went up Kate's spine. "Really?"

"Yes, the smell has pretty much disappeared, but it turns out we were right. The lady who wrote the journal mentions it several times and the piece she'd placed in the volume was given to her by… Well, you'll find out shortly. He said it was so she'd not forget him…as in—"

"I know," Kate interrupted. "'*There's rosemary, that's for remembrance. Pray you, love, remember*,' Ophelia says to Hamlet. Sounds like whoever he was, he was a cultured gentleman. Goodness, what was that?" A shock of electricity had shot up Kate's arm as she took the diary from Ruth's hands.

Ruth looked at her bemused. "What do you mean?"

"Didn't you feel it?" Kate rubbed her arm and held the volume away from her. "I got a shock when I touched it. You know, like an electric shock."

"Why would an old book give you a shock? It must have been from my tunic, I think there's some polyester in it. That can give you a shock sometimes. Static, you know?"

Kate wasn't convinced, but decided not to argue. She didn't want Ruth to think she was completely barking. "Yeah, you're probably right. Well, what have you discovered?"

The next hour or so was spent going over the transcription that Ruth had made of the journal. It was gripping reading. Written by a young lady in 1804, it covered a period of about twelve months. It started off innocuously, describing trips into Falmouth and the surrounding countryside, the weather, and other mundane matters. A typical genteel young lady's account of a bland and sedate life. Then things got interesting.

By March, she had attended an assembly where she had

made the acquaintance of a gentleman, John, who had taken a house in Falmouth. Her parents, however, did not approve, and forbad her to see him again. But this young lady had an independent streak. She defied her parents, and with the aid of her maid, she maintained a correspondence with John. By August, things were moving apace. Although she had spent time away in Bath to visit her sister, the author wrote of running away with her gentleman. The final journal entry spoke of a midnight assignation on the following evening '*at our usual meeting place in the woods*'.

Kate grinned. "Wow. Wonder what happened?"

"Well, I've done some digging in our local archives and I was able to identify her as Annabelle Tracy. Her family owned The Beeches for many years before selling up and moving to London – several months after her disappearance, as it happens. I understand her father suffered what I guess we would call a stroke these days. There are a local physician's bills and notes, recommending that Mr Tracy's speech might be restored by consulting a renowned medical man in London." Ruth put on a mysterious voice. "But of Annabelle there is no further word. I've found records of her baptism, but I can't find any records of her marriage or death." Ruth grinned. "Bit of a dead end, I'm afraid." She giggled. "'Scuse the pun."

Kate grinned back at her. Ruth had a sense of humour just like Win; no wonder the two women had got on so well. Then she saw Ruth's frown. "What is it?"

"Well, I've been to the Record Office where the Tracy family papers are held, and while there are records of her sisters' marriages and deaths, Annabelle just disappears. It all seems a bit odd."

"What do you mean? She might have died when she was away visiting and been buried there." Kate had studied many cases where it appeared that someone had vanished, and then a record popped up elsewhere that solved the mystery.

"Mmm." Ruth didn't sound convinced. "Anyway, never mind that for now. The good news is that I have also identified John."

"Really? That's fantastic. Anyone of note?"

"His name was John Rufus Lanyon. As luck would have it, he was mentioned in the local paper for that year. He'd taken on the lease of a gentleman's residence on Dunstanville Terrace, shortly before the date Annabelle mentions meeting him. That's how I found him."

"Oh, I know where you mean, out towards Greenbank." Kate had often admired the the elegant houses with views across to Flushing. "That's where a few of the wealthy packet ship commanders lived, isn't it?"

Ruth nodded. "That's right. Built for the well-to-do. Still are, if you ask me. Anyway, his father, an Earl, had a large estate in Wiltshire, as well as other properties here in Cornwall. Seems John was quite eligible."

"Then I can't understand why Annabelle's father was so against a match." It didn't make much sense to Kate. Unless the chap was an absolute bounder, of course. Normally, any gentleman with an unmarried daughter would have regarded the son of an earl as ideal son-in-law material.

Ruth tapped the side of her nose. "Aah, I might have the answer. It seems that he'd fallen out with his father. He was a second son and destined for the Church. But he changed his mind, hence the disagreement – there were rumours that he was dissolute." Kate's eyes widened, and Ruth answered her unspoken question. "I've got contacts at the archives holding the Lanyon papers. My friend there is an absolute gem. She went through the Earl's diaries and letters. It was all there."

"How lucky was that?"

"Anyway," continued Ruth, "It looks like John had a taste for adventure and was intent on joining the militia here at Pendennis Castle as an officer. I assume it was his way of finding adventure without actually going to war on the Peninsula. It seems he also had connections with the local Preventive Waterguard."

Kate pulled a face, she'd never heard of it before.

"They tackled smugglers who evaded revenue cruisers and they only operated in coastal waters."

"Sounds like he was a busy boy."

Ruth nodded. "He remained in the area for a couple of years, and was commended for his bravery and skill in foiling smugglers. Eventually he was reconciled with his father, which was a good thing as it happens, because his older brother died without issue, making John the heir. He inherited on his father's death, but he never married, and the title eventually went to a cousin on his death. According to the family papers, John died of a broken heart. He's in the family tomb at the Lanyon estate near Bath." Ruth shook her head. "So there you are… It's all very sad."

"Wow, what a tale." Kate was staggered by how much Ruth had discovered and said so.

Ruth was dismissive. "Well, doing this has kept me occupied. I wanted to do it because Win asked me to. When she died and I couldn't get to her funeral because I had the flu, it seemed like one way I could pay my respects to her, you know? Besides," she gave Kate a cheeky grin, "I can now pass it all on to you."

Kate laughed, and watched as Ruth started to gather the paperwork together into tidy bundles. Was now the right time to raise the tricky subject of Win's state of mind?

"Win's death was a bit, erm, strange, don't you think? Was she all right…in her mind, I mean?"

Ruth tutted and sent Kate a look that made her quail. "Thought you'd know better. Sharp as a tack, she was." She paused, looking thoughtful, her brow creased. "She did say she'd had some bad dreams, and she mentioned that a few odd things had happened. Noises in the night, that sort of thing. I thought it was probably burglars. Anyway, there was a break-in. She got up one morning to find a window had been forced, but nothing had been taken. She thought it was someone after a portrait she had. They didn't get it though… She'd hidden it."

"So that's why it was concealed under a photo. I thought so."

Ruth gave Kate another sharp look. "You know about that? Win wouldn't tell me who she thought was responsible, in case I did anything 'silly' as she called it. Stubborn woman."

Ruth swiped her eyes with the back of her hand, sniffed, then ran her hand through her hair, making her spikes stand on end even more. "Anyway, I stayed over there with her one night." Ruth eyes darted round, as if checking that no one else could hear. "That was a bit peculiar." Her voice had dropped several octaves.

"Why? What happened?"

"A feeling I had, that's all." Eyes suspiciously bright, Ruth continued. "Win put me in a bedroom at the front of the house, and I woke up about two in the morning. Thought I heard a noise outside on the driveway, so I got up to look out the window. Could have sworn I saw a figure gliding down the drive." She gave an exaggerated shiver. "There was something else…" Kate wondered what was coming. "I went downstairs to make myself a drink and check the windows. And then I smelt it – rosemary it was – in the dining room. So strong…" Her eyes met Kate's and they both looked at the journal. "My God! You don't think…?" Ruth shook her head and answered her own question. "Nah, that's too fanciful."

Kate wasn't so sure. She swallowed hard, and muttered, "Yes, you're right. It's too fanciful."

Ruth continued. "I told myself I'd imagined things, so didn't mention it to Win. I didn't want to put ideas in her head, she was stressed enough. I told her to fit an alarm and get a dog – I didn't like the thought of her alone out there. But then…well, you know what happened." Kate put an arm round the older woman's shoulders and they shared a silent moment.

Ruth's head spun round to face Kate. "Are you staying there on your own? I didn't mean to frighten you. You look a bit pale."

"Don't worry. I'm fine and I don't frighten easily." She gave Ruth's arm a squeeze. "I am on my own there, but the solicitors told me that all the locks have been checked. And I've done a self-defence course. I don't believe in ghosts and I'm not going to let anything or anybody frighten me away. I've always loved that house." Kate hoped she sounded convincing. She wasn't really sure what she believed. Her words must have worked, because Ruth's face relaxed.

"Good girl. Win wanted you to have the house. She always said you loved it as much as she did." Ruth carried on gathering the papers, then held them out to Kate. Before releasing them, she cocked her head to one side and gave Kate a speculative look.

"May I ask a favour, Kate?"

"Of course. You've done so much with this stuff. Saved me hours of work. What would you like me to do?"

"A lady I know needs help with some old family documents. Only, I've got so much on at the moment at work...and as you're a qualified historian, well, I thought you might be able to—"

"Of course I'll help. It'll give me something else to think about, and it means I'll get to know somebody else around here. What's her name and address?"

Ruth grinned. "You're a good girl, Kate. Win always said so. Sue Pellow is going through a bit of a tough time at the moment, so she'll appreciate any help you can give her. It might even take her mind off things. She's been such a support to the library in the past that I've felt bad about not being able to return the favour."

A little while later, with the journal, Ruth's copious notes, and Sue Pellow's contact details packed in her bag, Kate departed for home.

Chapter Eight

There was still no car outside Tom's cottage as Kate turned up her drive. She shook her head. Trust her to be living next door to one of the rudest men she'd ever met – well, nearly the rudest, she modified – some of the academics she'd dealt with had tried her patience. Not to mention that tech tycoon, whose family tree she'd done... he'd been well-nigh impossible with his demands. Maybe Tom was just an averagely rude person. She giggled and briefly enjoyed herself coming up with pigeon holes of annoyance that she could fit ex-acquaintances in.

Going straight to the study, she settled down to examine the journal in detail, comparing it with Ruth's transcription. By the time she finished, she knew Ruth had done an excellent job. There were no glaring mistakes, just minor errors with the odd word – not surprising, as some entries looked as if they'd been scribbled in haste and were decidedly difficult to decipher. Kate gathered the papers and placed them with the journal in the desk drawer. Stretching back in her chair, arms behind her head, she went over everything that Ruth had told her, especially the bits about Win and the scent of rosemary. She involuntarily sniffed the air... Nothing. It was just coincidence that the journal had contained a sprig of the same plant, surely? No, it had been Ruth's talk of the break-ins, and the attempted theft of the portrait that really made her feel uneasy.

Kate stiffened and jerked upright. The portrait. Where was it? It should have been in the drawer. She checked again. No, it wasn't there. Bloody hell! Had someone got in while she'd been out? She looked at the lock. It looked intact, no sign that it had been tampered with. *Think, think. Did I put it somewhere else?* She shot off her chair and raced across the small hallway to check the dining room, panic scratching at her insides. It wasn't there. She knew she hadn't moved it. Trying to control the growing sensation of nausea and fear, she sank down on to the sofa to take a few deep breaths, before recommencing her search.

She got up and started pulling open the sideboard drawers, shuffling the books on the shelves, even sweeping the cushions off the sofa in the sitting room. All to no avail. The portrait was not there. A further heart-pounding inspection of the entire ground floor confirmed that all the windows and the front door were locked and showed no signs of being tampered with. Had somebody got a key? The solicitor had assured her that she had the only set.

Frustrated and angry, and not a little frightened, Kate perched at the kitchen table while she waited for the kettle to boil. She needed time to think. The guy in the art shop, the previous attempted burglaries, being chased in Oxford – could they all be connected?

But Win had never reported anything stolen, Kate told herself. There was no sign of a break-in now…and there was still a niggling doubt that she might have moved it herself. With the meagre amount of sleep she was getting, she could be doing anything. It wasn't beyond the realms of possibility that it had been safely stowed away and she just couldn't remember where. A groan escaped her – upstairs was the place to check, a prospect that did not appeal at all. It would have to wait until tomorrow. With luck, a few hours sleep might even restore her memory of where she'd hidden it.

Kate poured the boiling water onto the herbal teabag and took the mug upstairs. She flicked the bedroom light on and stopped dead in the doorway. The portrait was on her dressing table, propped up against the mirror. Kate had no recollection of putting it there. Convinced that she was suffering from some sort of amnesia, she picked it up with a shaking hand. Her nose twitched… A faint smell of rosemary hung in the air. She frowned. If this sort of thing continued, she was going to have to see a doctor, to get herself something to help her sleep.

"How did you get here?" she murmured. "Did I move you?" The eyes of the gentleman in the portrait gazed silently back into hers. The mattress gave as she sat down on the side of her bed to sip her drink. She racked her brain trying to recall everything she'd done that morning. She knew she hadn't moved the portrait. Someone must have a key to the house. But if it was the portrait they were after, why hadn't they taken it? Nothing made sense.

Her lips pursed. Could someone be trying to scare her? Force her out. That was a possibility. Her knuckles whitened round the handle of her mug. Well, she'd soon put a stop to that. First thing in the morning, she'd arrange for a locksmith to come and change the locks. Nobody was going to spook her and drive her away. Feeling pleased that she'd worked it out, she replaced the portrait on the dressing table, secured the door of her bedroom with a chair placed under the handle, and left her phone within easy reach, before getting ready for bed.

Nobody's going to make a fool out of me.

Sleep, however, was fragmentary and elusive. There were more disturbing dreams of being trapped, of stumbling in woodland in the dark, of needing to meet someone – but that someone was always just out of reach. By five o'clock Kate decided to call it quits and got up. A glance at the dressing table told her the portrait was still there. She let out a breath. She was not going mad, and no hands – ghostly or otherwise – had moved it. Before going downstairs, Kate moved it into the top drawer of the dressing table, hiding it carefully beneath a layer of folded tops. Her conviction grew that someone up to mischief was playing games with her.

Crunching the last of her toast and marmalade, and coffee mug in hand, she padded to the study to look up local locksmiths on the internet. There were several in Falmouth. As early as she dared, she rang the one she liked the look of, and after a brief conversation, the lady at the other end assured Kate that her husband would be able to sort things out.

"Don't worry, dear. My Joe will get round to you by lunchtime. We always make our lady customers a priority." Although delighted that it could be sorted so quickly, Kate cynically concluded that business must be slow.

Her next phone call was to Sue Pellow, the lady Ruth had asked her to help. Sue sounded nice, though a little harassed. She said it would be wonderful if Kate could come round the following day, and that she would have everything ready for her. Pleased that she'd sorted two pressing matters, Kate settled down to work in the study.

Joe Rawlins bowled up in his transit van as Kate was about to make herself some lunch. He didn't need to knock, the spluttering and bangs coming from the exhaust announced his arrival well before he knocked on the front door.

"Sorry about that; getting a new exhaust fitted tomorrow." He grinned, wafting away the pungent diesel fumes with his flat cap. He was a slightly built, middle aged chap with a cheery, comforting manner. "Don't you worry, miss. Soon have this sorted. Mind you, this lock looks pretty secure to me," he said, examining the front door.

"Oh, I haven't had a break in. I think someone's got a duplicate key and has been getting in when I'm out." Kate thought she'd better tell him straight what she thought the problem was.

"That's not good, is it?" He tutted and shook his head. "Right, I'll do this one first and…did you want the back door doing?"

"Yes, and the patio windows in the drawing room."

"Leave it with me. Couldn't make me a cup of tea, could you, love? Fair parched I am. Been out since eight and the previous job was a commercial property over in Penrhyn, so I haven't had a drink since I left home."

"No problem," said Kate, grinning to herself as she left him to get on with things. She'd make him tea all afternoon if he sorted the locks out, and she could begin to feel safer.

A couple of hours later, six new keys lay on the kitchen table, two for each door. Joe had also replaced the bolts on the front and back doors. To Kate's untutored eyes they looked more substantial than the previous specimens. The bill he handed her was also substantial, but she reckoned it was worth it for peace of mind.

I'll have to cut down on a few luxuries like food, books, and gin. Never mind.

Feeling a lot happier, she made herself some supper and settled down in the drawing room to read. The TV was on, but the sound was muted so she could read in peace. For some reason, she always enjoyed the sense of company it gave her, even if she was ignoring it. Her lack of sleep the night before meant it wasn't long before her eyelids drooped. When she woke up her neck was stiff. Falling asleep on the sofa was not a good idea. Her book was on the floor, and in the corner, the screen was silently flickering. A glance told her it was an old episode of *Friends*. She rolled her eyes when she saw the time on her phone. Had she really been asleep that long? It was two in the morning. But she should be grateful that she'd got any sleep at all. She stretched, trying to get the feeling back into her feet. *Better get upstairs to bed. No point staying down here.*

She heaved herself up and hobbled over to unplug the TV, wincing at the pins and needles in her feet. A movement outside caught her eye. The curtains were still undrawn and moonlight illuminated the driveway and front garden. She slipped behind the curtain and peered out. In the trees at the edge of the drive something moved.

Kate held her breath as a figure stepped out of the trees.Whoever it was moved in a furtive way, stopping and starting, as if afraid of being discovered. But what set Kate's pulse racing was the fact that the figure appeared to be wearing a cloak – it was as if a drawing from a history book had stepped off the pages and come alive. The cloaked figure moved into a shaft of moonlight and that's when Kate gasped. She could see straight through the apparition to the trees and shrubs beyond. As if aware that it was being observed, the figure turned and an arm beckoned, gesturing Kate to follow. Kate swallowed. *Not bloody likely.* She blinked hard and looked again. The figure had vanished, and the driveway was deserted.

Kate stepped back from the window and drew the curtain across, still not quite believing what she'd seen. It had to be someone playing a trick. She considered calling the police and reporting a prowler, then decided she'd be better off waiting until morning. Whoever it was wouldn't be able to get into the house, not with the new locks, and besides, if they tried again she would be ready for them. She checked one more time that everywhere was secure and headed up to bed. Once upstairs, she placed the chair against the door again, and after preparing for bed, switched off all the lights. Going over to the window, she peered through the curtains, but couldn't see very much, the moon now being obscured by clouds. Her hearing told her that nothing was stirring outside, only the odd hoot of an owl in the distance a reminder that some creatures were awake. She shivered and returned to her bed. It was some time before she fell asleep.

Chapter Nine

Stifling a yawn, Kate stood on the doorstep of the imposing house on the outskirts of Falmouth, gazing around while she waited for someone to answer her knock. Set in its own grounds, the house was surrounded by shrubs and trees, with a large lawn to the front. The gardens looked rather more manicured than those of The Beeches, the uniform lines on the lawn indicating that it had recently been mown.

That morning, she'd woken up late for a change and had embarrassedly telephoned Sue Pellow to apologise, telling her she would be around in half an hour. Thankfully, Sue had been very understanding and had told her not to worry. In the cold light of morning, Kate had also decided not to notify the police of the weird sighting of the night before. She was sure they'd write her off as an over-imaginative female. Besides, there was no sign of an attempted break-in. She told herself to forget it. *I was half asleep anyway. Probably did imagine it.*

The door behind her opened, and she turned to see a trim, casually-dressed woman about the same age as her own mother, in her fifties, at a guess.

"Mrs Pellow? I'm Kate." She held out her hand to the lady, who was now smiling broadly.

"Oh, Sue, please... Mrs Pellow makes me feel quite ancient. Do come in, Kate. I'm so glad you were able to find time to help me. I hope this is not too inconvenient for you, only the mornings are best for me at the moment." As she spoke, she ushered Kate down the hallway into a large, pleasant kitchen that opened out into a conservatory, where two faded sofas faced each other across a large wooden coffee table. "I thought we might be more comfortable in here. This room catches the afternoon sun, so it's nice and cool in the mornings. My daughter Laura enjoys sitting here when she's feeling well enough."

"Oh, is your daughter ill, then?"

Sue nodded. "Yes, that's right, I'm afraid. Poor Laura has ME. I don't know if you've heard of it?" She sent Kate a challenging look through narrowed eyes.

Kate vaguely remembered reading something about it in the press. "Isn't that what they call yuppie flu?"

Sue sucked in her cheeks and Kate knew she'd said something to upset the older woman.

"That name is part of the problem. Nobody takes it seriously, not even doctors."

Kate shifted in her seat. "I'm terribly sorry. I had no idea. Is she very ill?"

Sue's face immediately crumpled. "It's not your fault, dear. You weren't to know. Most people are unaware of how serious it is." Sue sat down on one of the sofas and gestured for Kate to sit beside her. "Poor Laura has had to deal with a lot, on top of feeling really ill. Anyway, she's living here with me and my husband at the moment." Sue sighed. "Laura can't do much for herself, bless her. She's had to give up her job. She was a teacher and a bloody good one too. Now she's pretty much house-bound. On her rare good days you wouldn't guess she was ill just by looking at her. But if she overdoes things, she pays for it later. She's so ill she can't talk or stand any noise or light. It's terrible." Sue rubbed at her eyes.

"Good grief, it sounds awful. How do you manage? Is there any treatment?"

Sue shook her head. "No, no treatment yet. But we're hopeful. Thankfully I'm retired and Martin will be retiring soon...and we get a lot of support from our son now he's moved back down here. He's very close to his sister, which is nice." She smiled apologetically. "Anyway, that's enough of my problems. Sorry for my little rant. Shall I make us a cup of tea, or would you prefer coffee, and then we can make a start?" She leaned over and picked up a box from the side of the sofa and placed it on the coffee table. "I'm sure you're anxious not to spend too long on my silly little project."

"Nonsense, no need to apologise. I'm looking forward to seeing what you've got for me. Tea, please, white no sugar." Kate pulled the box towards her as Sue stood up to make the tea. Before she made it to the kitchen, Sue's phone rang.

"Will you excuse me a moment, Kate? That's Laura. She needs me to help her with something. I won't be long."

"Not a problem. Shall I put the kettle on?" Kate put the box down.

"Will you, dear? I'll be two ticks."

Sue disappeared upstairs and Kate went into the kitchen to find the kettle. She gazed round for a moment – it was sleek but cluttered and reminded her a little of the kitchen at the Beeches. The cupboards were done in a similar farmhouse style, but these were more modern, painted a fashionable pale grey. A black range cooker stood in an alcove. Kate eyed it enviously. On the wooden countertops stood a blender, a food processor and a large Dualit toaster – all evidently well-used. Stainless steel pans hung from a rack above the central island. It was obvious that the lady of the house enjoyed cooking.

Kate was filling the kettle when the sound of the front door slamming, followed by hurried footsteps coming nearer, made her stop what she was doing. She wondered if it was Sue's husband returning home and turned, ready to greet him.

"What the bloody hell are you doing here?" Tom's eyes sparked with anger as he stalked towards her.

Kate looked up and her mouth fell open. *What's he doing here?*

Before she knew it, he'd wrenched the half-filled kettle from her hand, and pointed to the door. "Get out. I don't know what your game is, but it's over, lady. Did *she* send you?"

Kate, dazed by this sudden verbal attack, and intimidated by his towering presence, was in the hallway before she found her voice. "Look. I don't know what you think, but I'm not going anywhere."

The whole situation was bizarre. What was he even doing in the house? She decided to call Sue.

"Mrs Pellow! Sue! There's a strange man in your house. He's trying to get me to leave."

A head appeared over the bannisters from the upstairs landing. "Tom! For goodness sake, what are you doing? Kate, are you all right?"

Sue hurried down the stairs and glared at Tom, who was still sending Kate glowering looks from the kitchen doorway. It dawned on Kate that Sue knew Tom's name. Did he normally go bowling into people's houses manhandling their guests? Was he the local eccentric that everybody knew, but no-one mentioned?

"Kate, I'm t...t...terribly sorry." Sue looked stricken. "This is my son, Tom. Tom, what were you thinking?"

"Mum, you don't know who she is." He was still angry and apparently not a whit embarrassed by his mother's admonition. His eyes blazed into Kate's. "I've bumped into her three times this week, that's more than coincidence. I think Eve is behind this."

Kate was trying to puzzle out who had actually bumped into who, and wondering who Eve was, when Sue spoke. "Tom, Ruth Morris at the library asked Kate to help me. She's a historian. Win, that nice lady who lived at The Beeches, mentioned her name to me once at one of the fundraisers for the library. Why on earth would you think Eve is behind this?"

Kate squared her shoulders, annoyed with herself that she'd been about to head to the front door, when she saw Tom's expression change from anger to uncertainty. He glanced at Sue, who was shaking her head.

"Oh God." He slumped against the doorframe. "I'm... I'm so sorry. I don't know what to say."

"Do you mind if I sit down? I've had a few too many surprises recently." Kate's legs were shaking, and her heart was thumping in her chest.

Sue took her by the hand and led her back into the conservatory, pushing her gently but firmly down on the sofa.

"Sit there, dear. I'll make some tea, and when Tom is recovered he can come and explain. I don't know what came over him." She shook her head. "That awful woman has a lot to answer for."

Sue returned to the kitchen and Kate was left on her own to wonder who 'that awful woman' was. The sight of Tom looming over her, his face like thunder, kept replaying in her mind. *What the hell was he thinking?* The sound of whispered conversation in the kitchen drifted through to where she was sat. Sue's soothing tones could be heard, apparently trying to reassure her son that Kate was not a threat.

Who on earth does he think I am?

Ten minutes later, Sue bustled in, followed by a sheepish Tom.

"Here we are. A nice cup of tea and some biscuits. They're homemade, Kate, please try one." Sue gave wobbly smile as she offered Kate a plate. It was obvious she was desperate to make amends for her son's behaviour. Sue was a sweet lady with enough problems, Kate told herself, so she resolved not to make a fuss in her presence...but she would have a word or three to say to Tom in private.

They all drank their tea, Sue gamely trying to chatter as if nothing was the matter, while Tom sat taciturn near the window.

After a few minutes of laboured conversation, Sue put her cup down on the table. "I'll just go and check on Laura."

Kate was grateful for her diplomacy. As soon as she'd gone, she tackled him. "Do you mind telling me what that was all about?"

"It's a long story." He had his head down, as if he didn't want to meet her eye.

"I've got all day." *Bloody man.* He wasn't going to wriggle out of an explanation for his atrocious behaviour.

He shifted in his seat. "I saw your car on the drive – I recognised it as yours from the other night. Couldn't think why you'd be round here, you having just moved in and all. And then... Well... I thought my ex-fiancée was putting you up to tricks. It's the kind of thing she would do."

"I can assure you, nobody has put me up to anything." Kate words came out through clenched teeth. "But I agree, we do seem to have been falling over each other since I arrived. I think you're quite rude, if you really want to know. I'd be perfectly happy to avoid you, even though you are my nearest neighbour."

He looked up then, with something like shock in his brown eyes. Kate was gratified that her words had had some impact. *Probably used to girls fawning over him all the time, if what the waitress had said was true. Conceited sod.*

"Look. I've apologised," he said. "In my defence, I can only say that I'm under a lot of stress at the moment, what with Laura, and Mum, and Dad, and everything."

"Well, you're not the only one under stress, mate. So think on." Kate considered his excuse feeble in the extreme. She was having to deal with break-ins, creeps following her, and bloody ghosts, for goodness' sake. "Anyway," she continued before he could reply, "I'm going. Please tell your mum I'll come back tomorrow, if that's all right with her. She's got my number if she wants to re-arrange." She pulled herself up to her full height and stalked out. He made no attempt to talk her out of it. She was still fuming when she got to her car.

"Bloody men!"

Chapter Ten

Kate woke up early the following day. She'd suffered another disturbed night of bad dreams, which she now put down to being churned up by Tom's irrational behaviour and her lingering guilt at leaving without giving Sue an explanation. Even though she'd telephoned Sue when she'd got home, and Sue had been very understanding, it rankled that she'd been impolite.

"I know what it's like to be under stress, Kate, so don't worry. It would be lovely if you came round tomorrow, but don't feel you have to. Tom wasn't himself this morning. All I can say is that he doesn't normally go round trying to throw out my visitors. I thought he was getting over things…" Kate heard Sue sniff, then she continued. "I can't say too much, Kate…only that he went through a bad time not long ago. I promise you, he really is a very nice person."

Yeah, right, was the first thought that popped into Kate's head. But she couldn't ignore the hidden plea in Sue's voice. "Of course I'll come back, Sue. See you tomorrow." She would put the whole stupid episode behind her. It would take more than Sue's obnoxious son to stop her from helping someone out. The puzzle was, she'd seen a whole different side to him when he'd called round the other night – a softer, caring side. What had happened that made him mistrustful and downright rude?

Kate arrived at Sue's on the dot of ten. There was no sign of Tom. In fact, the morning went quickly and after initially feeling edgy in case he appeared, Kate relaxed and enjoyed Sue's lively chatter as they went through the documents and letters. The papers were mostly to do with Sue's father's army career, and being legible and in reasonable condition, they were easy to read and organise.

"There's a lot more up in the attic. Stuff of my grandmother's and even older. I'm not even sure it all relates to my family. I've never gone through them. Do you think...?" Sue bit her lip and looked guilty. "Oh, I shouldn't presume, I'm sorry."

Kate grinned. "Tell you what. Why don't you dig them out and bring them round to mine? I'll catalogue them on my computer and give you printouts, or copy them to a memory stick, whichever you prefer. I can't promise I'll be quick though, but if you don't mind waiting?"

Sue's eyes lit up. "Oh Kate, you're an angel. Are you absolutely sure? I feel I'm taking terrible advantage of you. There must be some way I can repay you."

"You could invite me round for Sunday lunch sometime." Kate was aghast that Sue was considering paying her. She was doing this as a favour for Ruth's hard work.

"Are you sure?" Sue looked uncertain. "It doesn't seem much."

"Yes, of course. I miss Mum's cooking and I'm hopeless at making gravy."

"Well, Tom and Laura always say I do a decent Sunday roast, so I'll be happy to have you round."

It was getting on for two o'clock before Kate packed her things and headed home. As she turned up the drive to The Beeches, she saw that Tom's car was again absent. *He must be keeping clear of me*, she thought, feeling smug. Her eyes widened as she saw what was propped up against her front door.

She parked the car at the side of the house, then hurried round to the front to retrieve the large bouquet of flowers, wondering who had sent them. It wasn't her birthday, so they weren't from Mum and Dad. She opened the card and shook her head. The message was short and to the point.

Sorry for being a dick. Tom.

Hmmm, he'd delivered them knowing she'd be out, so he wasn't prepared to apologise in person. She blew out a breath. It would take more than a bunch of flowers to convince her he was not a dick. Nevertheless, they were too good to put in the dustbin. She took them in, found a vase, and plonked them in the hall.

Next morning, Kate woke up around seven, feeling much better, and prepared to face the day. She'd only woken once in the middle of the night, disturbed by the recurring nightmare of being trapped. She checked the drawer on the way to the bathroom, as she'd done every morning since hiding the portrait. Yes, it was still there. At least one thing that had been bothering her now appeared to be sorted.

Dressed and ready to do some work, she skipped downstairs to get some breakfast, then halted in the hallway. She sniffed – the scent of rosemary was so strong it made her screw her nose up. *Good grief.* She examined the bouquet in the vase thoroughly, but found nothing that pungent nestling amongst the artfully composed stems of roses, anemones, and ranunculus. She must be imagining it. Either that, or Win had secreted something that she hadn't managed to find yet. But why did the scent come and go? She couldn't think of a valid reason. Feeling slightly rattled, Kate hurried into the kitchen and started to make herself some breakfast. Her mind was going round in circles.

Outside, the sound of car wheels crunching on the gravel drew her attention. Through the window, she saw a large Volvo estate pull up behind her Mini. Sue climbed out. She went round to the car's boot and started to heft what looked like a large bag. Kate could tell it was heavy by Sue's strained expression, so she rushed out to lend a hand.

"Hi! How are you?" She hid her surprise at the unexpected visit.

Sue looked up and stopped what she was doing. "Hello, Kate. Sorry to barge in on you so early. I was going to call in on Tom first, but his car's not there, so I came straight to you. Don't suppose you've seen him, have you?" She hauled the bag out and was starting to drag it along the ground. "I stupidly added more stuff to this after I'd got it into the boot." She paused to take a breath. "Didn't realise it would be so bloomin' heavy."

Kate grinned and grabbed one of the handles. "Here, let me. We'll manage it between us. No, I haven't seen Tom at all." Together they got the bag up the steps and into the hall, Kate thinking it curious that Tom hadn't told his mum how acrimoniously they'd parted. "I haven't seen him since... well, since he tried to throw me out." Kate saw the fleeting look of disappointment on Sue's face. Had she been expecting them to now be the best of friends? *Fat chance.* "Come in and I'll make you a coffee. By the time you've finished he might be back." She wasn't going to let Sue know either. The poor woman had enough problems without being told what an arse her son was.

Sue looked unsure. "I was just going to drop this stuff off. I don't want to be a nuisance."

Kate touched Sue's arm. "Come on, I was just making myself a drink. Five minutes." It would be nice to have some company for a change.

"All right then, though I must be home by half-nine. Can't leave Laura for too long." Sue followed Kate into the kitchen and sat down at the table. "This is nice," she said, looking round. "I've always wondered what it was like inside. Seventeenth century, isn't it?"

"Mmm, yes, mostly...though one wing is more recent, eighteenth century." Kate had a sudden impulse. "Would you like a tour?"

"Oh, yes please." Sue's enthusiastic agreement told Kate she'd done the right thing.

She left the coffee to brew and took Sue round the ground floor. They'd just entered the dining room when Sue commented. "What a lovely smell... Rosemary, isn't it?" Sue was looking out of the the window, and she turned when Kate didn't reply. "Are you all right, Kate? You've gone white as a sheet."

Kate pulled out the nearest chair from the table and sat down with a thud. *It must be real if Sue can smell it.* The thought hit her like a punch to the gut.

Sue moved nearer and crouched down on her haunches. She frowned and took Kate's hand. "You look as if you've had a bit of a shock. Stay there and I'll fetch a glass of water. Try putting your head between your knees if you feel faint." Kate watched numbly as Sue stood up and rushed off to the kitchen. A minute later she was back and handed Kate a glass. Kate managed a few sips, but she was shaking so badly, most of it went on her jeans. Sue was watching her, her brow furrowed and a questioning look in her eyes. Kate decided she needed to say something, but was not entirely sure what she could say that would not make her seem like a complete idiot. An apology might be a good first step.

"Sorry about that, Sue. Didn't mean to give you a fright. I'm ok now, honest."

"Well, there's a bit of colour coming back into your cheeks. But I think you might want to see a doctor if this happens a lot. I thought you were going to pass out there. You might be anaemic. Or," Sue's cheeks flushed, "you don't think you might be…"

Kate almost choked. "Definitely not. I haven't— Well, never mind." She was not going to give Sue specifics about her lack of a love life. "It's just that…it's just that…" She paused as a wave of fear swept over her, overwhelming her resolve to stay strong: the smell of rosemary, the strange figure on the drive, the guy in the shop, the break-ins. "Oh bugger."

Kate dissolved into tears.

Half an hour later, Sue knew everything.

"But why didn't you report that chap to the police? They'd have put a stop to all this nonsense he's been putting you through. Though at least you had the sense to change the locks."

Kate felt like a five year old – it all sounded so reasonable when Sue put it like that.

"It wasn't quite that simple." Kate felt compelled to justify her inaction. "I didn't know the guy in Oxford was connected to any of this. I only spotted him in Falmouth a couple of days ago, and I'm not completely sure he's linked to the break-ins here – though it does all seem a bit too coincidental. I've been tired too, not thinking straight."

"Why's that?" Sue cocked her head to one side, like a mother hen observing one of her chicks. They were now sitting at the kitchen table, both clutching mugs of hot sweet tea, courtesy of Sue; she'd insisted it was the best thing for shock

"I've been having terrible nightmares. I've barely had an unbroken night's sleep since I got here." Kate grimaced, certain that Sue would think her a complete wimp. It was such a pathetic excuse.

"You poor dear. Is there anywhere else you can stay?" Kate gave her a rebellious look. "Just for a night or two, see if it helps. It's worth a try if you're nervous about staying here."

"I wasn't nervous at all to begin with. That's what's so odd. It's just…" Kate thought about it. Maybe Sue had a point. "I suppose I could stay at Mum and Dad's flat in Falmouth. But only for a night. Nobody is chasing me away from my house." She was adamant about that. Once she was rested she'd be able to deal with things, she told herself.

"I tell you what, Kate. I've had an idea." The gleam in Sue's eyes made Kate wonder what she was about to say. "I'll ask Tom to stay here tonight, if you're going to be away. He'll sort out anyone who turns up. He's got a black belt, you know."

Kate's heart plummeted. She was pretty sure Tom would not want to get involved in anything concerning her, and she wasn't too sure she wanted him wandering round her house either. The less she had to do with him the better. Then she remembered the flowers.

But that was an easy gesture, she told herself – meaningless, and probably prompted by his mother.

"Oh, no need to bother him, Sue. I'm sure he's far too busy." Kate's protest landed on deaf ears.

Sue grinned back at her, obviously pleased with her solution. "You leave it with me."

Chapter Eleven

By mid-morning, Sue had sorted everything. Kate had never known someone so managing before, not even her own mother, who could be pretty dictatorial when she wanted. Sue wasn't unpleasantly domineering – she just had a way of persuading and cajoling that, before Kate knew it, she'd agreed to do exactly what Sue suggested. To her dismay, she'd also been inveigled into accepting an invitation to Tom's for dinner.

"He insisted, Kate. Said he'd be happy to stay over tonight while you're away. He'll bring a sleeping bag and camp on the sofa, so no need to worry about making up a bed for him. And he said he'll cook you a meal before you go off to your flat, to make up for the other day's unpleasantness." Sue looked very pleased with herself as she put her phone away.

Kate had listened with growing horror as Sue had outlined her plans to Tom, and apparently he had not objected. She hadn't heard Sue ask more than once, that was for sure. Why was he being so helpful, even inviting her for dinner, when they couldn't stand the sight of each other?

After Sue left, Kate filled the rest of her day trying unsuccessfully to do some work. Several times she'd been on the point of calling Tom to cancel their evening appointment. Each time, she'd remembered the look on Sue's face as she'd left, blissfully happy that Kate and her son had apparently smoothed over their misunderstanding. She was only doing it for Sue's sake, Kate told herself. She'd give him one last chance.

Kate slung her overnight bag into the boot of the Mini and drove the short distance down to Tom's cottage. *This is a big mistake*, she thought, getting out of the car and heading for the front door. Through the leaded windows she glimpsed Tom moving about in the front room. He looked up, saw her, and had the door open before she reached the front step.

"Welcome to my humble abode." He waved her in with a mock bow. Kate rolled her eyes. Now he was making fun of her. She almost turned and went back out again. He must have sensed her antagonism, for he added, "I think we got off on the wrong foot the other day."

Well, that's an understatement. "*We* did, didn't we? What on earth did you think you were doing, trying to throw me out?"

As he guided her forward into the living room, she was gratified to see he was looking a little sheepish. Perhaps he wasn't as confident as he was trying to appear. "Come in and let me explain. I feel pretty stupid about it."

Kate gave a grunt of disbelief, then paused in the living room doorway as she took in her surroundings… Stone walls, beams, large inglenook fireplace, and comfortable sofas. It was her idea of the perfect cottage.

"This is…lovely." Her words were inadequate, she knew. The room was delightful, expensively furnished, but comfortable, and if she'd had the design brief, it was exactly what she would have chosen.

His face flushed with pleasure. "It is nice, isn't it? Living in London, I got bored with soulless, minimalist apartments, so I went for something with a bit of character. I thought if it was going to be my workplace and my home, it might as well look exactly how I wanted it to be."

Blimey, looks like Mr Grumpy actually has taste… My taste. The thought gave Kate a jolt. She was not going to succumb to his charm just because they shared the same opinions on interior design. That would be stupid. She reminded herself that he still not forgiven. Then her eyes widened. "Wow. You've got some really nice pieces." She was drawn like a magnet to a magnificent oak book case taking up nearly the whole of one wall.

"My parents let me root through their attic. I got some bits and pieces from them, and that came from an antique shop in London. It cost a shed-load, but I love it." Pride was evident in his voice. "One of the lads I went to school with has a second-hand furniture business – not quite antiques, but not rubbish either. He lets me know when he's going to a house clearance. I got my dining chairs that way."

Something clicked in her brain. He'd said parents. Or had she got it wrong?

"Why is your surname different to Sue's? Has she remarried? I'd no idea you were her son."

He bit his lip and ran a hand through his hair. "It's a bit embarrassing, actually. Carbis is Mum's maiden name. I use it to try and make it difficult for my ex to find me. Of course, she knows my parents are in Falmouth, but she doesn't know I came down here to help out with Laura. She's a bit of a nightmare, my ex. To put it mildly."

Kate's jaw dropped. "Good grief, really? Was Eve your ex?" She remembered Sue had mentioned he'd been through a tough time. Things must be bad, if he was resorting to changing his name. And it explained a lot about his behaviour.

He sucked in his cheeks, then nodded. "Yes, took me a while to realise what sort of person she was. But anyway..." He looked away, and for a moment Kate thought he was going to confide some more details, but when he turned back there was a smile on his face – a devastating smile that caused butterflies in Kate's stomach. "That's enough of her, come with me and I'll show you round." His tone was firm, even though there was the hint of a twinkle in his eye.

Kate decided not to pursue the subject; talking about his ex was definitely out of bounds. On the plus side, Kate thought that if he continued to remain this charming, she would be perfectly happy to leave that subject alone.

He led her across the flagstone hall to the dining room. This too had an inglenook. Furnished in dark woods, and with plastered walls painted a deep red, it oozed atmosphere.

"This was originally two cottages," he explained. "I think they were knocked into one about fifty years ago. The couple

I bought it off spent a lot of money upgrading it and used it as a second home. Luckily for me, they decided it wasn't quite big enough, and when it came on the market, Dad rang me and I came racing down. Made my mind up the same day."

"Are you always that impetuous?" Kate grinned. She was seeing a whole different side to him.

"Occasionally. When something feels absolutely right." He looked at her sideways. "Sometimes, it just hits you, doesn't it? As soon as I stepped in the door it felt like home, even though the furnishings were all 'Footballers' Wives', you know?"

Kate giggled. "Gold taps?"

"Not quite, but the original floorboards were covered with carpet. White, would you believe? Chrome-embellished coffee tables, and the largest leather sofa you've ever seen. It swamped the room, so it's no wonder they thought the house was too small."

Kate looked at the polished oak floorboards, lovingly restored, yet still showing the nicks and scratches of great age. She shook her head. "How could they?" She wandered across the room to examine the books on the shelves. Books could tell a lot about a person. Maybe here she'd learn a bit more about the real Tom.

Her eyes scanned the spines. There were, unsurprisingly, a large number of technical computer manuals and business books – she spotted *Devil Take the Hindmost,* and *Extraordinary Popular Delusions,* and had no clue what they were about. But there were many that she did recognise: the classics of Dickens and Trollope, plus a complete set of *Rebus* novels shelved alongside volumes by Reginald Hill and Val McDermid. *Hmmm, something else we have in common.* The bottom shelf was filled with auction catalogues, a copy of *Art and Illusion,* and various other volumes on art history. Well, it was eclectic, she'd give him that.

While she'd been engrossed in deciphering his character through his reading materials, Tom had disappeared.

"Well, I hope you like steak."

His voice broke into her thoughts, and she abandoned her perusal of the shelves to go and find him. Standing in the doorway to the kitchen, she saw him frowning at two sizeable pieces of meat. He turned a panic-stricken face to her.

"Oh God... I forgot to check. You're not vegetarian, are you?"

Kate burst out laughing. "No, I'm not. What would you do if I said I was?"

"Looked for some eggs to go with the chips and salad!" He was smiling now. "I've opened a bottle of red to let it breathe. May I pour you a glass?"

"Yes, please, but just a small one as I'm driving." She looked at the black granite worktop, where two small plates of tomato and mozzarella salad were already prepared. The smell of basil was divine. "These look good. Shall I take them into the dining room for you?"

"If you don't mind. I'll bring the wine."

The evening is going far too well, thought Kate an hour or so later. Tom had cooked an impeccable meal, they'd chatted and joked, and he'd been the perfect host. If she wasn't too careful, she'd be another of his temporary conquests, she warned herself. No, she was not going to let that happen. She'd seen him surly and angry, she wasn't going to allow herself to be bowled over by this charm offensive. *And, my God, he can be charming.*

Tom was making coffee, and lost in her thoughts as she toyed with her almost empty wine glass, Kate didn't hear him return until he spoke, almost in her ear. "Here you are, one flat white, no sugar." Brushing close to her, he placed the cup on the table. She caught an appealing whiff of fresh soap and the slightest tang of aftershave. *He smells nice.*

With an effort, she turned and gave him a business-like smile. "That was a lovely meal, Tom. Thank you. I'd better just drink this and be on my way. Now, are you still set on spending the night at The Beeches? I know Sue must have bullied you into it, but please don't feel obliged. Lack of sleep made me a bit jumpy, that's all, and your mum caught me at a bad time."

He plonked down in his seat, gave her a hard stare, then shook his head. Kate just knew he was thinking 'stupid woman'.

"Look," he said, "I promised Mum I'd check things out and I will. One night on a sofa won't kill me. If someone is mucking around we'll know, and I'll report it to the police." His jaw tightened; she knew he meant what he said. "And by the way…Mum did not bully me." These last words were said in such a way that Kate understood there was a depth of hidden meaning behind them, but what that meaning was, she had no idea.

"Well, if you insist." Kate knew arguing would be futile. She scrabbled in her bag, found what she was looking for, and pushed her kitchen door key across the table to him. "Here you go, that's for the back door. Help yourself to tea and coffee, and anything you can find in the fridge if you get hungry."

He gave her a superior smile as his fingers closed round the key. "I'll post this through your letterbox if I don't see you tomorrow. Now let me clear these cups away and I'll see you out." He'd only been gone a moment when she heard him call from the kitchen. "Hey, are you expecting visitors? I can see lights over at your place."

She jumped up and joined him in the kitchen, where she found him leaning over the sink, peering out of the window. Through the trees of the woodland that bordered the end of his property, she caught a glimpse of a car's lights heading up the drive to her house. Kate looked at her watch. Eleven o'clock.

She frowned. "It's a funny time to call, wouldn't you say? My parents are away and besides, they would have called me first. So would anybody else for that matter." Then a thought struck her. "You don't think it could be…?" She didn't get a chance to finish.

"Right, phone the police. I'm going over there." Tom was

already reaching for a jacket hung behind the door, his face grim.

"No!" Without thinking, she grabbed his arm. "You might get hurt." He didn't pause to discuss it with her, but just removed her hand from his arm and pointed at the phone on the wall before heading for the door.

"Telephone now! I'll be fine."

Gobsmacked, she watched as his dark shape slipped through the garden, vaulted the fence and loped off into the trees. Trembling, she punched in the numbers, nine, nine, nine. She gave her location and explained the situation. The operator assured her that a car would be sent straight away. She waited, panic rising in her chest. What must have been only minutes felt like hours. She was on the point of setting off after Tom when there was a squeal of wheels. A car shot down the drive, headlights blazing as it turned up the road and down Penjerrick Hill towards Roscarrack Road. Would the police see it and stop the driver? There was no sign of Tom.

Kate pelted out the front door and, using her phone as a flashlight, stumbled her way up the drive. "Tom! Tom! Are you OK?" Her voice cracked. What if something dreadful had happened to him? Twigs snapped and a shape came staggering out of the darkness.

"Buggers got away," Tom growled, rubbing his knuckles. "Mind, one of them will have a black eye. I definitely made contact with his face when he was trying to jemmy your back door, but I didn't realise there were two of them. His mate caught me from behind, hit me with something."

Kate's shoulders sagged. Thank God, he was all in one piece. He rubbed the back of his head and by the light of her phone she saw his fingers glistening with something dark and wet.

"Let's get you inside and wait for the police." She grabbed Tom's arm and guided him to the front door. This time he didn't protest or try to escape her grip. Once inside, she pulled him down the hallway and into the kitchen, where he slumped down into a chair. There was some Dettol under the

77

sink, and soon she was dabbing at his head with a clean tea towel soaked in the pungent-smelling liquid. He winced as she touched him.

"Sorry. I'm afraid it'll sting." Once she'd taken a good look at his injury, she could see it wasn't as bad as she'd feared. Whoever had hit him, had caught him more on the neck than his skull.

"I suppose I'll survive. I've had worse on the rugby pitch. Some physios can be a bit brutal." He turned apologetic eyes up to her. "It's a pity. I didn't manage to catch them for you."

"Don't worry. I'm sure the police will be able to deal with it." She made her words brisk, not wanting to let him know how upset she was, when what she really wanted to do was wrap her arms round him. He'd taken a big risk trying to help her, and things could have ended up so much worse.

A flashing blue light and the sound of a car engine alerted them to the fact that the police had arrived. The two policewomen didn't stay long, but when Kate looked at her watch as they left it was nearly twelve thirty. They'd made a cursory tour of her house to check there was no-one hiding, and taken a few details from Tom. An abandoned crow bar had been discovered outside the kitchen door and bagged for fingerprints.

"Though they were probably wearing gloves," explained one of the policewomen, giving Tom a winsome smile. "Still, it's worth a go, just in case."

Unfortunately, Tom hadn't seen the car's registration number, but was almost certain it was a Mercedes. Kate's expectations of the culprits being caught plummeted.

"Look. There's no need for you to stay now. They're not likely to come back again tonight," she said, when she and Tom were on their own again. To be honest, she was also nettled by the policewomen's fawning over Tom – not that he'd encouraged them.

Bloody hell! I'm getting jealous. Get a grip, girl.

"Hmm. Think I'll stay in any case. Could be those burglars were someone else entirely."

"That'd be a bit of a coincidence, wouldn't it?"

78

The set of his jaw told her he would not be budged. "Well, I'm going to get my sleeping bag. I said I'd stay and I will. You go and get a good night's sleep in Falmouth."

"Oh have it your way then."

Arrogant man. Impossible man. Bloody gorgeous man.

Chapter Twelve

Wiping the sleep from her eyes, Kate scrabbled for her phone amongst the clutter on the bedside table and looked at the screen. She jerked upright. Good grief, she'd slept for nearly ten hours! She threw back the duvet and swung her legs over the side of the bed. How had she managed to sleep for so long? She'd arrived at the flat shortly after one, gone straight to bed…and enjoyed an undisturbed night of sleep, the first in some time. She definitely felt better for it, there was no doubt about that.

She picked up the glass of water from the bedside table and took a thoughtful sip of the now tepid liquid. The events of the previous day clamoured for attention in her mind – for one day, there had certainly been a lot of them. The biggest surprise for her, apart from the burglars of course, had been Tom. He'd shown a completely different side to his character, and in fact, she'd enjoyed his company far more than she'd been expecting to – although he did have a tendency to think he knew best. She clenched her jaw, remembering how he'd gone charging up to tackle the burglars. It could have gone badly wrong. Then he'd still insisted on staying for the night. Her stomach gave a lurch. How had he got on? Had he seen the figure on the drive, or smelt rosemary? Putting the glass down, her hand went to reach for her phone. She itched to call him. But something stopped her. Calling him might make her appear weak and needy… Besides, he might think she was ready to be another conquest if she sounded too eager. Better play it cool, she decided.

Kate padded across the thick-pile carpet to the bathroom, still pondering about Tom. It was impossible to get the bloody man out of her head. His cottage hadn't been at all what she'd expected, in fact, she wasn't really sure what she had been expecting – something designed by an expensive interior designer, she supposed – not the warm, comfortable room filled with furniture, and items with special meaning for their owner, that had greeted her eyes. Stripping off her pyjamas, Kate dropped them on top of the wicker linen basket and stepped into the shower, letting the hot water stream over her hair and body. With her eyes shut, Tom's smiling face became clearer, his even white teeth and dark eyes that held a hint of mischief and laughter; how had he managed to keep that side of him hidden on their previous encounters? Last night he'd been funny, engaging, and she'd enjoyed his intelligent conversation.

She leaned back against the tiles and cracked open her eyes to locate the shampoo bottle. She poured some out, and lathered her hair, gently kneading her scalp – the gentle rhythm sent her thoughts running again back to Tom. What would it be like to kiss him, to feel his arms around her?

Kate was enjoying these thoughts when a sudden change in the water temperature put a halt to them. Damn! She'd forgotten how temperamental the shower thermostat could be. Her skin reacted to the now icy-cold water drenching her head and body and she quickly flicked the shower switch to the off setting. The waitress's warning about Tom rang in her head as she waited for the temperature to re-set, chilling her nearly as much as the cold water had done. She'd have to be careful or she'd be falling for him. She'd already been burned by her stupid involvement with Robin, though he hadn't been commitment-averse, rather the opposite – the problem being he was already committed to somebody else.

Tom's been engaged, so he's not always avoided commitment.

What had changed him? She remembered what he'd told her, albeit obliquely. Was his ex-fiancée the cause for his present aversion to long-term relationships?

Finishing her shower, Kate towelled herself off, brushed her teeth, and headed back into the bedroom to dress. She put on the jeans she'd worn the previous day and teamed them with a fresh linen top. Judging by the sight of the passers-by on the street below, most of them sporting skimpy tops, shorts, and sunglasses, it was going to be a scorcher of a day. She tucked her pyjamas back into her overnight bag and squinted out the window again, before cracking it open to let in some air. The quiet room was suddenly filled with the sounds of the busy street below, jarring her ears. The efficient double-glazing had sealed the bedroom from the noise – the flat being across the road from a lively pub, this was a necessity, especially at weekends and during the holiday season. A decent night's sleep had worked wonders on her nerves. She took a deep breath and leaned out to gaze up the road that led to the High Street and Jevson's shop. Her knuckles curled round the window ledge as she scanned the milling crowd. There were plenty of people about. She'd let things slide for too long.

Her mouth set in a firm line. It was time to tackle the guy in the art dealer's. What could he do in broad daylight?

After a breakfast of coffee and toast, made with bread she found in the freezer, she set off before she could change her mind. It didn't take long to reach the shop. It was open for business according to the sign on the door, and the painting that she'd admired had been changed for a sombre still life of fruit and flowers. Kate hovered on the opposite side of the road, considering her tactics. *First, check that the guy was in, then hang around until lunchtime.* She hoped he went out for lunch – she was not sure what she'd do if he remained in the shop all day. She wasn't keen on going in on her own, and would have to re-consider her options if he didn't come out. Kate strolled past once, head down under the brim of her straw sunhat and large sunglasses perched on her nose. She paused by the window, her heart hammering when she caught sight of him, or rather his profile, as he positioned a painting on the wall. He was engrossed in what he was doing, he didn't turn at all. She moved away quickly, heart still thumping in her chest as she planned her next move.

It was then she spotted the Phoenix coffee shop. It was a little run-down, but its location was ideal, being almost opposite Jevson's. She pushed at the door, whose paintwork looked as if it could do with some TLC, and went in. It was not quite what Kate was expecting. No one could accuse the decor of being trendy, and the equipment behind the counter had definitely seen better days. Gritting her teeth, Kate decided to go for it. She ordered a coffee from the woman behind the counter, and settled at a table from where she had a clear view of the art dealers' opposite. Despite the crowds outside, the cafe was not busy. Besides herself, an elderly couple at the next table were the only patrons. As she took a sip from her cup, Kate understood why. Stifling her grimace, she pulled her phone out of her bag and pretended to be engrossed.

The time crawled by, half an hour stretched to an hour. Kate was beginning to think the guy would not budge from the shop. After three cups of disgustingly bitter coffee and a round of tuna mayonnaise sandwiches, which were more mayonnaise than tuna, she was considering abandoning her post, when a familiar figure came striding down the road. Her heart gave a lurch. What was he doing here?

Tom was frowning when he stopped in front of Jevson's. Mesmerised, Kate watched as he shielded his eyes from the glare to peer through the glass into the shop. Then, evidently making his mind up, he marched through the open doorway. Kate gasped when she saw the door close behind him and the sign turn from open to closed.

"Everything all right, love?" a voice asked, jerking her out of her trancelike state. It was the woman who had served her earlier. Her straw-like, permed hair bobbed up and down as she scrubbed at the now empty adjacent table.

"Oh, yes thanks. I…err…thought I saw someone I knew, but I was mistaken. Nice coffee, by the way." God, why was she lying?

"Don't like coffee myself." The woman continued to spray the table with her cleaning fluid, in a futile attempt to erase the ingrained ketchup stains. "Prefer tea. But the boss says we have to have it these days. Says it's the future, he does."

"Mmm, really?" Kate was distracted by the sight of Tom

hurtling out of the shop door and marching back up the road. He was rubbing his knuckles. She gathered up her bag and grabbed her phone off the table.

"You haven't finished your coffee, love," called the woman as Kate made for the door.

Outside she hesitated. She wanted to follow Tom, whose dark head she could see getting further away amongst the crowds heading towards the Maritime Museum, but the door to the art dealer's had opened. The guy with the long hair was peering up and down the street. Interestingly, he was clutching his nose with a bloodstained handkerchief. Even more interesting was the fact that one of his eyes was black and bruised. That hadn't just happened.

Kate squared her shoulders and crossed the road towards him. It was now or never.

It took a few seconds before he noticed Kate heading in his direction. She'd taken off the hat and glasses and knew immediately when he recognised her, for his eyes widened in something like horror before he whirled round for the safety of the shop. She picked up her pace and stuck her foot in the door before he could slam it shut.

"We're closed." His public school vowels held a hint of panic.

"Not for me, you're not." There must have been something in that awful coffee, Kate thought. She wasn't normally this assertive. Or was she just being reckless? "I want to know what's going on, and you're going to tell me, or I'm calling the police."

"No, don't do that." The impression of good looks now vanished – close-up, his weak chin and insipid eyes, albeit that one was swollen, bruised, and nearly closed, were clearly evident. "Let me lock up and I'll come with you." His Adam's apple bobbed convulsively. "I don't want the police involved. I'll go inside if they find out, and Mummy will kill me."

Not wishing to point out the chronological impossibility of these events, Kate just grunted her affirmative, tapping her foot as he prepared to lock the shop. Her eyes lit on the neat pile of business cards on the counter, so she helped herself to one:

Rupert Gormley-Smith, Manager Falmouth Branch, Smith and Jevson, Art Dealers and Valuers.

Her insides started to jump. *Well, Rupert, are you going to spill the beans?* She watched as he picked up his suit jacket from behind the counter, slinging it over his shoulder. By its quality, she guessed it came from Savile Row. He plucked a bunch of keys hanging on a hook with his free hand, his other was still occupied staunching the blood dripping from his nose.

"Come on." Kate grasped his arm and directed him up Market Street, towards the Prince of Wales pier. Reassuringly, there were no hard muscles hidden beneath his shirt sleeve. Rupert it seemed, was no gym bunny. Nevertheless, she thought it wise to remain where it was busy, the pier should be the ideal location. She wasn't sure how she'd manage if he turned nasty, but with any luck he would not try anything in public. And steering clear of Tom also seemed a good idea – she'd tackle him later.

When they reached the pier, the St Mawes ferry had just departed, so while it was still fairly crowded there were a few vacant benches where they could sit and talk undisturbed. Kate chose one facing out across the inner harbour towards the Carrick Roads and distant views of St Mawes Castle over the sun-speckled sea. In any other circumstances it would present a charming view, but Kate was too churned up to appreciate it.

"Well, Mister Gormley-Smith, if that's your name, tell me what you've been up to. You followed me in Oxford and you've broken into my house. Why?" She glared at him as he shifted away, increasing the distance between them, his head down and shoulders slumped.

He started to mumble. "Yah, I'm Rupert. Rupes, actually, to my friends." Kate didn't try to hide her sneer. He caught her eye briefly and looked down again before continuing.

"David Smith is my uncle. It wasn't my idea… He made me do it. Him and his partner, Reggie Jevson." His words had a nasal twang, no doubt due to the misshapen state of his nose, which he dabbed at again before stuffing the stained handkerchief into the pocket of his trousers. He lifted his head and squinted at Kate with his one good eye.

"Why did they make you do it? I don't understand." Kate was getting impatient. Was she going to have to drag it out of him? His public-school drawl indicated an expensive education, but she'd already formed the impression that he was not the sharpest tool in the box.

"Uncle David wanted the painting – said he had to have it, it would make his reputation. The painting in that big house. Belonged to an old woman."

"Which big house? You mean Mrs Saunton's house?" Kate wondered what was so special about the painting; it hadn't looked anything out the ordinary to her. But then again, she was no art *aficionado*.

He nodded. "That's right. Anyway, the old biddy wouldn't sell it. Unc's main shop is in Truro, but he wants to get a foothold in London…where the big boys are, he says. Promised me a holiday in Verbier if things went well. Said he'd forget about the drugs thing if I helped him out. It was only a bit of coke anyway, nothing heavy. Think the judge just wanted to make an example of me. How was I to know it was his granddaughter?" He shrugged, a gesture which gave Kate the strong urge to shake him. Instead, she balled her fists in her lap.

"Never mind that. What did he do when Mrs Saunton wouldn't sell?"

"Oh yah. Broke in, didn't he? Said it was easy." He sniggered. "But he couldn't find it. The old bat had hidden it. She wasn't daft." Kate, only with great willpower, kept her balled fist in her lap. "Anyway, next thing we knew, she'd died, so Unc tried again, but no luck. Then he heard that you'd inherited the house, found out where you lived and wanted me to get friendly with you." His mouth twisted as if remembering something unpleasant. "That's the bit Cesca didn't like when I told her – said she'd never invite me to another of her daddy's shooting weekends if she found out I was messing with someone else." His eyes darted around as if mentioning his girlfriend's name might risk conjuring her presence.

"So you bottled out of talking to me?" asked Kate.

"Yah," he said, a sheepish look on his face. "Saw you go into that bar with your pals. But you were surrounded all the time. Thought it would be better if I followed you when you left and sort of, erm, bump into you."

"You do realise I was scared out my wits, don't you?" Was he a complete moron?

"Yah. Sorry." He hung his head. "When I lost you, I rang Unc. He told me to make myself scarce. Said I'd get done for harassment or something. So I drove all the way back home."

Kate pursed her lips and glared at him. "Go on. What next?"

"Well, Unc thought we should try the house again. Last night. That's when I got this." He pointed to his eye. "Unc managed to get that chap off me. The chap hadn't seen him, you see. Unc'd gone round the back to check for an easy window. I was having a bit of trouble with that door."

"Good, serves you bloody-well right," said Kate. "But what about all the other times?"

"What other times?" He frowned, giving a convincing impression of being confused. "Only went there the once, and as far as I know, Unc only got in twice – once when the old girl was out, and once just after she died. He waited until the all the hoo-ha with the police had died down."

"You're lying." Kate prodded an accusatory finger into his chest. "What about moving my stuff around, and trying to scare me in the middle of the night?"

His face registered total incomprehension. "I don't know what you mean. Unc said he was going to leave it after last night. Said he wasn't taking any more risks. Thought the police were going to stop us when they went racing past. Didn't half give me a fright." He sighed. "Won't get my trip to Verbier now. Pity."

Kate swallowed her revulsion and looked away towards the water. However obnoxious and pathetic, he did seem to be telling the truth. But if it wasn't him, who was it? She felt a pull on her arm and turned back to face him.

"Here, you won't let that chap of yours hit me again, will you? I promise I'll never do anything like this again. Mummy says she'll cut me off without a penny if I get into any more trouble."

Kate got no pleasure from hearing him grovel, he was beneath her contempt.

"I'll think about it," she said at last, determined not to let him off the hook too easily. "If I have any more mysterious visitors, though, I'm going straight to the police and it'll be you I'll be pointing the finger at." She gave him the sort of glare she normally reserved for readers caught using pens in the Bodleian's manuscript reading rooms.

"I promise," he nodded earnestly. "Cesca says she might think about marrying me if I make a good impression on her daddy. He's got stables, lots of horses." His face took on a dreamlike expression. "I like horses. Know where you are with horses. Never understood all the fuss about paintings."

"Just one more thing." Kate grabbed his sleeve. "Why was your uncle so anxious to get his hands on the painting?"

"Oh, yah, think I remember." Rupert scratched his head. "That's right, he thought it was done by that chap... Whotsisname?" At Kate's puzzled look he added, "You know...some painter chappie who did portraits?" He screwed his eyes up in concentration. "Cesca's daddy has got one." He shook his head. "No, that's a Gainsborough, not him. Some other chap." He frowned apologetically. "'Fraid I can't remember."

Right, thought Kate, it definitely wasn't a Gainsborough. *As if.*

Rupert was still speaking. "May I go now? I won't bother you again. Unc won't either. Nearly getting caught last night was enough for him... Had to have two snifters before he could breathe properly. Thought he was going to fall off his twig. Mummy would not have been happy at all."

Kate gave him what she hoped was an intimidating look. "Go on then, get lost. But don't forget: any more trouble and I'm reporting you."

Rupert didn't wait to hear any more. Before she could blink, he'd sprung up and was making his way back down the pier towards the street, jacket slung over his shoulder and head bobbing from side to side. Kate could only wonder at what Cesca saw in him.

She turned back and gazed out over the water. Now what should she do about Tom? What did Tom think he was doing, going in and punching that idiot? And how had he found out? She bit her lip, trying to fathom it out. She could only conclude that Sue must have told him about the incident in Oxford and how she'd recognised Rupert earlier that week. She certainly hadn't. But what was Tom doing interfering? He didn't think he was protecting her... Did he?

But most puzzling of all...if Rupert and his dratted uncle weren't responsible for the weird goings on, who was?

Chapter Thirteen

Kate ambled back up the pier. She should have been feeling elated, but instead she felt confused. Of course she was relieved to discover Rupert was no real threat; never had been, in fact. And his uncle's misguided belief that the portrait was valuable had been the cause of the break-ins. But there shouldn't be any more trouble on that front – she'd meant it when she said that she'd go straight to the police with their names if there was.

That just left the unexplained figure on the drive and the weird atmosphere in the house. She frowned. Had she just imagined it all? Stress, an overactive imagination, no sleep… and all primed by Win's troubled chat with her shortly before she died. She inwardly squirmed at the thought of Tom confirming that he'd had an undisturbed night. Bugger! What an idiot he'd think she was! What she needed was some time to unwind. She remembered her swimming kit in the boot and smiled. It was a hot day, what could be better than chilling out at the beach? Besides, she wanted to put off for as long as possible the sight of Tom's smug expression when he told her that she must have imagined things.

The key she'd given Tom was lying on the mat in the hall when she got back. She grinned. He was reliable, she'd give him that. Running one hand through her salt-encrusted hair, she swept it up on her way into the kitchen for a much-needed glass of water. Thirst quenched, she pulled open the fridge door and quirked an eyebrow at the sight of the bare shelf that had previously contained the leftovers she'd planned on having for supper. She only had herself to blame, she reminded herself, recalling that she'd told Tom to help himself. She spotted a packet of bacon and located the last small wedge of parmesan. All was not lost. Soon the kitchen was filled with the tantalising aroma of frying onions and tomatoes – she wouldn't be going hungry after all.

Appetite sated and dirty dishes stacked in the dishwasher, she wandered into the drawing room. Everything was in its place. There was no sign that Tom had spent the night there – apart that was, from the note lying on the coffee table.

Hi Kate. Hope you had a better night's sleep in Falmouth. I've got to go to Exeter today, so won't be back till very late. Perhaps we can have a catch-up tomorrow, if that's ok? I suggest you stay over in your flat tonight, just to be on the safe side. Mum says to come over for dinner this Sunday, no excuses. Tom.

She frowned. What did he mean by *'just to be on the safe side'*? Did he really think that Rupert or his uncle would come round again, especially after he'd warned Rupert off with a bloody nose? She thought for a minute. Tom was unaware that she'd witnessed his bout with Rupert. Was he just trying to keep her out of the house for longer? Why? What was his game?

She decided she was staying put. She'd slept soundly last night and felt much better, and she was ready for any idiot who tried to frighten her. Not that she really expected Rupert or his uncle to turn up again. No, the question was, would somebody else rock up?

Kate spent the rest of the afternoon and evening in the study. She was growing to love the small wood-panelled room with its old-fashioned keyhole desk, crowded wooden bookshelves, and view over the front garden. She leaned back in the swivel chair – the only concession to modernity, apart from the computer.

There was some really interesting stuff in the bag that Sue had left with her, she concluded. Earlier, she'd flicked through the assorted letters, deeds, bills, and account books, rapidly sorting them into separate piles on the desk, before settling down to go through them methodically. Concentrating on a task helped take her mind off her problems.

She yawned and rubbed her eyes, rolling shoulders that were stiff from sitting in the same position. She checked her phone. Had she really been there over three hours? She stood up to stretch, getting a full view of the mass of materials covering her desk and the adjoining table. Kate was pleased with the result. Not bad for someone who'd played truant for the best part of the day.

She'd learned a lot about Sue's family. Sue's grandmother and parents had lived in a house not far from Bath – a house that had been in the family for many years, until Sue's brother had been forced to sell because of death duties. Sue had confided that her brother had given her the task of sorting all the family papers; something she'd never quite got round to. And with her current problems, she's never likely to, thought Kate wryly.

Kate decided a pot of tea was required before she did any more work. She was determined to make a rudimentary list of everything before she went to bed. Not quite a catalogue, but at least she would be able to account for every item. She stirred the pot absentmindedly as she gazed out the window; it was getting dark now. The oven clock told her it was nearly ten-thirty. Perhaps another hour and she'd be done, there was after all, only one small bundle of letters left to check. Mug in hand, she returned to the study, settled back down in her chair and picked up the bundle, which was tied with a faded blue silk ribbon. Struggling with the knots, she eventually managed to untie the ribbon and rolled it up tidily before turning to examine the letters.

There was a loose sheet on top of the bundle, and in an elegant but faded, copperplate hand were the words:

My letters to AT

It looked like the bundle had not been opened since they had been tied up in the ribbon – an exciting prospect that sent a tingle of anticipation down Kate's spine. As she lifted the top letter off the pile, a sprig of rosemary concealed amongst the letters rolled onto the table, its desiccated fronds crumbling on the desktop.

Kate sniffed and caught only the faintest of aromas. She carefully unfolded the first letter. The paper was fragile and frayed at the edges, the creases of the folds torn in places, and it looked as if someone – the sender, perhaps – had read them many times over. Kate started to read.

My dearest heart,

It has been so long since I held you in my arms, I am in torment. Each night, I gaze at your face, knowing that you too gaze upon mine. Your likeness seems so real, sometimes I even think I can smell your presence. Soon we will have no need of those painted facsimiles, my darling, we will be together in truth, never to be parted. Next time we meet I will be the happiest of men. I will wait in our trysting place and pray that the fates will be on our side.

Be brave, my darling Annabelle.

Yours always and forever,

J

Kate's eyes widened as she read. This was unbelievable. A letter addressed to an Annabelle, signed by someone whose name began with J, and the sprig of rosemary. She checked the top sheet again. Her conviction grew that the initials AT stood for Annabelle Tracy. It was too much of a coincidence. And they'd obviously been returned to the sender.

Why?

The J could only be John Lanyon, a man desperately in love. What were they doing in Sue's family papers? Was Sue related to the Lanyon family? Kate's trembling fingers opened the second letter. It was another brief note from J, saying that all had been arranged and instructing Annabelle to be no later than two hours after midnight or they would miss the tide.

So, the couple had planned to run away together, but

something must have happened to foil their plans. According to Ruth, John Lanyon had never married, and was rumoured to have died of a broken heart. There was nothing to say what had happened to Annabelle.

Kate sat back in her chair, folded her arms behind her head, and closed her eyes. Her mind was far from relaxed, however. What a fluke that she had been the one to discover the letters – one of the few people to have read Annabelle Tracy's journal and able to make the connection. Sue would be delighted to hear the whole intriguing story and she might be able to shed light on why the letters were amongst her family papers. If only the puzzle of Annabelle's disappearance could be solved.

Kate wracked her brain. John spoke of a portrait in his letter, an image of Annabelle – his words implied that she also had one of him. What had happened to them? Something clicked in Kate's brain. There had been a receipt for two portraits somewhere in the documents she'd listed. Seizing the mouse, she clicked it, and her computer screen came to life. There had been so many bills and invoices, but she was sure she'd seen one.

"Bingo!"

She hurriedly found the pile devoted to receipts, and started to methodically go through it until she located the one she needed. Her heart was pounding with excitement. She loved it when something serendipitous occurred when she was trawling through archives. It didn't happen that often, but when it did... Of course, punching the air and yelping were frowned upon in most academic reading rooms, but in her own study that was a different matter.

Once she'd calmed down, she scrutinised the paper, checking the foliation number she'd given it earlier to ensure it matched the one on her screen. She'd foliated the sheets as she'd entered them, pencilling a twenty-seven at the top right-hand corner of this particular bill, with a heading engraved across the top:

Mr Vaslet, paintings in oils, miniature, crayons, etc,

Argyle Buildings, Bath

Underneath was handwritten:

For two portraits in crayons, complete with frames, twenty guineas.

Could this be what she was looking for? Where were the portraits now? Kate scrabbled around in the bag in case she'd missed anything. A few old diaries and almanacs, but no portrait. She would ask Sue about it when she saw her. It would be wonderful if the portrait of Annabelle was also still with the family.

She remembered Annabelle's journal, almost certain that there was mention of a trip to Bath somewhere. She moved her desk light so that it illuminated the pages. The ink was very faded in places, and in others it had bled through the paper making it difficult to read. With a shaking hand, she turned the leaves, scanning each entry for the word she was looking for, until at last she found it.

"Yes."

Annabelle wrote of a trip to Bath to visit her sister. Skimming the pages, Kate saw that the visit lasted several weeks. More than one entry mentioned excursions to view the shops.

What made Kate's heart beat faster was the minute initial J in the margin next to each of these entries. Ruth hadn't said anything about them, and Kate herself hadn't really noticed them before. Now their significance screamed out to her. Could they be what she suspected – code for a secret assignation? And possibly appointments with a portrait painter? What other explanation could there be?

Kate checked the receipt again. The date fitted, the same year as Annabelle's visit, and several weeks after she had returned to Falmouth. Kate had no idea how long it took to complete a portrait, but it was all looking pleasingly and entirely feasible.

Fired up with adrenaline, Kate had an urge to share her

discovery, despite the late hour. She checked the time. It was too late to phone Sue – who wouldn't thank her for being woken up. What about Tom?

She had to admit that he'd been good company the other night, and she felt guilty for the bump on the head he'd suffered on her behalf – she could use this as an excuse to check he wasn't suffering any after-effects. But would he appreciate her sharing her thoughts about this discovery? Kate quelled her doubts. *It concerns his family after all.* And he'd said in his note that he would be back late, so he was sure to be up if he had returned.

Mind made up, Kate carefully enclosed the receipt and letters in a folder which she placed in the drawer with the journal. Keys jangling in her hand, and her jacket slung over her shoulders, she skidded out the kitchen door, only pausing long enough to lock it behind her. In her rush to share, it didn't occur to her to text Tom first. The gravel crunched beneath her feet as she hurried down the drive, drowning out the rustlings of night creatures going about their business in the undergrowth of the nearby shrubs and woodland.

She knew before she got there that he wasn't back. The cottage lay in darkness and his car wasn't on the drive. Her shoulders slumped and she shivered, suddenly aware of the chilled night air, now she was no longer buoyed by adrenaline. She turned back the way she'd come, feeling annoyed with herself for rushing out without checking first. A rustling in the shrubs to her left gave her a start. Probably a mouse or hedgehog, she told herself. Not a rat. Definitely not a rat. Rats gave her the shivers.

In the half-light something moved, a shape detached itself from the trees to her left. She froze mid-stride, heart thudding in her chest. Automatically, her fingers closed over her keys, forming a fist with her hand, with the end of each key protruding through her fingers. Something she'd learned in her self-defence classes.

Setting off again, more quickly this time, but trying to keep her footsteps light, she hurried up towards the house. Perhaps whoever it was hadn't realised she was there; they didn't appear to be moving in her direction. If only she could get to the kitchen door and inside before she was noticed. She didn't hear the car engine until it was too late – turning only when the blazing glare of headlights were speeding straight towards her.

Chapter Fourteen

Kate held her breath, squeezed her eyes shut, and braced for the impact. There was a squeal of wheels skidding in the gravel, a rush of air and...silence. She heard the sound of a car door being flung open and opened her eyes. Spinning round, she nearly fell into Tom's arms.

"Oh my God! I almost ran you over. What are you doing out here in the dark?" He had her by the shoulders. "What are you doing here at all? You should be in Falmouth." His voice cracked. He sounded shaken and angry.

"Oh. It's you," she managed to say. Three words totally inadequate for conveying her relief. His arms wrapped round her, and in that moment she felt safe. His breathing was audible, like someone who'd been running hard. Then his words registered, and she dragged herself out of his grasp.

"I live here, in case you hadn't noticed. Just because you think I should spend another night in Falmouth, doesn't mean I have to. I have a mind of my own." How did he manage to get her so riled up every time? Why did she let him?

"Never mind that," he snapped back, grasping her again by the shoulders. "Let's get inside. We've both had a shock."

On shaking legs, Kate allowed herself to be led back up the drive, resenting that he was making her feel like a naughty schoolgirl. As they passed his car, parked askew and the bonnet embedded in the bushes, he slammed the door shut with one hand and pointed the ignition key at it. The car's lights flashed, then they were in darkness.

"I think we could both do with a drink." Once inside, he started to fling open the kitchen cupboard doors. Kate sank into a chair and indicated the door to the pantry, where she'd placed her supplies of alcohol. He came out clutching a bottle of gin in one hand and a bottle of single malt whisky in the other, his face still grim.

"Which do you prefer?"

"Gin for me, but you have whatever you want. There's some tonic in the fridge. Don't bother about ice," she answered through clenched teeth.

"Gin it is. If you don't mind, I'll have some of this malt."

He poured her a generous measure of gin, then she watched as he poured two fingers of malt for himself, adding a mere splash of water. Begrudgingly she approved his taste. Her father only drank single malt, diluting it with just a few drops of water.

Tom put the glass of gin and the bottle of tonic down in front of her. "I don't want to upset you again. You'll probably accuse me of putting too much in, so do it yourself." He still sounded angry.

Kate had to bite her lip to stop herself from laughing. Now he was being ridiculous. She reminded herself that they'd both had a shock, so she didn't respond. Instead, she took a sip of neat gin, savouring the hit of alcohol and botanicals. It felt pleasantly warm as it went down her throat. She poured some tonic into her glass and watched the bubbles explode before taking another sip.

"Well, what were you doing outside in the dark?" At his question, she looked up to see him frowning at her. "God, if I'd been going any faster." His hand trembled as he lifted his glass to his lips. A twinge of guilt nagged at her. He was upset, really upset. A nerve twitched in his cheek.

"I'd just been to see if you were home." All anger now knocked out of her, her words came out in little more than a whisper.

His eyes widened. "Why?"

"I've discovered something…in the papers your Mum left with me. I just got all excited and wanted to share it with… someone." She stopped. God, she sounded ridiculous, like some overexcited schoolgirl. She'd probably just confirmed all his negative opinions of her.

He was looking at her strangely. "What did you find out?

It must be pretty important to send you down the drive in the dark." There was now a spark of interest in his eyes and what looked like the beginnings of a smile.

"Well, I thought it was." His warm expression was definitely having an effect on her, she smiled back at him. "It was just something that linked up with something I've been researching – about somebody who used to live in this house, in fact. A real case of serendipity, if you like."

"Now you've got me intrigued." He leaned forward – close enough for her to see that, despite his smile, he looked tired. It was very late. He'd probably been awake most of the night, then he'd had a long drive to Exeter and back... Not to mention the punch-up with Rupert. She risked a quick glance at his hand clenched around his glass. His knuckles were a nice shade of purple.

Kate reigned in her desire to share. "Never mind for now, it'll wait. I'll reveal all when I see your Mum for lunch tomorrow."

"Now that does sound exciting." His grin became decidedly wicked.

Kate kept her face blank, she didn't want to let on she'd caught his innuendo; couldn't let him know how easily he turned her into a quivering mass of longing. "Yes, I hope she'll find it interesting. Will you be there?"

"Now I know you'll be revealing all, I'll definitely be there. Not that I'd miss one of Mum's roast dinners." He winked as he took another mouthful from his glass.

It took an effort for her not to react. He had the most devastating smile... And his eyes!

She dragged her mind back.The best form of defence was attack. She narrowed her eyes. "Anyway, what were you doing coming up the drive at this time of night? I assume you thought, like a good little girl I'd obeyed your instructions to stay in Falmouth and the house would be empty?"

The look he gave her spoke volumes. "It wasn't an instruction, merely some well-intended advice. I thought you being an intelligent woman and all, would recognise that I had some issues when I stayed over. I didn't have time to spell it all out in my note."

"Why? What happened?" She dropped her cool tone, blurting out her question.

He cupped his face in his hands, then ran his fingers through his hair. For someone who always appeared very sure of himself, he was looking uncertain now, and attractively dishevelled. "I don't know. My guess is that it's someone playing silly buggers, trying to scare you. I think I've sorted it out but..." He took another swig from his glass.

"Yes?" she urged.

He shrugged. "I don't know how he managed it. I was asleep and something woke me up. Round about two. I saw something out the window... Someone moving about near the drive. I was out the window like a shot, but they'd completely disappeared. Scarpered. Looked everywhere and couldn't find any trace. I even went down as far as the road to see if there was a car parked nearby. Nothing. Not a sound either, that was another odd thing."

A shiver went down Kate's spine. It all sounded horribly familiar. But what did he mean about sorting it out?

"Who did you suspect and how have you sorted it?" She could guess what he was going to tell her.

"Aaah...yes. That." His eyes slithered away from hers. That nerve was twitching in his cheek again. "I suppose you'll find out anyway...when he reports me to the police. Surprised they haven't arrested me already. I went to the art dealers and sorted out that chap. Mum told me what you'd said to her. Couldn't help myself, I was so angry. And I'm pretty certain he was the chap I nearly caught the other night trying to break in. Same long hair and he had a black eye this morning."

Kate couldn't contain her laughter.

"What's so funny?" Tom frowned at her, he was almost growling. "I've never hit anyone unprovoked before."

"Oh Tom, I saw you. I was in the café opposite, biding my time. I'd decided I was going to face up to him, and was waiting for the right moment when you came bowling along." She giggled, shook her head, then reached across and stroked his bruised hand. "Is it very sore?"

"I'm afraid I still don't understand what's so amusing." He ignored her question, but did not pull his hand away.

"I went in after you'd left." His eyes widened, so she hurried on before he could start telling her off again. "He's not going to report you... Too frightened everything will come out about the attempted burglary. He's terrified of going inside. You see, he's got a suspended sentence hanging over his head." She sent him a triumphant grin and watched as Tom slumped back in his seat.

He expelled a breath. "Thank God. But you took a hell of a risk. What if..."

"He was a wimp, actually." Kate hurriedly went on to explain how a cowed Rupert had allowed her to drag him up to the pier for her interrogation. By the time she'd finished, Tom's shoulders were shaking with laughter.

"Anyway, now we know the reasons for the break-ins. And he's promised he won't try anything again. Says his uncle has given up too."

"Hmm." Tom wiped the tears of laughter from his eyes. "And you believe him?"

"Well, he'd be a bit daft to try anything now, wouldn't he? If he tried again I'd be straight onto the police with his name."

"I suppose so," agreed Tom. "There's just something niggling me." Kate rolled her eyes and he backed down. "Oh, I expect you're right, but give me a call if anything bothers you." He checked his watch, a rather nice Rolex. "I'd best be on my way." He drained the last of the malt, rinsed the glass under the tap, and gave Kate's shoulder a squeeze on his way to the door. "Call me if you're worried, right?"

Kate looked up to see concern in his eyes. "Sure."

"Mum says can you be there for twelve thirty? I'd give you a lift, only I'm going over early. Dad wants a hand with something."

"Thanks, I will... Be there at twelve thirty, I mean. I'm sure I won't need to call you. Don't worry."

The intense look in his eyes almost made her insides melt.

It was nice having someone who cared about her again.

"Not worried about you." His wolfish grin appeared again. "Sorry for the poor sod who you'll probably terrify and frogmarch to the police station." He'd closed the door behind him before she could think of a suitable retort.

She grinned to herself. That was another thing in his favour. His sense of humour. Oh dear. If she wasn't careful, she'd have her heart broken again.

She got up to rinse her own glass and suddenly remembered the figure she'd seen on the drive. In all the terror and excitement of nearly being mown down, and seeing Tom again, it had been wiped from her mind. Tom hadn't mentioned seeing anything.

Probably my imagination.

Chapter Fifteen

Kate arrived at Sue's house dead on twelve thirty. She was not feeling her best. The same nightmare of being trapped had returned to waken her up in the early hours, and she almost regretted not taking Tom's advice about returning to Falmouth for the night. When she pulled up on the drive his car was already there.

"Thought I heard an engine. You're very punctual. Mum'll be pleased."

She turned to see Tom grinning at her as he emerged from the path at the side of the house. Kate stared – in fact it was difficult to tear her eyes away, for he was bare chested, and glowing with perspiration. The shape of his torso told her that he was no stranger to physical work – something that she'd deduced from seeing him fully clothed, but now definitely confirmed. He wiped a grimy hand across his face to flick away a lock of hair, leaving a black streak across his cheek.

"I think you need to wipe your hands, and you've got something across your face." She smiled. "Anyway, why wouldn't I be punctual?"

"Thought you might not have slept very well and been too tired." His eyes narrowed, scrutinising her. "By the look of your eyes, you didn't sleep well, did you?"

Blast, why was he so observant? She shifted from foot to foot, not wanting to admit he was right. Fortunately, she didn't need to reply. Tom was looking at his hands.

"Bother. Been helping Dad to service the lawn mower. Oil everywhere." He rolled his eyes. "Anyway, may I give you a formal welcome to the house, especially after what happened here the first time?" He cocked his head to one side and gave her a repentant smile so intense that it set butterflies off in her stomach. "My only excuse for being incredibly rude then is to say that I was being incredibly stupid."

How could she not forgive him? "Forget about it. I have."

He gestured over to the gardens and she spotted an impressive treehouse just visible in the far corner of the garden, behind the shrubs and flower beds; it looked like an exciting playground for small boys. "Anyway, this is where I grew up. I used to spend hours in the tree house over there with my mates, pretending to be pirates."

"And how often did you fall out of it?" Kate was beginning to get her butterflies back under control.

His laugh was like a warm caress. "Only the once. I learnt my lesson after that. It wasn't much fun having my arm in plaster for what seemed like ages and not being able to swim or climb."

His eyes twinkled as he spoke and she forced herself not to grin inanely back at him. She felt like a rabbit in the headlights when he looked at her like that.

Just then the front door opened, breaking the spell, and a grey-haired gentleman, dressed in cords and a check shirt, ambled out towards them. Kate guessed this was Tom's dad, which he confirmed when he introduced himself.

"You must be Kate." Her hand was clasped in a firm grip. "I'm Martin, this reprobate's father." Martin grinned at his son. "I hope you're going to have a quick shower before lunch, Tom."

"Just going, Dad. I've put everything back in the shed. The mower should work ok now, but if it doesn't, give me a shout. See you in a few minutes, Kate. Don't let Dad intimidate you." Tom chuckled as he strode off back through the garden.

"He's a cheeky beggar," Martin said with a laugh as he guided Kate to the front door and ushered her inside. "Come in, come in. Lovely to meet you at last. Sue's told me all about you, and I know how helpful you've been." He stopped, took her gently by the arm, and looked her in the eye. "She's been a bit low recently, what with Laura and everything, so it's really good to see her enthusiastic about

105

something again. It's made a big difference."

The sincerity in his face gave his simple words added meaning, and Kate's cheeks reddened at this unmerited praise; she'd barely done anything, and what she had done had helped her far more than Sue.

"Honestly, I haven't done that much. But I have found out something quite exciting... Well, I think it's exciting."

"Hoho. That sounds interesting." It was easy to see where Tom got his twinkling eyes and good looks from, Kate thought when she saw Martin's smile. He continued to lead her up the hallway. "Anyway, come into the conservatory. We'll have a drink before dinner while we wait for Tom. You can meet Laura. She's feeling well enough to sit downstairs with us today. Tom carried her down. I'm sure she'll appreciate seeing a new face."

They went through the kitchen, where the smells of a roast dinner tantalised Kate's nose, and on to the conservatory, where Sue sat with her daughter.

Sue leapt up to give Kate a hug, reminding her of her own mum – all affection and warmth, and a faint whiff of *Dioressence*.

"Hello, Kate. It's lovely to see you. This is Laura. She's feeling a bit better today, so it's nice that you two can meet. Laura, this is Kate."

Kate smiled at the pale young woman reclining on one of the sofas. Laura had the same strong facial features as her brother, but in her they were softer and more feminine. Her skin was almost transparent, as if she hadn't seen the sun for a very long time, and lines around her eyes told of pain. As their eyes met, Kate could have sworn an expression of surprise passed over Laura's face before being replaced with a smile.

"Pleased to meet you." Kate extended her hand.

"Hi. Sorry, I can't get up. Requires a bit too much energy." Laura's voice was low pitched, but pleasant.

Kate could easily imagine her standing in front of a classroom and holding her pupils' attention. Sal, who'd been snoozing at Laura's feet, woke up and, bounding towards her, greeted Kate like a long-lost friend.

"Blimey. You're privileged. She usually ignores visitors." Martin bent down to ruffle Sal's ears. "Now, what would everyone like to drink?" Sue opted for a sherry, so Kate did the same. Laura was drinking water. "Right, I'll have a beer and I'll pour one for Tom." Martin headed back towards the kitchen.

"And I'll just go and check on the meat." Sue stood up. "You girls can get to know one another. Sit over there, Kate, make yourself comfortable."

"Your Mum told me about your illness," said Kate as she sat on the sofa opposite Laura. "She said you'd been to Belgium a while back for some treatment. Has it helped?"

Laura pulled a face. "Who knows? But I'll try anything. Well, almost anything." Her voice had a cynical tone.

"Come on. Laura. I thought you were feeling quite positive about the treatment." Tom's voice made them both turn. Kate watched as he went over and knelt down on the floor by the sofa and took his sister's hand. His still damp hair glistened and his white linen shirt made him look even more bronzed. He really was quite devastatingly handsome.

Kate realised she was staring and dragged her eyes away. What was she doing mooning over him? She forced herself to concentrate on what Laura was saying.

"Oh, I am really. But the consultant said there were no guarantees." Laura shook her head and looked sideways at Kate. "I'm just fed up not being able to do anything. Life's passing me by, and yet some people have the nerve to say this illness is imaginary, and that anyone who has it is an attention seeker. Bloody hell! Attention is the last thing you get. The world has forgotten I exist."

Kate could see Laura was trying hard not to cry, and in the ensuing uncomfortable silence turned away. She got up and went over to look out at the garden, where a pond covered in waterlilies sparkled in the afternoon sun. She heard Tom whispering, guessing he was trying to reassure his sister. A moment later, she felt Tom's presence next to her. He'd obviously decided to give Laura time to compose herself.

"What a lovely garden. Are there fish in the pond?" She looked up to see Tom's grateful smile at her attempt lighten the mood.

"Yeah," he answered. "I'll show you around later, if you like. I'll just go and give Dad a hand with the drinks." In a whisper he added, "Could you have a word with her? She might listen to you."

Kate wasn't sure she had anything useful to say to Laura, and she was positive that Laura would be justified in telling her to get lost – they'd only just met, for goodness sake. But at the pleading in Tom's eyes, she reluctantly nodded her head. Looking relieved, Tom gave her arm a brief squeeze and disappeared to find his father.

Kate returned to her seat, perching on the edge. She had no idea what to say. Laura was pulling at the fringed hem of the tartan blanket covering her legs, in a world of her own. Something seemed to be bothering her. At last she looked up, regarding Kate from beneath lowered lashes. "Sorry about that. I didn't mean to make you feel awkward."

Kate relaxed and smiled back. "Don't mention it. It must be frustrating for you to go from leading an active life to this."

"Mmm. That's right. I keep thinking of everything I'm missing. But hell…we are where we are." She shrugged. "Anyway, enough about me. What about you? Mum has been singing your praises, and even Tom…" Laura stopped speaking and her eyes narrowed. "You're not going to hurt him, are you? He's been through enough."

Kate frowned. "Sorry? What do you mean? Hurt Tom. No. Why would I?" She didn't have a clue what Laura was talking about, but before she could say anything else, Tom and his Dad returned with the drinks, closely followed by Sue.

"This is nice," said Sue, flopping down on the sofa next to her daughter. "It's been ages since we all had Sunday lunch together. And it's lovely of you to join us, Kate. Laura gets bored just seeing our faces all the time."

"Oh, Mum. I'm not bored with you," protested Laura.

"Take no notice, Kate. Mum has told me you've sorted out all her papers, and Tom said you'd got some news?"

Still puzzled by Laura's previous question, Kate tried to order her thoughts, as she was now the focus of everyone's attention. She knew she was blushing. But it wasn't Sue and Martin's scrutiny that caused this reaction, it was the look that Tom was sending her as he leaned nonchalantly by the window, out of everyone else's view.

"Yes, I have, but...but it's quite a complicated story." Her voice faltered. She'd given confident presentations to prestigious academics and multi-millionaires, so how could one guy turn her thoughts to a complete muddle?

"Don't worry. The dinner won't be ready for another twenty minutes." Sue's friendly reassurance gave Kate the jolt she needed, so keeping her eyes away from the corner where Tom lounged, she concentrated them instead on Sue's face which was rapt in anticipation.

Kate had been talking for some minutes about her discoveries, outlining her hypothesis about the possible connections between an aristocratic family and the writer of 'her' journal, and the puzzle of the portraits, when Laura interrupted. "Mum, isn't there...?"

"Yes, yes, I know what you're going to say." Sue's face had an excited expression as she gestured to her son. "Tom, run upstairs, there's a love, and bring Flossie down. She's in the back bedroom."

Kate watched in bewilderment as Tom heaved himself off the window sill and sprang into action. When she shot him a questioning look, he just tapped his nose and smiled.

"Wait and see." He disappeared to fetch whatever it was.

Martin smiled at her. "You'll see in a minute." He turned to his daughter. "Clever of you to remember, Laura. Though how we'll ever confirm anything, I don't know."

Kate didn't have a clue what they were talking about and hoped Tom would not take too long to fetch the mysterious Flossie.

At last Tom's footsteps sounded on the tiled floor. She turned to see he was carrying a framed painting. Strangely, it was similar in size to the one she'd found in Win's bedroom. A tingle of excitement went up her spine. Tom held it up and turned it round so she could see.

"Well, what do you think?"

Kate's jaw almost dropped to the floor. Looking at her with an enigmatic smile was a young lady, her head turned to gaze over her left shoulder at the viewer. Vibrant green eyes, glossy chestnut curls, a small but determined chin, and a straight pert nose. She was a beauty. More to the point, even to Kate's unpracticed eye, the painting was remarkably similar in style to the portrait of her gentleman. The frame was identical.

"Good grief! Who is she?" Kate managed to get out at last. Her heart was thudding. Pieces of the puzzle clicking into place in her brain were almost audible. Could it be?

"That's just it," said Martin. "We don't know."

"We've always called her Flossie," said Sue. "She actually came with the family papers that my brother sent. There was nothing with the painting to say who she was, and I just liked her so much I put her in the back bedroom. It doesn't get much direct sunlight so I didn't think it would cause any damage. Do you think she could be...?" She looked expectantly at Kate, who wished she knew more about art in order to give Sue the answer they both wanted. Tom had now placed the painting on the coffee table so that they could all examine it.

"I should've remembered this when I saw that portrait of yours, Kate," he said. "The frames are similar. And the sitter's dress looks to be from the same era. What do you think?"

"What's that, Tom? Another portrait like this?" Sue interrupted.

Kate took a moment before answering. She was almost certain, but didn't want to raise everyone's hopes before getting everything confirmed by an expert. "Yes, Sue. I have one very similar. It's a portrait of a gentleman – young and good looking. They do appear to be from the same period, but I'm not an expert on dress...or art, for that matter." She turned to Tom. "It could be the same artist. We need to get them looked at. Something else I need to tell you...about Annabelle and John." All eyes swivelled to her. "Sue, as I said, in the papers you left with me, were letters from someone who signed himself J, addressed to someone called Annabelle. I'm sure they are the same people. Somehow they were returned to him. But more importantly, there is a receipt for two portraits...done in Bath." For once she was lost for words.

"Gosh, this is exciting." Sue's face was glowing. "The papers and portrait all came originally from Grandma, according to my brother. By the time I got them all the details were very muddled, understandably as Grandma was very confused in the years before she died."

"Now, your Grandma lived near Bath, didn't she?"

Kate was totally unprepared for Sue's next revelation. "That's right. We're distantly related to the Lanyons, you know...the Earls of Batheaston."

Kate took a sip of her sherry, wishing she had something stronger. Yes, it was all slipping into place, the coincidences were too numerous. But she needed to get the paintings authenticated. Someone at the Holburne Museum should be able to confirm whether the artist of both was Vaslet. She looked at the portrait again – the young woman smiled enigmatically back at her.

Hello, Annabelle. What happened to you?

Chapter Sixteen

After all the excitement died down, Sue shepherded everyone except Laura into the dining room. Kate had noticed how Laura's initial animation over the portrait diminished and was therefore not surprised when Laura tugged on Sue's sleeve to say she was going to have a rest in her room.

"I'll save some dinner for you, love. Let me know when you want to eat." Sue gave Kate a brave smile as Tom carried Laura upstairs. "Never mind. I thought she was trying to do too much. Next time you come round, she might be feeling a bit better and you can spend some time together, get to know one another. It's done her good to meet someone new." Sue slapped a hand to her mouth. "Oh dear. There I go again. I haven't even asked you whether you'd like to see her again. I do beg your pardon, Kate."

Kate patted Sue's arm. "Of course I'll come and visit Laura. And not because I feel sorry for her; I'm sure we have a lot of common interests." It was true. Beneath the constraints of ill health, it was clear that Laura possessed an intelligent mind and a lively sense of humour. Kate thought in other circumstances they would get on well together. But she was not entirely sure about risking an involvement with Laura's brother.

Tom had been utterly charming once they'd cleared up that awful misunderstanding, so charming in fact, that she was in great danger of falling head over heels for him. But she didn't want to get hurt and she also sensed a remaining wariness on his part. There were areas of his life that he was reluctant to share or discuss with her. And what had Laura meant with her warning not to hurt him? Surely he could take care of himself? He could be very intimidating when he wanted. She wasn't looking for a new relationship this soon, Kate told herself, and neither, if what the waitress had said was true, was he.

Kate took her place at the table, Tom was seated across from her, with his dad at the head and Sue at the other end. An empty place setting next to Kate indicated where Laura would have sat, if only she'd remained well enough to join them. Sue, however, seemed determined to make the best of things. It was obvious to Kate that this meal was more than just a normal Sunday lunch. There was a starter of smoked salmon, served with salad leaves and a vinaigrette, followed by a main course of roast pork with the usual accompaniments of stuffing, apple sauce, roast potatoes, carrots, green beans, and lots of gravy. By the time Kate had cleaned her plate she didn't think she could find any room for dessert.

"That was wonderful, Sue. I really enjoyed it. I think I've eaten so much, I'll have to walk home to work it off."

Sue glowed at Kate's praise, and Tom patted his mum on the shoulder as he started to clear the dishes. "Me too, Mum, that was really good. That's another reason I moved back down here, you know. I missed your cooking."

"Nonsense, Tom, but it's very nice of you to say so." Sue bit her lip and looked down at the table, but Kate caught the brief look that passed between mother and son, a mixture of embarrassment and…she wasn't sure what.

She wondered about the real reason for Tom's return home. Would he ever tell her? Was she just some passing fancy, to be charmed into his bed and then abandoned? Looking at him from across the polished dining table, Kate couldn't quite believe that he would put on the charm – and he had been very charming, showing an interest in her studies and her life in York and Oxford – just for a casual fling. He certainly didn't strike her as shallow.

After a suitable interlude, chatting and sipping the excellent Bordeaux, Sue announced it was time for dessert, and brought in a large bowl of fresh fruit salad and a dish of clotted cream.

"I hope you don't mind, Kate, I didn't have time to do a proper pudding…"

"Blimey, Sue. I don't know how you found time to do that wonderful roast, with all you have to cope with. Don't apologise."

Tom mouthed a "thank you" to Kate, then spoke aloud to Sue, "Stop beating yourself up, Mum. You're running the house, looking after Laura, researching treatments for her… not to mention helping out with the library committee."

Sue shrugged then gave a weak smile and everybody turned to their dessert; it was several minutes before conversation started up again.

It was agreed that Kate would contact a curator at the Holburne Museum to arrange a date when she would take both portraits there for identification. After dinner, Sue had packed the portrait in bubblewrap, whilst she and Tom cleared away the rest of the dishes and washed up. Martin had made his farewells to Kate before going upstairs to check on Laura.

Sue handed the portrait to Kate as she was leaving.

"It will be so exciting to have her name at last."

"Well, they might not be able to give a definite answer about that," cautioned Kate. "At best, we should hope for identification of the artist, though it does seem that, as they are so similar, the likelihood that the same artist painted both is pretty good. Only then might we have a case for saying that the sitters are the people we think they are." She didn't want to raise false hopes.

"Let me know when you get a date for the appraisal. I'd be interested in coming along." Tom's words took Kate by surprise. He must have noticed her look of shock, as he quickly added, "Only if you don't mind, of course."

"That would be nice." Sue cut in before Kate could reply. "Then you could call in to see Uncle Pete. He'd be interested to hear all about our discoveries, I'm sure."

"Mum, Kate might want to go on her own. She hasn't answered my question yet."

Sue bit her lip, looking put out.

Kate knew she was backed into a corner; if she said no, it would make her look churlish. Besides, she couldn't think of a valid reason to refuse his request – apart from the one of becoming even more attracted to him. How dangerous could a long car journey in his company be?

"No, I don't mind at all," she said at last. His eyes twinkled back at her. Damn him, he knew she'd had no option. "I'll let you know when I get a date."

Kate drove back home, hands clenched round the steering wheel. It was a good job it was Sunday and the roads were quiet – her clutch control had gone to pot, the gears crunched, and the Mini bunny-hopped on the hill start out of Falmouth.

She had the distinct impression that she'd been manipulated. Tom could easily have asked to accompany her to Bath out of his mother's hearing…and she would, of course, have refused. That's why he'd done it when he had, making any refusal impossible. She just couldn't fathom why he was determined to spend more time with her.

As soon as she got back, she headed straight to the study. If she sent an email to the Holburne straight away, they would get it first thing in the morning, and she might be able to arrange a visit before the end of the week. She really wanted to move this along. Of course, if they could see her at short notice, Tom might not be able to come with her. That would be a result, she thought with some satisfaction as she pressed send.

Tuesday arrived and Kate awoke to the sound of banging. Someone was hammering on the kitchen door. As she flung the covers off, the hammering stopped and her phone started to ring. She scrabbled on the bedside table till her fingers closed round it, and through sleep blurred eyes saw it was Tom calling. What did he want?

"Hello." It came out as a croak, her mouth was dry.

"Hi, it's me… Tom." He sounded remarkably chirpy. "Where are you? Have you had lunch yet? Thought you might like to go to Swanpool as it's such glorious weather. We can both play truant for the day."

"Errr, what time is it?" She tried to buy herself time to consider his invitation.

"Are you all right? You sound a bit...groggy. It's just after noon."

It was no wonder she was groggy – the last two nights she'd barely had any sleep, thanks to disturbing dreams of being trapped. The single night she'd spent in Falmouth had not been enough to break the pattern, and she was seriously considering going to stay at the flat for longer, to see if it made a difference. It was all in her head anyway, she just needed a strategy to deal with it – either that or see a doctor.

"I'm fine. Just woken up. Is that you I heard banging on the back door?"

"Sorry, yes. Didn't realise. Late night, was it?" There was a pause. "Don't worry. Give me a call if you fancy meeting up." The phone went dead.

Without stopping to think, Kate swung her legs out of bed and raced over to open the window. Tom was stalking back down the drive, shoulders slumped and hands in pockets.

"Tom, don't go. Hang on a minute and I'll be right down."

He stopped in his tracks and turned back. Even from that distance she could see his grin. Without stopping to question what she was doing, she scuttled down the stairs to unlock the back door. He was leaning on the doorframe, eyes creased in a smile – a wicked smile that made her insides curl.

"Nice pyjamas."

She rolled her eyes. "Come in. Put the kettle on will you, while I get dressed? Won't be a minute."

It took her fifteen minutes to shower and get ready... Fifteen minutes during which she repeatedly wondered if she was doing the right thing. He was getting pretty hard to resist. She had to remind herself how obnoxious he'd been at their first couple of encounters; encounters that were rapidly fading from her mind, to be replaced by far more pleasant ones.

She dragged a comb through her hair as she went

116

downstairs, where a welcome smell greeted her as she entered the kitchen. Her eyes widened at the sight of the table – in the centre was a plate of hot, buttered toast, and places laid for two. Tom was leaning against the kitchen counter, legs crossed, crunching on a piece of toast, and – she had to admit – looking very attractive. He seemed very at home there.

"Thought you might not be able to wait for lunch," he said, seeing her. "Shall I be mother?"

"Yes, please. Thanks for doing this. You didn't have to." She gave him a suspicious glance. "So you fibbed the other night when you implied you weren't domesticated?"

"I might have exaggerated a little." He grinned back at her, as he poured tea into her mug. He put the teapot down and gave her a searching look as he handed her the mug, a frown creasing his brow. "Have you been burning the candle at both ends? You've got shadows under your eyes." She didn't have time to reply before he went on, "Don't tell me Rupert whatsisface has been back? I'll have to go and sort him out, get the police involved."

"No, no, nothing like that… It's…it's something else." She didn't really want to tell him, but the look in his eyes told her he wouldn't be easy to fob off. It was also very flattering that he cared so much.

"What then?" He was leaning towards her, arms braced on the table, bringing him nearer. He'd have made a good detective, she thought; he'd be great at interrogations. She tried to play for time.

"You won't believe me if I tell you," she said, taking a gulp of her tea.

"Try me."

She shrugged, trying to appear nonchalant. "I'm not sleeping very well. Nightmares, that's all." Her tactic didn't work.

"What sort of nightmares? Do you normally have them?" He hadn't laughed. In fact, he sounded concerned. He moved round the table and now he was standing so close she could smell him – a clean smell of soap, and something indefinable, but definitely him.

"You know, the usual...running away...being trapped." Her heart was racing and it wasn't caused by the memory of her nightmares.

"Hmmm, you poor thing." He put his arm round her shoulder. "How long have you been getting those?" He put his hand under her chin and tipped her head gently, so that he was looking into her eyes. "Just since you moved here?"

Kate couldn't speak so she just nodded. How could he have such an effect on her, turning her insides to jelly with those dark, intense eyes, and a voice like chocolate?

Tom blinked, and then, as if remembering where he was, he moved away from her. "Well, about my suggestion of going to Swanpool. Do you fancy it?"

Relieved not to be interrogated further, but somehow disappointed that he'd pulled back...how close had they come to kissing? What had stopped him? And shouldn't she be glad he had? She was thoroughly confused. But she couldn't think of a reason to refuse his invitation, and besides, it would do her good to get out of the house for a few hours.

"I'll just get my things."

Why not have an enjoyable afternoon with him, she asked herself. She was obviously not his next target for a one-night-stand, judging by the way he'd pulled back from kissing her. As she ran upstairs to get her sunglasses and swimming things, she indulged herself by thinking what he might look like wearing swimming shorts. Well, she'd soon find out.

It was a perfect afternoon. Tom found a place to park not too far from the beach, and turning off the main road, manoeuvred his Land Rover into the car park. Fortunately, there were several vacant spaces – peak holiday season was still a couple of weeks away.

"This is Laura's." Tom pointed to one of the two paddleboards strapped to the car roof. "I thought I'd bring it, in case you fancied a go. Do you?"

"I'd love to, but I warn you, I'm a novice at this." Kate

hoped she wouldn't make a fool of herself. She was an excellent swimmer, but had never used a board before.

She needn't have worried. Tom patiently taught her the finer points of paddle boarding until she got the hang of it; before long she was able to both lie and kneel on the board, and move forward, without tipping into the water. He was good company, there was no doubt about it. She discerned no sign of arrogance or bad temper from him when she failed to keep her balance, just a steady hand to help, and encouraging words. It was a pity she wasn't looking for a serious relationship and neither was he. She'd just enjoy the day for what it was: two friends spending some time together.

Swanpool wasn't too crowded, and the families on the beach were mainly older couples or families with toddlers, as the schools hadn't yet broken up for the summer holidays. Halfway through the afternoon, older kids and teenagers started to appear. The bay filled up, and as she bobbed around on her board trying to avoid a particularly boisterous pair of young lads who were trying to duck each other under the water, she heard Tom call her.

"Kate! Fancy something to eat? Let's head over to the café."

Kate gave a thumbs-up sign and started to paddle after him. As he glided across the water to the beach, his shoulder muscles rippled, reminding her of an ancient sculpture of a Greek athlete she'd seen at the Ashmolean. She wondered what impression she made. She kept herself reasonably fit, but was definitely more soft curves than gym bunny toned – too many hours in the library and on the computer had seen to that.

The café was crowded but there was one free table outside. Kate sat down, glad to be in the shade of the awning, while Tom went to order the food. Feeling pleasantly exhausted, she looked out across the now crowded bay, shading her eyes from the sunlight and watching the waves as they broke on to the shingle beach. She felt lucky to live so close to the sea, it was practically on her door step. She was still lost in her thoughts when Tom returned, bearing a tray laden with baguettes, cake, coffee, and bottles of water.

"Gosh, didn't realise I was starving," said Kate, sometime later, guiltily wiping her mouth with a paper napkin. "Mind you, all I've had to eat today is a slice of toast, thanks to you."

"Thought I'd better feed you up." His brown eyes creased in a smile as he gazed at her from across the table. "You looked a bit wiped-out earlier. Now, you've got some colour in your cheeks."

They were relaxed and on neutral territory. It was the perfect opportunity to discover a bit more about him, so Kate took the plunge. "Where did you study? I assume you went to uni?"

He leaned back in his seat, increasing the distance between them across the table, but his smile didn't falter. "Yeah, went to Warwick. Shared a house in Leamington – it was great fun, despite the rats."

Kate grinned at him. "I lived in a house like that once…in York, though. It must be compulsory for student landlords to supply rats or mice for all their tenants." He chuckled and she dared to probe further. "Where did you go after uni?"

A nerve twitched in his cheek and his eyes darkened. He took a swig from his bottle of water before answering. "Moved to London. Got a job with a large consultancy firm. They had a graduate scheme, so it was a great opportunity for me to acquire a few more skills. Studying computing, you tend to meet the same sort of people, so it was good to get out into the real world." He fiddled with the bottle top, twisting and twirling it between his fingers. "After a couple of years, I moved on to another firm, an investment bank. Stayed there, made some money – enough to set me up here and try my hand at working for myself." He removed his sunglasses, and started to clean the lenses with the edge of his teeshirt as he squinted over at her. "How about you?"

Kate guessed that wasn't the whole story – in fact it all sounded so boring and innocuous, that he had to be keeping something from her – but satisfied for now with what he had shared, she decided to let it go. She told him about her career so far, working in libraries and archives round the country, sometimes even abroad, when her clients had foreign roots. "It's a bit like '*Who Do You Think You Are?*' but without the cameras and celebrities," she said with a wry grin. "And it takes a lot more hard work than they make out, where everything seems to fall into their laps." She wrinkled her nose, thinking for a moment. If they were to be friends it would be normal to share. "My real passion is illuminated manuscripts. In fact, I'm writing a book about them. My thesis was based on the subject, so a lot of the work has already been done and I've published academically, but I wanted to write something more accessible, you know?" She glanced over to see if his eyes had glazed over with boredom. Amazingly, they sparkled with interest.

"Wow! Very ambitious. Have you got a publisher?" He was now leaning towards her across the table. She'd go so far as to say he looked impressed, and a feeling of pleasure curled through her.

"Nah. Too soon to think of that. I think I'll wait until I've got the structure of the book and what I want to say sorted, before I start pitching."

They continued chatting as they ambled back to the car. She was feeling quite pleased that they were on an easier footing. Maybe it would not be too long until he felt able to confide in her. She climbed in beside him and started to fasten her seatbelt. Tom gripped her hand and her eyes met his. She was not expecting his next words.

"Now, about those nightmares?"

Chapter Seventeen

Kate froze. He was supposed to have forgotten what she'd told him this morning. Obviously, he hadn't. Now what should she say? "Oh, they were nothing. Probably been watching too many horror films."

"Yeah. Right," he said deadpan, turning the ignition. "I told you what happened when I stayed."

She interrupted before he could continue. "But that's been sorted. The art dealers have given up their stupid games, and I believe what Rupert said." If she said it out loud she might convince herself that nothing else was going on – no weird smells in the dining room, pictures not moving of their own volition, no drops in temperature.

His jaw clenched. "I think you're under a lot of stress. You need more than one night away to sort this out. It's all still playing on your mind."

"We'll see," she answered noncommittally, determined that she would sort it out herself without his, or anyone else's interference.

He grunted, but didn't say anything. They drove the rest of the way in silence.

As they pulled up on her drive she heard him take a deep breath and knew he wasn't going to let the subject drop. "Look, I'm not trying to bully you – I'd be the last one to do that – but I am worried about you. Mum told me how upset you were the other day." His eyes searched her face as he spoke, she could see he was really concerned.

She told herself it wouldn't hurt to be generous. "Why don't you come in and I'll see if I've had a reply from the Holburne. While I'm checking, you can go round the house, make sure everything's as it should be. I'm sure I'll sleep soundly knowing you've done that." She injected some levity into her voice, and smiled at him, hoping that would do the trick. It might indeed help her to sleep easier if Tom checked things, and it also might convince him she was a reasonable person, and not some hysterical head-case.

She was in the study as Tom began to go round the house. Before long, the floorboards above her creaked and she knew he'd gone upstairs. She forgot about him as she methodically went through her emails. As usual, there was lots of junk mail, quickly deleted. Then Kate spotted a long message from her mother and she became engrossed in reading about the great time she and Dad were having, now that the conference was over and they were travelling round. Kate smiled to herself – her mum and dad both worked hard, and it was the first real holiday they'd had in years.

At last she came to the message she'd hoped to see, from the Holburne. The curator there was happy to meet her and look at the portraits, but it would have to be either tomorrow or in two months' time, as she was taking a short sabbatical. The alternative was to take them to London and the curator gave the name of another expert, who Kate could contact.

Kate chewed her lip. She could get across to Bath tomorrow if she got up extra early – whichever route, it would take around four and a half hours. She should really check with Tom. Remembering him, she looked up. Where had he got to? It had all gone quiet. She cocked her head and listened. A muffled rhythmic thudding met her ears. It seemed to be coming from somewhere upstairs. She leapt out of her chair and headed off to find the source of the noise.

She paused at the bottom of the staircase. "Tom! Tom, are you up there?" The thudding stopped momentarily, then started again. Was that Tom's voice she could hear? She pounded up the stairs and halted on the landing.

"Hallo. Tom, are you there?"

"At last!" A muffled but unmistakably angry voice came from the front bedroom, the one where she'd been trapped on the first day. Feeling apprehensive, she reached out and grasped the handle, half expecting it not to budge. It moved easily. She pushed the door open and peered in to find an unsmiling Tom, his arms crossed and legs apart facing her. He did not look at all happy.

His voice was brusque. "How did you manage that? Is it your idea of a trick? I've been trying for the last fifteen minutes to get that handle to turn and it wouldn't give at all…and it's got bloody cold in here too." He moved forward, bundling her unceremoniously out of the bedroom and across the landing. The door closed with a bang behind them, making them both jump.

Kate started to shake, and Tom's body language changed from belligerence to concern. His arms went round her. His head turned towards the door then his eyes returned to rest on her. She was now shivering in his arms.

"Kate," he whispered. "What's going on?"

She vaguely remembered him guiding her downstairs and into the kitchen, where he pushed her down into a chair at the table. She watched as he put the kettle on and made them both coffee. She was still trembling.

He thrust a steaming mug into her hand, then went into the pantry and came out with the bottle of whisky. He tipped some into her mug, and did the same for his own. "I think we both need this. That was totally weird."

"I know," answered Kate. "The same thing happened to me on the day I moved in. I got trapped, the handle wouldn't turn." She gave a brittle laugh. "I'm afraid I very nearly panicked – I don't like enclosed spaces, you see. Can't do lifts, not unless someone is with me, and even then it's still an effort not to go to pieces." If anything was going to convince him that she had a propensity for hysteria then these embarrassing admissions would, she thought bitterly. So much for their burgeoning friendship. She wouldn't see him for dust. Instead, to her relief, his hand closed over hers and stayed there. It was funny, she thought, normally his presence induced either fury or butterflies… Now, the touch of his hand calmed her racing nerves.

"I thought you were mucking about at first," he admitted.

"Thought you'd locked me in. The curtains started flapping about, but the bloody window was closed. Then it went really cold. Bloody spooky. No wonder you're having nightmares." He squeezed her hand.

The whisky had done its job and she was beginning to recover her nerves. Of course it wasn't just the whisky – the fact that Tom still held her hand made her feel better. "Most of the time everything is fine. I avoid that room," she said. "But there is a smell of rosemary that comes and goes in the dining room...and that figure on the drive. I don't believe Rupert and his uncle are responsible for that."

"Hmm," he muttered, releasing her hand and taking a gulp of his coffee. He didn't sound convinced.

She wondered if she should say what she really thought. Would he think she was completely barking? He'd definitely been shaken up, she'd seen it in his eyes. Perhaps he'd be open to the idea that something unearthly was responsible. She decided to risk it. "I think it has something to do with Annabelle Tracy."

A flash of disbelief crossed his face. "What? A ghost you mean?" He rolled his eyes and shook his head. "I suppose stranger things have happened, but I can't help thinking something much more mundane is responsible. I know I was spooked, but maybe it was my imagination. You can convince yourself of anything given the right circumstances. Believe me, I know." His words were spoken with some vehemence and she wondered why. "I probably just didn't turn the handle the right way," he said finally.

"What about the curtains and the drop in temperature?" she shot back, determined to prove her point. She'd previously been disbelieving, trying to explain away irrational occurrences. "Besides," she added, "Win thought there was something weird going on too. What other explanation is there?"

Tom shook his head again. "A draught from the chimney? There's also some panelling in that room. Draughts could be coming from anywhere." He was being totally rational now, determined to deny the existence of anything unnatural. He took hold of her hand again, his tone soothing, as if she were a child. "Why on earth do you think a girl who has been dead for nearly two hundred years is responsible for some odd goings-on? I think you've probably been working too hard on Mum's papers, and what with the break-in and everything…"

"You think I'm mad, don't you?" Her words came blurting out as she whipped her hand out of his. If she didn't get a grip on her temper she was going to give him a few home truths. Why would he not believe her?

He groaned and pulled a pained face. "No, of course I don't. I've told you, I think you've been under some stress." He gripped her hand again. "You've admitted working till all hours. And you've just moved house. Good grief, that's one of the most stressful things you can do, isn't it? Look at me, Kate. You know I'm right. I know the mind can play awful tricks on you."

She looked up to see him pleading with his eyes – a look so intense it almost frightened her. She wondered briefly how he knew so much about the mind. Her shoulders slumped and her anger dissipated. He was correct, blast him.

Seeing his words had had the desired effect, he took the now empty mugs and made two more coffees, this time omitting the whisky. He sat down again, looking thoughtful, and pushed Kate's mug towards her. "Tell you what, I'll stay here with you tonight. Don't worry," he quickly added, seeing her eyes widen, "I'll sleep on the sofa."

Kate decided not to argue. "Whatever." He'd soon find out there was something unnatural going on. Either that or he'd be advising she see a shrink. It would be for the best if she knew one way or another. She couldn't let things carry on as they were.

"That way, I can confirm that Rupert and his uncle have abandoned their attempts to scare you and find out what's really going on here. Tomorrow, I'll look at that door handle, and we can also go round that room checking for draughts." He sent her an encouraging smile.

"You'll see. We'll soon get to the bottom of things."

Bless him, he did care and he was doing his best to

reassure her, she thought.

"OK, you're on." She remembered the email from the Holburne. "I'll have to get up quite early. The curator at the Holburne can only see me tomorrow afternoon, otherwise it means waiting for three months or taking the portraits to somebody else in London."

Tom grinned back at her. "Great! I fancy a trip to Bath tomorrow. I'll come with you. I can give the old girl a blow-out."

Kate frowned. Surely he was not referring to her Mini. It was almost new. "I'm happy to drive in my car."

"No, we'll use mine, I insist." She opened her mouth to protest, but he cut in before she could say anything. "Honestly, you'll be much more comfortable in mine. And it's not the old Land Rover. I mean my other car... Don't get the chance to drive her much since I moved down here." He gave her an enigmatic look. "If you think you'll be all right on your own for about twenty minutes, I'll go and collect my things." He grinned and had already disappeared out the door before she answered.

"Of course I'll be fine," she said to an empty room.

A couple of hours later they were back in the kitchen devouring the takeaway Tom had ordered. It had seemed like a good idea to eat something that wouldn't require a lot of washing up – not when they had an early start in the morning, and assuming they had a peaceful night.

Kate had also taken the opportunity to shower while Tom had gone to collect his things and, by the look of his damp hair and change of clothes, he'd done the same.

"I'm so glad you like curries," Tom said, as he helped himself to more nan bread. "My ex couldn't stand the smell, and wouldn't entertain cooking or buying anything remotely spicy." His tone became bitter. "I was only able to eat them when I had to meet a client for lunch...and when I got home I'd be in trouble because she could smell it on my breath." There was silence.

Kate looked up from her own plate of biriyani and saw the

look on Tom's face. His mouth had clammed shut, and his eyes refused to meet hers. He grabbed his glass of lager and took a swig. Her fork halted momentarily midway to her mouth, as she took stock. He'd spoken about his ex-fiancée and now it seemed he was regretting his disclosure. Tom's rigid posture told her not to probe. What had the woman done to make him so comprehensively wary of further relationships? It had to be more than banning the occasional curry. Whatever it was, there was no rush to find out, she decided. If their friendship grew, he would tell her in his own time.

"I'll let you into a little secret," she said. "I don't normally buy curries either."

He looked up, brow creased in a frown. "Oh... I thought you said you liked them. Was that a fib?"

Kate giggled. "Of course not. I don't buy them 'cos I make my own. I'm told my rogan josh is particularly good. Mix all my own spices and everything." She winked at him and felt glad when his face relaxed into a smile.

"You'll have to promise to make one for me," he said. "It's been ages since I've had a really good rogan josh. This one's not bad," he pointed to his nearly cleared plate, "but it's not quite the same as home-made."

"I'll need to stock up on some of my spices. I haven't done a proper shop yet. But, yes, I'll make us a curry if you bring the beer."

Tom raised his glass. "Deal."

There wasn't much washing-up, and what there was didn't take long. Tom insisted on doing it and Kate dried the plates and put them away. Like we're an old married couple, she thought, as she hung the tea-towel up to dry, before joining Tom in the drawing room. The spare duvet and pillows she'd brought down earlier lay piled up on the armchair, so she went over to join Tom on the sofa. It's going to be weird sleeping upstairs knowing he's down here, she thought. Weird, but quite nice and reassuring.

He shuffled up to make room for her as he played with the TV remote. "Why don't we watch TV for a bit, then I think you ought to go up to bed. We've an early start in the morning."

Kate arched an eyebrow at him. "Yes, Dad."

He gave what sounded like a snort. "Don't be like that. I'm only trying to be practical. You look done in, and you had a bit of a shock earlier."

She didn't need reminding, and a wave of guilt swept over her. He was only trying to look after her. It'd been a long time since a bloke had cared for her, and she just wasn't used to it.

She pulled an apologetic face. "Sorry, didn't mean to snap. You're right, I am a bit tired. Let's see what's on, then I'll make us some hot chocolate in a while, and we can both try and get some sleep. Are you sure you'll be comfortable on this?"

"Apology accepted." He grinned and bounced up and down on the sofa cushion. "See? Don't worry about me. It's fine, and in any case, I can sleep on a washing line."

"Is it me or is it getting a bit chilly in here?" Tom was rubbing his arms. Kate placed the two mugs of chocolate she was carrying down on the coffee table and nervously looked at the clock on the mantelpiece. It was almost eleven.

"It's a bit early for anything to start." Her insides were beginning to churn and she knew it wasn't because of the curry. She'd only been out the room a short time, but the temperature had dropped considerably in her absence.

"Don't be daft, woman, that's not what I meant." Tom's words were reassuringly bracing. "Now it's dark outside, the temperature's bound to be lower. There's nothing to worry about." He pulled on her arm. "Here, sit down. Let's pull this duvet round our shoulders, and you snuggle up next to me while we drink our chocolate and watch the rest of this film."

Kate shook her head and smiled. It was good that he was rational, it helped her regain her own scepticism. Maybe being on her own had made her prey to stupid ideas, letting her imagination run away with her. She sat down and he pulled her closer, tucking the duvet round her. She relaxed and rested her head on his shoulder. On the screen Katherine Hepburn and Cary Grant were arguing, but it was obvious that their characters' real feelings for each other were something quite different.

Tom took a sip from his mug and settled back, putting his arm around Kate's shoulder. "Mmmm, this is nice," he whispered, echoing Kate's own thoughts.

They watched on for several minutes until, with no warning, the TV flickered then died, and the room was plunged into darkness.

Kate froze and felt Tom pull his arm away. "Bloody hell!" He cursed. "A power cut. Just when I was going to…kiss you."

"Oh." It was all she could think to say. She'd been rigid with fear that something overwhelmingly creepy and supernatural was going to occur, but his matter-of-fact oath and logical reason for the blackout brought back her normal scepticism for other-worldly occurrences. She shouldn't let her imagination run away with her. The power failure was just a coincidence. Then his words sank in. "Were you?" She whispered.

"Well, yes. But if you'd rather we didn't…? I'm sorry. I thought… "

She'd quite liked to be kissed. Had been longing for him to kiss her, if she was honest.

"No. I mean, yes. We can kiss in the dark, can't we?" She reached out and put her arms round his neck, and he pulled her onto his lap. The wool of his Aran jumper rubbed her cheek as she snuggled close and he nuzzled her neck. She caught a whiff of his aftershave: something subtle, fresh citrus and hints of bergamot. She moved her head to angle her lips near to his, opening her eyes briefly to make sure she didn't collide with his nose. For a fraction of a second she had a clear view over his shoulder through the window behind.

She froze.

"What's the matter, Kate? Only a kiss, love. We won't go further; not unless you want to …"

She must have been making some sort of sound, for he stopped murmuring and nuzzling, and turned his head to look where she was looking. She knew from the way he tensed beneath her that he'd seen the same thing.

"Good grief, what's that?" he hissed in her ear.

They untangled themselves and Tom grabbed his phone off the coffee table. The room was freezing now, their breath condensing like mist in the frigid air.

Kate found her voice at last. "If you open the sash, we can climb out that way, it'll be quicker."

Tom was already at the window, sliding it upwards. He slung one leg over the sill and there was a crunch of gravel as he landed. Kate, nerves jangling, scrambled after him, grabbing his arm before he set off without her. There was no way she was going to be left behind. She shivered in the cold night air and looked to the spot where the ethereal figure was still just visible, gliding down the drive. Her fingers dug into Tom's arm, making him stop, as she'd intended. "Is it…is it…beckoning us?" she hissed.

"Looks like. Come on, we'll catch the beggar." Tom started off again, his hand now firmly clasping hers. "Look, it wants us to go into the woods. It seems to be glowing. Some sort of clever trick, it must be. No such thing as…" his voice trailed off as whatever it was suddenly plunged off the drive and into the tangle of trees and shrubs.

The beam from Tom's phone played over greenery. "There he is. I'm going after him. Go back to the house, Kate. This looks as if it might be tricky in the dark."

"Don't be stupid. Of course I'm coming with you," she growled back at him. Blimey, did he think because she was female she was going to wimp out?

Their pace got slower the further into the woodland they got. Branches tore and scratched at Kate's bare arms and she cursed inwardly. If only she'd remembered to pick up her fleece before leaping out the window. Stumbling on, they made some progress into the overgrown shrubs and woodland that led down towards the coast. Tom was in front and his hissed curses could be heard as he tripped up over a fallen branch. Kate caught up with him as he disentangled himself and stood up. She bent forward, resting her hands on her knees, trying to get her breath back. She felt Tom's hand on her shoulder and swivelled her head to looked up at him.

"I think we've lost him," he said through gritted teeth. "I just don't know how he managed to move so fast through this stuff." He waved the beam from his phone over the tangle of fallen branches, tangled ivy, and shrubs gone mad. "I'm pretty fit, but there's no way I could get through this lot at speed. They must know a path through it that we missed in the dark."

Kate straightened up. She'd never been in this part of the woodland before, even as a child. Win had always warned her that it was unsafe and therefore out of bounds. She strained her ears, trying to catch the sound of their mystery figure crashing through the woods. Surely a real person would make a noise, unless they'd stopped too... Or they weren't human. All she heard was the hooting of a distant owl, and the long doleful blast of a ship's horn as it departed Falmouth docks. She shrugged and rubbed her hands up and down her arms.

"Here, take my jumper." Before she could protest, Tom put his phone down, stripped off his sweater and was pulling it over her head. It was deliciously warm and smelt of him.

"What about you?" Her voice was muffled by the Aran's bulk, until she found the opening for her head.

"I'm fine. My shirt covers my arms. Yours must be scratched to bits, you daft girl." She could tell he was smiling as he said this. "Why didn't you put something on before coming on this wild-goose chase?"

"What? And let you go off without me? No chance!"

He moved towards her and gently tugged her hair out of the jumper where it had got caught up. He gave her a quick decisive kiss.

"There," he whispered, "all sorted." He picked up his phone from where it lay on the ground. "Come on, no point in us trying to break our necks out here any more. Let's get back. Only we'll go a bit slower this time." He clasped her hand. "I'll lead the way. We'll get to the bottom of this, Kate. There's someone behind all this, I'm sure. Someone real. Stop worrying, we'll sort it out together."

Chapter Eighteen

It had gone midnight and Kate lay in bed staring at the ceiling. Sleep would not come. How could she sleep knowing Tom was curled up on the sofa downstairs, adamant that he would protect her from some human mischief-maker, when she was now convinced that no human was involved? It was stretching things to ask someone like him to consider the possibility of a ghost, or more precisely, the ghost of Annabelle Tracy. A shiver ran down her spine. It was the only explanation. Win had believed it, and with all the strange goings-on, she too believed a restless spirit haunted the house and grounds. The question was why?

It had all started with Win finding Annabelle's journal. Perhaps if she could discover what had happened to Annabelle, it might explain things. The portraits were another link. Hopefully, tomorrow would answer more questions.

I'll find you, Annabelle.

Thinking of tomorrow brought Kate's mind back to Tom again. Even if he didn't believe in ghosts, and perhaps thought her a tiny bit mad, she had to admit, he was being very protective of her. A frisson of excitement shot through her, remembering their nearly-kiss on the sofa – the one in the woods had been too quick to count. She'd been tingling with anticipation; it had felt so good to be curled up on his lap, running her fingertips over the stubble on his cheeks, breathing in his smell of fresh soap, bergamot, and him. If only she hadn't looked out the window. She sighed. Never mind, there would be other opportunities.

She'd enjoyed being with him yesterday. He'd shown her an entirely different side to his nature. She should have guessed that a man who cared for his family, and whose family was protective of him, was bound to be a decent human being. Again, she wondered about Laura's warning not to hurt him and his inadvertent admission of the way his ex had exercised control.

Kate frowned. There must be a lot more to it. What else had the mysterious Eve done to damage him so badly?

And could she be the one to convince him that not all women were the same?

By six o'clock they were on the road. The other car turned out to be a two seater Mercedes roadster, normally kept in the garage by the side of Tom's cottage. It smelt of leather, its seats an impractical cream colour, but gloriously comfortable.

Kate couldn't resist surreptitiously running her fingers over the edges of her seat, a contrast to the cloth covers in her own beloved Mini. The portraits had been carefully stashed in the boot, and they were driving, at Tom's suggestion, with the roof down. To her surprise, it didn't feel like being in a wind tunnel. Tom had assured her that if she did get chilled he would stop and put the roof up.

"And we shouldn't get wet; no rain is forecast. It should be sunshine all the way." He patted the steering wheel lovingly. "It's ages since I've had her out for a long run."

Kate smiled to herself at Tom's enthusiasm for his car. Despite her father's best efforts to educate her in the finer points of car engineering and styling, she'd only been interested in how reliable and economical they were to run. She didn't get men and their cars – as far as she was concerned, a car was just an efficient way of getting from A to B.

Dad would probably get on very well with Tom, she thought. She swallowed. What on earth was she thinking? It was more likely that the two would never meet. Tom was surely only sticking with her as a friend to solve this mystery. She must remember that. She couldn't see a long-term future for them… But a short-term fling might be nice.

The roads were fairly clear – what traffic there was

consisted of trucks and farm vehicles, the holidaying hordes had not yet awoken, so the miles slipped by. To her surprise, Kate found that she enjoyed travelling with the roof down, the breeze riffling her hair, cooling her cheeks, and the feeling of being somehow more connected to the environment. Stopping at traffic lights brought snatched conversations of passing pedestrians, the calls of children cycling on the pavement, dogs barking, the pungent smells, tempting and otherwise, wafting out of takeaways. The whole experience was for her a stark contrast to the disconnected sensation of driving in a conventional car. She began to understand why Tom preferred it.

It did however, make conversation more difficult. After exchanging pleasantries for the first few miles, she and Tom both lapsed into silence, the effort of raising their voices, to be heard over the noise of the traffic being too great. She consoled herself with the thought that there would be other opportunities later that day.

She turned puzzled eyes to Tom when he pulled off the road shortly after passing Exeter, turning up a well-tended driveway towards a rather posh-looking country-house hotel.

"I don't know about you, but I'm feeling hungry. I thought we might stop here for breakfast," Tom said as he pulled up in one of the parking bays.

"Sure. I am a bit peckish." Kate picked up her leather tote bag and swung her legs out of the car. "Mmmm, that feels better," she said after stretching her arms above her head and tipping her face towards the sky. "What's the matter?"

Tom was staring at her, an appreciative glint in his eyes.

"Nothing at all, from what I can see." He walked round to her side of the car and took her arm. "Come on, follow me."

They went up the stone staircase and through the impressive doorway into a large tiled entrance hall, from which several corridors led off. Kate was impressed, it looked like a very expensive hotel.

"I've used this a few times before," said Tom, interrupting her perusal of the framed prints on the walls, and which explained the porter's familiar greeting.

"I'm having the full English. What would you like?" Tom closed the breakfast menu and smiled at Kate across the table. They were seated in a pleasant conservatory, overlooking a manicured garden. The only other occupants were an elderly couple, who looked like hotel residents, at a table in the far corner.

"The same, please," answered Kate, inwardly vowing to spend more time swimming in the coming days to work off all the calories. She wasn't going to turn down a full English breakfast this time in favour of a croissant, she wasn't that daft. In any case, croissants made outside France never really tasted as good as genuine French ones, she told herself.

"I'll just ring Uncle Pete. Let him know we're coming." Tom pulled out his phone and checked the time. "He should be up by now. Blast!" He frowned. "Have to go outside. I might get a signal there." He stood up. "What time are we scheduled to see your expert again?"

Kate checked the note on her phone. "Dr Kemble said any time after one thirty."

"I'm hoping we'll get there well before then. How long do you think she'll need?"

Kate shrugged. "Not sure." There'd been no mention in the email from the curator. "She might be able to tell straight away or it could take longer. But she did say she would only be there until four."

"Right." Tom ran a hand through his hair. "Let's assume we'll be finished by four. I'll tell Pete we'll be with him by four thirty."

She followed him with her eyes as he strode out the dining room, phone clamped to his ear, and grinned at the appreciative look the waitress gave his jean-clad derriere.

True to his words, they arrived before noon and found a vacant space in the car park near the Royal Victoria Park.

"We're the wrong side of town for the Holburne, but I didn't want to try the smaller car parks. Bath's so crowded this time of year, they're bound to be full," said Tom, pressing the button for the roof to close.

Kate got out and did her stretches again, while Tom sorted out the parking fee on his phone. The final part of the journey had been the worst. Bath was horribly congested and it had been a crawl through the town. It felt like they'd been driving round forever.

"We've got a bit of a walk, but I'll carry these," said Tom, lifting the holdall with the portraits out of the boot, and hefting it onto his shoulder. "And I think we should have time for a coffee first. There's a nice little Italian I know."

"Sounds good to me." Kate saw his outstretched hand and, after the briefest hesitation, reached out her own. His fingers clasped hers and...somehow, it felt right. It had been a while since she'd walked hand in hand with a guy. She hadn't realised till now how much she missed it.

If the roads had been busy with traffic, then the pavements were even worse. Kate decided that the world and his wife were spending the day in Bath. Groups of disinterested students, shepherded by anxious-looking teachers thronged in the main thoroughfares, blocking the entrances to the Abbey and the Pump Rooms. Voices in different accents and languages assailed the air. Kate and Tom had to shout to make themselves heard. After threading their way through the crowded streets for what seemed like ages, Tom led a now hot and perspiring Kate down a narrow alleyway lined with shops. About halfway down he halted in front of a crowded café. All the tables outside were taken, and peering through the window, Kate saw with disappointment that it was just as busy inside.

She arched an eyebrow at Tom. "It looks pretty full to me."

Tom shook his head. "Don't give up yet. Come on, they might have room upstairs." He went through the door and to Kate's relief, the guy behind the counter gestured them towards a narrow winding staircase.

"Thought so," said Tom, a hint of smugness in his tone.

Kate rolled her eyes and followed him up. Ten minutes later she sipped her aromatic coffee and gazed round the room, filled with the pleasant hum of hushed conversations. There was air conditioning so it was cooler than outside and far more comfortable than on the congested streets. She watched as waitresses clattered up and down the stairs, carrying trays of food and drinks from the kitchen to the customers at the mismatched tables and chairs. Their cheerful chatter was a mix of Italian and English. Smartly dressed office workers sat cheek by jowl with students and pensioners in the small space that made up the first floor. It was a world away from the gleaming modernity of the Ubiquitous Bean.

Kate looked down and forked another generous portion of the most decadent and delicious chocolate cake into her mouth. It melted on her tongue. "Mmmm, this is good," she said, licking her lips. "So good, in fact that it probably has a million calories."

"I thought you were going to do that thing from '*When Harry Met Sally*' then," said Tom, a wicked twinkle in his eye. "I think I'd quite enjoy hearing you groan…in pleasure."

Kate glanced round, her cheeks burning, to check that no one else had heard. "Shhh, you're embarrassing me." She giggled. It was fun being flirted with. She knew he wasn't serious.

Tom winked at her. "Now admit it, don't I know the best places?"

"You do indeed," she admitted. "How do you do it?"

He tapped the side of his nose. "My secret. I like things to be absolutely right."

He held her gaze as he spoke, his eyes not laughing now, but serious and intense. Her pulse started to race. Somehow she knew he was not referring to the coffee or the cake. He'd said something similar at the cottage and looked at her in that same way, turning her insides to jelly. Was he hinting that she meant something to him? No, she was reading too much into what was probably a flippant remark.

She tore her eyes away and checked her phone for the time. "One o'clock. Shall we head off?"

He gave her another smile that sent her insides fluttering. "Just when I was beginning to enjoy myself," he said with a wicked twinkle in his eyes.

They arrived at the museum on time and, after their identities had been confirmed, they were ushered into the curator's office. A smiling silver-haired woman – Kate guessed she was in her sixties – came forward to greet them. June Kemble had sounded friendly on the phone, and this impression was not dispelled on seeing her in the flesh. Through large black framed glasses, her blue eyes sparkled with interest and her fuchsia red painted lips twitched into a welcoming smile.

"Professor Kemble, thank you so much for agreeing to see us," said Kate offering her hand. "This is Tom Carbis. His mother is the owner of one of the portraits."

"How do you do, Dr Wilson and you, Mr Carbis? It's nice to meet you both at last." Professor Kemble shook both their hands enthusiastically, and beamed at them, showing teeth that were gapped and slightly prominent. She reminded Kate of an inquisitive squirrel. "I must say, I'm very intrigued. This will be a really exciting find if what you have are genuine Vaslet portraits. There are so few that we know of, and most of them are in Oxford, at Merton College. Please call me June, and if you'd like to put the portraits there," she indicated two empty easels, "I'll examine them."

There was a deep inhalation of breath from June when Kate and Tom unwrapped the portraits and placed them carefully on an easel each. The curator paced this way and that, crouching down and surveying them through a magnifying glass she'd pulled out of her jacket pocket.

"Mmmm," was all she said for several minutes, before starting her perusal again.

Kate's hopes began to fade. How long would it take for the curator to confirm that they were not what she thought? After what seemed like ages, June straightened up, sucked in her cheeks, and turned to face Kate and Tom.

"Well… I'm happy to stake my reputation that these are indeed by Vaslet. The strokes are quite characteristic."

Kate let out her breath and heard Tom's own sigh of relief.

She dug out the invoice from her bag and passed it to June, who peered at it for a moment before exclaiming,

"That's wonderful.This adds to the provenance. It's like the icing on the cake. I must do a paper on this." There was no doubting that June was one very happy bunny.

"Is there any way that the sitters can be identified?" Kate asked tentatively, crossing her fingers.

"Hmm, that might be a little more difficult." June's vivid red mouth twisted. "He didn't leave many records so we don't know all his patrons. If you have an idea who they might be, and there are other extant portraits of them... well...that might be a way to make identification."

"Kate thinks her portrait is John Lanyon, the Earl of Batheaston," Tom put in, "and the portrait of the young lady came to my mother via her grandmother. That side of the family are distantly related to the Lanyons, but Mum hasn't been in touch with them for years." He frowned. "I suppose I could contact them and see if they have a portrait of John." He turned to Kate. "It might mean another trip over here."

June looked thoughtful. "Well, the current earl is a great patron of the arts, and has supported this museum most generously. I could give him a call and explain the situation. I know he's at Lanyon Park at present because he phoned me yesterday about a fundraiser we're holding next week." She trotted over to her desk. "Give me a moment." She began to flick through a large notebook.

Kate still hadn't uncrossed her fingers. *Oh please let there be a portrait of John Lanyon.*

Ten nail-biting moments later and it was confirmed. Kate unlocked her fingers and inwardly thanked the god of researchers. She was so overwhelmed that everything seemed to be working out, that she nearly missed the small detail of the appointment Professor Kemble made on their behalf. She and Tom were expected to visit Lanyon Park the following day.

Tom waved away Kate's muttered protestations as they finally made their goodbyes to an ecstatic June, who was itching to telephone her colleagues at the Royal Academy to inform them of *her* discovery.

"Don't worry, I'll sort something out," hissed Tom under

his breath as he smiled and nodded to June who ushered them to the door.

Back outside in the sunshine, Kate let her exasperation show as she followed him down the path through Sydney Gardens.

"We'll have to find somewhere to stay now. I didn't plan on this." She shouldn't be grumbling, but she hated being bulldozed into things. Was he reverting back to type – the arrogant bully she'd first encountered? "Why on earth did you agree? I could easily come back another time."

He didn't stop walking, nor did he answer. Kate pulled a face behind his back. Did he have an ulterior motive? Bath was always packed in the summer months, and they'd be pushed to find a hotel. Perhaps he was hoping they'd have to share a room. She frowned to herself as she hurried to catch him up.

No, he'd spent the night at her house sleeping on the sofa – if he'd wanted to get more intimate he'd have tried then. She was not entirely sure she would have refused, if he had tried. Good grief, she was confused!

He stopped suddenly, grabbed her arm, and pulled her over to a bench. "Stop worrying. I know you want to get this mystery sorted, and I want to help you. You can easily pick up a toothbrush and anything else you need."

"Yes, but—"

"Yes, but nothing," he interrupted. "Uncle Pete invited us to stay over when I called him this morning. At the time I told him we didn't plan on stopping, but I'm sure he'd still be happy to put us up." He folded his arms and his face had that irritatingly smug expression that she'd come to recognise. His eyes twinkled, and she knew any further complaint on her part would be irrational and churlish. "I'll give him a call now and let him know we're on our way."

She stayed on the bench as he stood up and walked a few paces away to make his call. Frustration welled up inside her. Kate hated not feeling in control, and Tom had wrong-footed her again. She took a deep breath. *Get a grip, Kate!* June had identified the portraits as Vaslet's work, and they were

142

another step along the way to identifying the sitters. She should be over the moon.

Tom had been the perfect companion all day, looking after her and generally giving the impression that he enjoyed her company and wanted to get to know her better. But that was the problem. On the face of it, he was perfect – any normal, hot-blooded girl's dream of a boyfriend, but the waitress's words still rang in her head – he didn't go in for commitment. And she didn't want to get involved only to get dumped the next day. He was so bloody attractive, physically and intellectually, and hard to resist. What was a girl to do?

"That's all sorted." Tom's words broke into her reverie as he flopped beside her on the bench. "We'll call in on Uncle Pete just now. His apartment is only down the road. Then we can go and pick up a few things for tonight and collect the car. Auntie Rose has driven to Salisbury to visit a friend and won't be back until late tomorrow, so we can use her parking space." He nudged her with his elbow. "You look a bit glum. What's up? I thought you'd be pleased to have the artist confirmed."

Kate looked up and saw the concern in his eyes. It was time to bite the bullet. She could no longer cope with the roller-coaster of feelings he provoked in her. She had to tell him what was on her mind.

Chapter Nineteen

Kate shifted uncomfortably, not knowing how to start, and unable to look him in the eye.

"What's the matter, Kate?" He squeezed her arm. "I can tell you've got something on your mind. Is it something to do with what's going on at The Beeches? I've told you I'll help to sort it out."

God, he was being so nice. It was a temptation to fling herself into his arms and ignore all her doubts. Instead she steeled herself, lifted her chin, and looked him in the eye.

"It's about us, actually."

His eyes narrowed in confusion. "What do you mean? I thought we were getting along well. I really like you, Kate." A nerve twitched in his cheek. "I…I thought you liked me."

Instinctively, she stretched out her hand and gripped his arm. "That's the problem. I do like you…a lot. But…" She hesitated for a fraction, before blurting out, "I've heard you're not into commitment."

"Who told you that?" He shrugged off her arm, the nerve in his cheek twitching like mad.

"It doesn't matter who." She wasn't going to tell him. Before he could object, she continued, determined to explain herself. "You see, I've been hurt…badly. When I moved to Falmouth I'd decided to avoid getting involved, at least for the time being. Then you came along." She shrugged. "And…well…I'm frightened of being hurt again, Tom. If you're only interested in a quick fling, then I'm afraid you'll have to look elsewhere."

His face had turned pale, his eyes two black hard marbles, bleak and soulless. She was frightened at the effect her words had had on him. All she could think about was how she would get back to Falmouth. Had she destroyed their friendship? Was he really just a cold-hearted bastard?

Then something inside him seemed to break, and he took her in his arms. "Oh Kate. I'm so sorry." His voice was muffled in her hair. She felt him shiver and knew he was trying to regain control of his emotions. "You're the first person I've allowed to get close to me in ages. I never even considered that you might be cautious about a relationship." His warm breath caressed her ear. "God, I've been very selfish, focussing on myself, and I'm not surprised you heard I was only after one night stands. That's what I did for a while when I moved back." He pulled away and looked her in the eye. "There weren't that many, I promise you, but in a small place like Falmouth...well...word gets round. I just didn't trust anyone."

"Why not?" Was he ready to tell her about his ex-fiancée? His eyes shuttered and she knew the answer to her silent question.

"Maybe another time." His eyes slid away from hers. "It's still pretty painful to talk about it, and I don't want to spoil the day." He looked up, was that a hint of fear in his eyes? "And...you might think differently about me."

"You can't be sure about that." Her stomach clenched. What was he worried about her finding out? "But I won't push you if you're not ready to tell me."

"Look." He took both her hands in his. "I will tell you soon, but not today. I do want more than a quick fling with you, Kate, believe me. I like that you don't play games. You're straightforward and tell it like it is." He chuckled. "God, when you yelled at me after I tried to throw you out of Mum's, it clicked somewhere in my brain that you weren't messing around. You said I was arrogant and rude and then you stomped out."

Kate was jolted into laughter. "I did not stomp."

"Alright, you flounced," he shot back. He was looking at her sideways, but she could tell he was grinning.

"That's even worse than stomping." She was glad to see he was more like himself.

He wrapped his arm round her again and she snuggled into him. A group of teenagers sniggered as they walked past. Kate didn't care. She and Tom had cleared the air between them and now she knew he was serious.

"Why don't we take things slowly, get to know each other a bit more before…before things get too intense?" He let out a deep breath. "I don't want to hurt you, Kate and, goodness knows, I couldn't bear to get hurt again."

"That sounds like a plan I could go along with."

He pulled her towards him and nuzzled her forehead. "Come on," he murmured into her hair, "Uncle Pete will think we've got lost."

Tom's uncle lived in an apartment on Great Pulteney Street, only a few steps away from the Holburne. He was tall, like Tom, and in his early sixties. His sharp, intelligent eyes assessed Kate as they sat in the impressively large living room, drinking iced water from tall crystal tumblers. The room was a cool respite from the heat of outdoors. Through the open sash window, the occasional vehicle could be heard as it passed by. Fortunately, although a broad thoroughfare, and important in its heyday, Great Pulteney Street was now mainly used by pedestrians heading either to the Holburne at one end or Pulteney Bridge and the city centre at the other.

Dressed in navy chinos and a white polo shirt, Pete leaned back against the cushions of the large cream leather sofa and smiled at Kate who was seated on an identical sofa on the opposite side of a polished maple coffee table. The seat was too deep for her and the leather slippery. She was worried she might slide off.

"So you're a historian, Kate? Tom tells me you're helping Sue with some of our family papers."

"That's right," Kate answered, setting her glass down on the table, making sure it sat neatly on its coaster. The whole apartment looked as if it had never seen a sticky finger or a speck of dust, and she didn't want to be the first to spoil its pristine condition. "I've already made a list of all the documents to do with your grandparents and sorted them into separate folders. It should be easier now to find anything you need. I can send you a copy of the catalogue once it's finished."

Pete nodded. "I'd like that, yes. Thank you. Like Sue, I just haven't had the time to sort it myself." He turned to Tom, who was lounging next to Kate. "How's Laura, Tom? Your mum and dad must be worried sick. Last time I spoke to her, your mum said they were off to Belgium to see a specialist. How did it go?"

Tom heaved himself up and paced to the window to gaze out. "Not too bad, actually. He said he could help." His voice was gruff, he cleared his throat. "Laura's very optimistic and that's what she needs, some hope that things will improve. But she's a very strong person – mentally, I mean." His hands clenched and unclenched. "If anyone can get through this illness, she will."

After finishing their drinks, Pete showed them to their rooms – separate, to Kate's relief. Tom must have explained that they were not sleeping together.

"I've put you in Jenny's old room, Kate. The bed's already made up. We never know when she's going to drop in on us, so Rose always keeps it ready. And Tom, you can go in the spare room. Rose'll be sorry to have missed you." He squinted at Tom. "Are you sure you can't stay over a second night? It's bad luck that I'd already made plans for tonight to meet an old colleague from work. Bob and I are going for a meal and a pint while Rose is away, so I won't be able to spend much time with you either."

"Don't worry about us, Uncle Pete." Tom patted him on the shoulder. "Kate and I will go out for a meal. It's really good of you to put us up at such short notice. We weren't planning on staying over, but the curator at the Holburne got us the appointment with Charles Lanyon tomorrow. We can't really afford to miss it."

"Good of him to see you, I suppose." Pete shook his head. "Haven't seen Charles in ages, our paths don't cross much. Grandma's funeral, I think. Give him my regards, won't you?"

A short time later, Kate and Tom left to go and collect the car. Pete had given them a key, and instructed them to help themselves to tea and coffee and generally make themselves at home. On the way, they'd called in to a supermarket for toiletries, and Tom had booked a table for later in the evening at a restaurant near The Circus.

"Don't tell me, you know all the best places," teased Kate as he put his phone back in his pocket.

Tom arched his eyebrows in mock condescension. "Of course. I like things absolutely right." If she didn't know him better, she'd think him quite impossible. She smiled as she followed Tom into the car park. Apart from the unsettling experience of baring her soul to him earlier and listening to his own partial confession, she hadn't enjoyed herself so much in ages, and the day wasn't over yet.

The drive to back to Pete's apartment was another frustrating crawl through Bath's busy streets. "Why is it called rush hour?" wondered Kate out loud, as she sweltered in the passenger seat. The temperature was still quite high, even for this late part of the afternoon.

Tom grinned back at her. "Bit of an oxymoron, isn't it?"

When they got back, Pete had already left. There was a note on the sleek black granite island in the kitchen telling them to help themselves to towels from the airing cupboard, and that there was plenty of hot water if they wanted to shower.

"Sounds like a good idea," said Tom. "We've got enough time to freshen up before heading off to the restaurant. It'll take about twenty minutes to walk there, and there should even be enough time for a drink in a nice little wine bar I know."

"You know a lot of places in Bath. Have you spent a lot of time here?" asked Kate, pouring herself a large glass of chilled sparkling water from one of the taps over the stainless steel sink. She'd had trouble knowing which one to use, until Tom had helped her, pointing out that one served chilled, the other boiling water. She made a mental note that, when she had money to burn, she'd install something similar at The

Beeches.

"Only flying visits over the years," he replied, helping himself to a glass. "Jenny – my cousin – used to drag me out whenever I came over." He leaned against the island, legs crossed, as he continued to talk. "She knows all the best places. I used to do the same for her when she came up to London. We used to meet up quite often until…" He closed his mouth, then quickly added. "You'd like her. Pity she's working in the States at the moment."

After showering, and making herself more presentable – it was amazing what washing one's hair and applying a little lipstick could do – Kate strolled arm-in-arm with Tom up Great Pulteney Street towards the iconic Pulteney Bridge. The evening air was warm and still, and they weren't alone in taking the opportunity to enjoy the sights and sounds of a Bath summer evening.

"I wonder if Annabelle and John managed to stroll like this while they were both in Bath," Kate wondered aloud. "Probably not, thinking about it." She sighed. "Annabelle would've been chaperoned most of the time and certainly not permitted out alone with a gentleman in the evening."

"You are fixed on this couple, aren't you?" said Tom with feeling. "I hope we get to the bottom of things, you've got me quite wound up about it too."

The meal was perfect as far as Kate was concerned. The food and wine were delicious, but above all, Tom was an entertaining and witty companion. They were getting on so well, that it was only when the waitress brought the bill, that they both looked round to see they were the only remaining patrons.

Tom looked at his watch. "Good grief! Is that the time? I'm terribly sorry." He checked the bill and handed over his credit card to the yawning waitress.

"I'll settle my share when we get back," said Kate. She didn't want him to think she was a freeloader.

"Nonsense. I'll get this. If you insist, you can buy lunch tomorrow." He shoved the receipt in his pocket.

"And I also want to go halves on the fuel costs." Kate

persisted. "It's not fair for you to pay for everything."

He rolled his eyes. "We can discuss it when we get back. Now, no more talk of money."

Light from the window of the apartment indicated that Pete had returned.

Tom grabbed Kate's hand as she reached for the doorbell. "Just a minute," he whispered, wrapping his arms around her. "I've been aching to do this all day, and if we go in, well…" He inclined his head towards hers, his lips parted, and she closed her eyes. She'd been anticipating this moment too. Inhaling, she caught a whiff of his scent, a combination of soap, sandalwood, and…Tom. Her skin tingled, and the first gentle touch of his lips on hers sent her pulse rocketing. She angled her mouth to accommodate his. This would be heavenly.

"I thought I heard the lift," boomed a voice behind her. Her eyes shot open. Pete stood grinning at them from the now open front door. "Come in, come in. We can have a nice catch up now you're back."

Tom retained a hold on Kate's hand. From his almost bone-crushing grip, she guessed he was as annoyed and frustrated as she. It gave the lie to the smile now plastered on his face.

"Hi, Uncle Pete. That'll be nice."

Chapter Twenty

Pete had kept them talking until the small hours. This, combined with the early start from Falmouth, the long drive, and several glasses of wine, had the resultant effect of sending Kate to sleep almost as soon as her head touched the pillow. It was just as well, really. She'd been eaten up with frustration and longing for Tom's kiss, and trying to make polite conversation took up the last of her reserves. She could tell by the intense looks he kept sending her way, Tom was feeling the same.

Pete insisted on making them a full cooked breakfast before they departed for Lanyon Park the next day, so it was mid-morning before he finally waved them off. As they rounded the corner onto Edward Street, Tom let out a deep breath.

"Uncle Pete, bless him, means well… But my goodness." He dragged a hand through his hair.

Kate laughed. "He was very kind, cooking us that breakfast. I'd have been perfectly happy with a piece of toast, 'specially after that meal last night." She was seriously contemplating a five mile run once she got back home. She had to work off some of the extra calories she'd consumed in the last couple of days.

Tom grinned as he put the car into third. "I know, it was very good of him to make us so welcome. I think he and Aunt Rose miss having Jenny around. That reminds me, I must tell Mum she should visit them sometime, though it is difficult, what with Laura and everything."

They cleared Bath without too many hold-ups, the traffic being light at that time of day. A few miles out of town, Tom took the signposted turn off for Lanyon Park, and soon they were cruising along a winding tree-lined drive. In a dip in the landscape the house came into view. It was impressive: a grand Palladian residence in the honey-coloured limestone the area was famous for. A home befitting an Earl.

Kate couldn't help herself. "Wow! Some house."

"Isn't it just?" agreed Tom with a wry smile. "Pity they're such distant relatives. I could quite fancy staying here for a few days." He parked the car on the wide gravel drive in front of the main entrance, and Kate got out to join him in admiring the view of the parkland and gardens, before retrieving the bag with the portraits from the boot.

"Hello! Is that Tom?" a voice called. They turned simultaneously to see a lanky figure standing at the open front door.

"Yes, I'm Tom Carbis," called back Tom, as he headed towards the speaker.

Kate was surprised to see it was a guy about their own age, dressed in a well-worn pair of jeans and a tired grey tee shirt. Despite his floppy blond hair, that he kept sweeping out of his eyes, and an accent that denoted a public school education, he was not what she had in mind when she thought of an earl. Kate hoped he had a few more brains than Rupert, who'd definitely not been an advert for an expensive private education.

"Hi, I'm Freddie. Dad said you'd be calling, but I'm afraid he had to go out, so he's left me to do the honours. Do come in."

Freddie beckoned them into a large tiled vestibule and smiled as he held out his hand to Tom. "Welcome to Lanyon Park. I understand we're related, is that right? Dad said you're some sort of cousin."

Tom took the proffered hand. "Yes, through my mum's family, the Carbises."

Freddie smiled, revealing even white teeth. "Oh yes, I've met Jenny Carbis a few times. She's in the States now, though, isn't she? Do her parents still live in Bath?"

"Yes, Uncle Pete and Aunt Rose are still there. Uncle Pete sends his regards to your father, by the way. He's Mum's brother. Jenny is my cousin."

Freddie turned to Kate, who'd been listening patiently to this exchange. "And you must be Dr Wilson. Pleased to meet you." He flashed her a dazzling smile and shook her hand.

Kate smiled back at him. "Please call me Kate."

Freddie pointed towards the staircase. "Well, I'll take you to the gallery. The portrait you need to look at is there. Then once you've had a good look, I thought we could have some tea or coffee on the terrace." He turned to address them as he started to climb the stairs. "You're welcome to look round the house of course. We're just getting it ready for the open days, so things are a bit frantic at the moment."

"That sounds great, thank you. I'd love to have a look round." Kate glanced at Tom for his reaction as they traipsed after Freddie.

Tom caught her free hand and winked. "Just think, but for an accident of birth, this could all have been mine," he said out of the corner of his mouth, then in a louder voice, "It must be quite a responsibility… This house I mean."

"You're not joking." Freddie spoke over his shoulder as he continued up the stairs. "It was in a real mess when Dad took over. Grandad didn't have much of a clue, I'm afraid. Anyway, Dad has put a lot of effort in, getting professionals to advise on the estate management, and ploughing funds into maintenance. We're obliged to open the house to the public for a certain number of days in the year, which is a bit of a nuisance, but a small price to pay for the privilege of being able to live here." At the top of the stairs he turned left. "Here we are. This is the gallery."

Kate gazed down a long corridor-like room, gently illuminated on one side by windows whose partially lowered blinds let in a diffused light.

She pointed to the blinds. "They look pretty special. We had similar blinds in Duke Humfrey's library at the Bod."

Freddie nodded. "Yeah, and expensive too. We have to keep the light levels in here reasonably low. Luckily, this is on the east side of the house, so it's only early mornings that we have to be extra careful." He headed down the room, past several large and extravagantly framed portraits, before stopping. "This is the earl you want, I think." He peered at the faded inscription on the bottom of the frame. "Yes, that's the chap."

Kate held her breath. Her pulse had been steadily rising since they'd entered the house, and it wasn't down to climbing a flight of stairs. This portrait would confirm whether her small pastel depicted John Lanyon – another piece in the puzzle of Annabelle's story. She moved back to get a better view. The painting was so large, it was impossible to view it properly at close quarters.

Tom took a sharp intake of breath. "I don't think there's any doubt, do you?"

She looked up and met the same beguiling eyes and sensuous mouth of the gentleman in her portrait. It must have been painted when he was somewhat older, but there was no doubt in her mind that it was the same person. She shook her head. "No. No doubt at all. Can I...?" She indicated to her bag and Freddie pointed her to the window.

"There's a table over here."

With slightly shaking hands Kate set her bag down, then carefully withdrew the portrait. After removing the protective covering she placed it on the table for Freddie to see. She was still pretty much speechless. The three of them crowded round, looking from the portrait on the wall to the portrait on the table.

"Definitely him." Freddie's words were superfluous. No one could deny the likeness between the two. "He was known as the Reclusive Earl. Only went up to London occasionally. Bit of an adventurer in his early days, by all accounts, before he became the heir. Never married, and when he returned home he devoted himself to his books. Most of the collections we have in the library now are down to him. He wasn't that old when he died, either."

Kate found her tongue at last. "We think we might know why he never married." She pulled the second portrait out of her bag, unwrapped it and set it down on the table next to that of John. "Look at this." Was it just her imagination, or did

Annabelle's smile seem more pronounced?

Freddie's eyes lit up. "Crikey, where did that come from?"

Tom frowned at him. "It's my mum's. Why?"

"I'd swear there's one very like it in the library. It's larger, and by a different artist, but I'm sure it's the same girl. The pose and the dress are almost identical. But we've never been able to identify her." Freddie was almost bouncing with excitement. "Come with me." He strode off down the gallery and Kate and Tom grabbed the portraits and hurried after him.

After retracing their steps and heading across the landing, they reached a set of polished double doors leading on to a large room, evidently the library. Book presses lined the walls, between each press were portraits and paintings of landscapes. In the gaps between the tops of the presses and the ceiling cornices were yet more portraits. Kate wondered just how many ancestors the family had.

Two comfortable-looking sofas faced each other either side of a large marble fireplace, and small occasional tables and chairs were arranged haphazardly around the room. Kate watched from the doorway as Freddie went to one side of the mantelpiece. She could see that the portrait hung there, though smaller than most of the other paintings in the room, was much larger than the one in her hand.

Heart beating like a drum, she crossed the room and peered over Freddie's shoulder. Kate felt Tom's warm breath on her neck and knew he was as nervous as she was. Edging closer as Freddie moved out of the way, she again met Annabelle's smiling eyes.

"Don't you agree? It's the same girl," said Freddie, not hiding his excitement. "I'll check with our archivist, but I'm fairly certain this was commissioned by John Lanyon, the third earl. Unfortunately, all we know are the sitter's initials: A.T.. In the catalogue, it's described as a portrait of an unknown lady. Who do you think it is?"

"Annabelle... Annabelle Tracy," stammered Kate. "It's definitely her."

A short while later, a still-trembling Kate was on the terrace, seated on a delicate wrought-iron chair, and enjoying a coffee. Freddie had been as excited as she and Tom to learn the identity of the girl in the portrait, and had emailed Ben Travis, the family archivist, with the details. He and Tom had worked out that the smaller of the two portraits of Annabelle must have passed into Tom's great-grandmother's hands on her marriage, and that's how it had come into Sue's possession.

"It's lucky that your branch of the family have it, otherwise if it'd stayed here, we'd probably be none the wiser to her identity," said Freddie, squinting his eyes against the sun as he took a sip from his cup.

Tom put his arm round Kate's shoulder. "Well, we wouldn't have known anything about her either, if it hadn't been for Kate here." He gave her a squeeze, sending delicious quivers through her body.

"I think the thanks are due to Win, actually." At Freddie's questioning look Kate went on to explain. "Win, my late godmother, discovered Annabelle's journal, and it all led on from there. Frank, her husband, had already purchased John's portrait some years earlier, but of course, they didn't have a clue as to his identity. They just liked the look of it. It's all been rather serendipitous…that, then me meeting Sue…and Tom." She quirked a smile at Tom, then returned to sipping her coffee.

Thanks were also due to Ruth. Her hard work on the journal had uncovered Annabelle's history, and the sad love story. It was a pity they'd been unable to discover Annabelle's fate. It would probably remain a mystery forever.

"Why the frown?" Tom's question interrupted her thoughts.

"I was just wondering what happened to Annabelle. It seems a pity that we'll never know. She vanished into thin air."

"I'll certainly ask Ben to check our records, and see if there are any clues this end," offered Freddie, pouring them all a second cup from the cafetière. "But, if she is mentioned somewhere, I'm sure he would already have spotted it, and made the connection between the name and the initials on the portrait in the library."

"That'd be great," said Kate, scrabbling about in her bag until she found what she was looking for. "Please give him my contact details." She handed Freddie her card.

Freddie glanced at it. "You're freelance? Any chance of you being available to check the archives yourself? Ben's only part time. You'll be paid, of course."

She opened her mouth to reply, but before she could answer, Tom cut in, "You're quite busy at the moment, aren't you, Kate? Sorting Mum's papers and settling in to your new house."

Kate gave him a sharp look. What was he up to? He wouldn't meet her eyes. She cleared her throat. "Tom's right, I wouldn't be able to do it straight away, Freddie. But I'd be happy to go over them once I have a bit more free time. That is, if Ben doesn't mind."

Tom's mouth was unsmiling, and that nerve was twitching in his cheek again, but he remained silent.

After a few more stilted words – the atmosphere between Tom and the others had cooled somewhat – it was agreed that Ben would contact Kate in a few weeks' time, and she would make a decision then, dependent upon how far she was with her current work.

Coffee drunk, they had a quick tour of the house before heading back to Falmouth. Tom hadn't spoken much at all since she'd agreed to Freddie's suggestion, but Kate decided to ignore his silence until they arrived back home. It wouldn't be good to argue while he was driving.

Chapter Twenty-One

It was late when they got back. They'd stopped briefly for a coffee at a little pub, with a pleasant, flower-filled garden overlooking a river. Tom seemed to have discovered his equilibrium, but Kate continued to feel a slight withdrawal in his manner. His conversation was more stilted, and there was something in his eyes that she couldn't quite read. What on earth could be bothering him? It had all started when Freddie had asked her to return and look at the archives.

A crazy idea occurred to her. He wasn't jealous, was he? That would be absurd. And surely he didn't think she was fickle with her affections? She'd made it clear to him that trusting him had been a big step for her, he must know she wasn't about to go waltzing off with anybody else. But he'd been badly hurt in the past. Had his ex made him so insecure that the slightest thing brought all his insecurities to the fore?

As they pulled up in front of The Beeches, Kate decided to take the bull by the horns. It went against the grain with her, but she swallowed her pride and turned limpid eyes towards him. "Do you think you could come in and check everything is ok? I'm a bit nervous." She injected a little breathless gasp into her voice and hoped he wouldn't think she was asthmatic. She hated being deceitful but it was in a good cause. Would he go for it? She'd never played the weak little woman before.

He rubbed his hand through his hair and gave a cough. "Well, I was going to leave you in peace for a bit...but if you're nervous, of course I'll check. You stay in the car, just in case."

She passed him her house keys and gave a tremulous smile. "Thanks. I appreciate it. It's nice to know there's someone I can trust." Inside she squirmed at her blatant pretence of female fragility. There was a flicker in his eyes and she hoped she was not overdoing it. He turned the key in the back door and went inside. Kate waited until the lights went on upstairs, then she leapt out the car, and raced into the house. She was in the kitchen with the kettle on the boil by the time he got downstairs.

"I thought you were going to wait in the car." He sounded disgruntled. "Anyway, everything's fine. All the windows are closed. No sign of anything disturbed." He hesitated for a fraction. "Erm – I didn't go in that front bedroom, by the way. The door was already open, and I could tell from the landing it all looked ok."

"That's fine, thank you." She smiled. "While you're here, why don't you sit down, and I'll make some supper? Scrambled eggs ok?" God, she would definitely need to go on a diet, but she couldn't think of anything else that would tempt him to stay. Not in his current taciturn mood...and they did say the way to a man's heart was through his stomach.

For one moment she was sure he was going to refuse.

"Oh, go on then," he muttered. "I am a bit peckish, come to think of it."

She crossed her fingers and went over to the fridge. *Please God, let there be eggs.* Five minutes later, she was stirring the eggs in a pan and bread was in the toaster. Tom buttered the toast when it popped up and brought the plates over for her to dish up. She piled the eggs on top of the toast, giving him the larger portion. She wasn't sure how she was going to manage to eat, she'd planned on not eating for at least a week. Still, she consoled herself, it was for a good cause.

She watched him surreptitiously as she ate. The tension had disappeared from his face, the taut lines round his eyes becoming less pronounced. Time for the next part of her plan. "Why don't we take our drinks into the drawing room?" She stood, mug of tea in her hand.

His head shot up. "I really need to be getting back. Early start tomorrow."

"Oh, yes?" She injected the words with disbelief. "I

thought we could tell your mum the good news together."

For a moment he looked totally confused. "Oh, you mean about the portrait? Sorry, I'd almost forgotten about that."

She was quite out of patience with him. What the hell was wrong? She lost all pretence and snapped. "Look, Tom. What's the matter? You've been withdrawn all day – ever since we were at Lanyon Park in fact – and I thought we'd been getting on so well. Please tell me what's bothering you. I'm afraid I can't continue to pretend I haven't noticed."

He groaned and slumped back in his chair, his head in his hands. "Oh bloody, bloody hell!"

She walked round and put her arm round his shoulders. "Tom, what is it? You can tell me."

The muscles in his neck and shoulders were taut, his head was still bowed…and she wasn't sure, but he might be crying. She gently stroked his neck, and was pleased when his hand came round and grasped hers. He turned to look up at her with eyes that were red rimmed.

"I'm sorry, Kate. I just can't do this now. Can we meet tomorrow, and I promise I'll tell you everything then? Is eleven ok? We'll go somewhere quiet."

She gave his hand a squeeze and nodded. "Yes, of course." She'd agree to almost anything to find out what was upsetting him so much.

"Now, are you sure you'll be all right here? As I said, everything looks fine, but if you get worried, ring me and I'll be straight over." He was using a brusque tone, as if everything was normal. She decided to humour him and ignore it.

"I'll be fine. You go home and get some sleep. I'll see you at eleven."

After locking up behind him, she climbed the stairs with leaden feet. It had all started so promisingly the previous day, now she felt so low she just wanted to curl up in a ball. It didn't matter about the portraits, it didn't matter about the weird apparitions in the garden, or the smell of rosemary in the dining room. All she wanted was to get to the bottom of what had gone wrong between her and Tom. Did she just attract the wrong types? Was the problem with her?

By the time she crawled into bed she was no nearer working it out. She switched off the light and let exhaustion flow over her.

The next day was a bit cooler than the last, not that it mattered. Kate had set her alarm for eight but awoke well before then, sticky with sweat. The nightmares had returned with a vengeance. Trapped in darkness, somehow she knew she was underground, but the walls surrounding her were made of brick. She knew, because running her fingers over them she felt straight lines and corners. It didn't add up. In her dream she was shivering, it was so cold her damp clothes clung to her, clammy against her skin. Waking up, her nightclothes were clinging to her, but wet with perspiration.

She threw the covers aside and went for a shower. It felt good to get into a clean set of clothes after managing in the same ones for two days. After a breakfast of fruit and tea, the start of her healthy regime after the previous two days' indulgence, she began to feel more human. While waiting for Tom to call, she went into the study to work.

He arrived at eleven sharp, knocking on the kitchen door, and with a barking Sal at his heels. He smiled, but she could tell his air of joviality was forced.

"I thought we could take Sal for a run," he said, leaning against the lintel. "Mum sends her love, by the way. Sorry, I had to tell her what we found out yesterday and I know you wanted to be there, but…well, you know what she's like?"

Kate nodded. Sue was nothing if persistent.

"She's over the moon about the portrait. She's christened it Annabelle now and said she never really thought of her as Flossie." He rolled his eyes.

"That's good. I thought she'd be happy." Kate scrutinised his face. Despite his grin, his eyes were bleak. "I'll just grab my bag. I've got a few things to take to your mum. We can do that when we take Sal back after her run, can't we?"

His mouth twisted. "I suppose."

That didn't sound promising. What was he going to tell

her that he thought would make her not want to be with him? She had no idea.

They parked up near a deserted stretch of beach, and Tom let Sal off her lead. She tore back and forth, leaping in the water and jumping over waves – she, at least, was having a great time. Tom stood, his hand shielding his eyes from the sunlight and watched as Kate threw a ball for Sal to catch. As Sal bounded away, Kate turned and took Tom's arm. Perhaps it was up to her to start the conversation.

"Laura is very protective of you. Why is that?" She bit her lip, wondering what his reaction to her opening salvo would be.

He slanted his gaze down to her, then looked away, that nerve twitching again in his cheek. "Yeah, she is." His mouth clammed shut.

Damn. Why won't you talk to me? She tried again. "In fact, she was very upfront. She as good as told me that I'd be in trouble if I hurt you. Said you'd been through a lot. What did she mean?"

"Interfering madam. Wait till I see her," Tom growled. He shook his head and huffed a breath. "I suppose I've got to tell you. It's…it's embarrassing. Guys are supposed to be the strong ones. You'll think I'm hopeless." He turned bleak despairing eyes to her. "You won't respect me anymore."

Exasperated, Kate couldn't help snapping. "For goodness sake, what do you take me for? Some sort of superficial bloody bimbo?" Why on earth would he think she'd suddenly change her opinion of him? Surely he knew she was not like that?

He winced at her words, then with a look of resignation, led her over to where a large flat rock jutted out from the sand. He slumped down and patted the stone for her to sit next to him. Kate looked round, the breeze whipping the hair round her face and bringing with it the tang of salt and ozone. Sal pranced about in the distance, occupied with chasing seagulls, and there was no-one else nearby to hear their conversation. She swept the sand off the rock and sat down, waiting for him to speak.

His voice when it came, was hesitant and low. "Three years ago I was in a relationship. It was a pretty toxic relationship, but I didn't realise at the time. Things…just seemed to creep up on me." He looked at the ground as he spoke, scuffing his deck shoes in the sand.

Kate clasped his hand. "Go on."

"Well, I… " He swallowed and took a breath. "She…she had this way. One minute she'd be nice, and everything was wonderful, then…then, she'd say something…something to undermine me, make me feel unsure about myself. I was overweight, or I was stupid, my haircut was wrong, why didn't I know how to dress? Things like that."

"She sounds like a complete bitch," said Kate. "Why did you believe her?" Inwardly, she was shocked. She'd heard of women being bullied by their partners, but men?

He shrugged. "Like I said, it was insidious. She was clever, she'd wait until she knew I was keyed-up about something at work, like a talk or a presentation – things that had never bothered me in the past. Then she'd hint that something wasn't quite right, and I'd start to worry. It got so bad I felt like a complete failure. I couldn't move without her approval, I got so dependent on her." He stopped for a moment, his mouth twisted. "But it's worse."

Kate's stomach clenched.

"She was violent too." His eyes darted to Kate's and in them she saw shame and despair.

Anger swirled inside her. How could anybody treat another human being like that? She knew it happened, everybody did. She'd just never met anyone who'd experienced it. He must have guessed her shock by her sharp intake of breath. "She knew I'd never retaliate. I'd never hit a woman." His head was in his hands, the very picture of despair. "God! We were engaged. I can't believe I nearly married her."

Kate kept her voice low. "How did you manage to finish with her?" She was still reeling from his revelations.

"It was Laura, actually." He was staring out to sea as he spoke, his eyes narrowed and focussed on the distant horizon.

163

"She came to stay for a week while she was on a course in London." He gave a grim chuckle. "Eve was against her staying from the start. She didn't like me visiting my family or them coming to see me. She'd always think of an excuse to either stop me going to see them, or to cut short a visit. I should have guessed she was trying to isolate me. It got so bad, I even stopped seeing the guys from the office socially. I was on my own."

He flicked a glance at Kate, then returned to gazing out to sea.

"Anyway, Laura came and stayed, God bless her. It was the first battle Eve didn't win. To begin with she played nice, chatted to Laura, made her feel at home. Then Eve started to try it on with her... Said something like, 'Don't you think some jeans can make you look fat?' when Laura came in one night wearing jeans." He grinned as if remembering the moment. "Laura, bless her, just turned round and said, 'Yeah, you're right, that pair you wore the other day – mmm, bit of a mistake.'"

Kate burst out laughing. "Good for Laura. What did Eve say?"

Tom chuckled. "Nothing. But if looks could kill, Laura would've been stretched out on the carpet." He turned round to face Kate, looking a bit more like his old self. "Anyway, that's when the scales started to fall from my eyes. Laura told me about a few more things Eve had said when I wasn't around. When I thought about it, I couldn't believe the man I'd become... couldn't understand how I'd let it happen. I'd been so besotted, that I hadn't seen the sort of person Eve was. Which in a way, made me feel a failure again." He sucked in his cheeks.

"Hey. You're not a failure." Kate prodded him gently with her elbow. "You're a very bright, talented man. Look what you've achieved: a successful career, your own property. The girl you went to school with, the one who owns the coffee shop, couldn't praise you enough."

She put her arm around his waist and leaned her head against his shoulder. He was trembling. Kate prayed Eve got her just deserts for what she had done.

"It's usually women whom one hears about in cases like this though, isn't it?" he mumbled. "Not blokes."

"It can happen to anyone. People like Eve come in all varieties. They just need to be in control. I bet she was a bitch at work too."

"Hmmm…" He turned to look at her. "Anyway, yesterday…when we were with Freddie…"

Kate frowned. "Yes?"

His eyes slid away from hers. "I saw the way he looked at you. Then he invited you back. I…I was jealous, frightened that you found him more attractive than me. The same old doubts resurfaced, wondering why you were with me in the first place. You're such a gorgeous girl, you could have anyone…"

She put her finger under his chin and turned his head so that their eyes met. "Tom, look at me. I'm with you, aren't I?"

"But for how long?" he said bleakly.

Chapter Twenty-Two

They sat together in silence for several minutes, watching Sal charge backwards and forwards, chasing the waves. Grey clouds were gathering in the distance, and it wasn't long before the first fat spots of rain started to fall.

Kate pulled her jacket on and smiled when she saw Sal at last lolloping towards them, panting, tongue hanging out. Kate leapt up, knowing she was going to get soaked whatever the weather, when Sal stopped to shake her coat. Her movement roused Tom from his introspection and he grabbed hold of Sal's collar and clipped on her lead.

Sal looked up at him expectantly. If a dog could be said to be smiling, Sal was smiling then, thought Kate. Avoiding Kate's eyes, Tom glanced at his watch.

"We'd better get going. This rain looks as if it's in for the day and Mum said she'd do us some lunch." He set off with long strides back to the car. Kate struggled to keep up with him. By the time she reached the car, Sal was safely back in her cage and Tom was behind the steering wheel, key in the ignition. Kate could tell he was regretting his confession. His back was rigid, and his hands gripped the steering wheel so hard his knuckles were white.

Kate decided to act as if nothing was wrong. If she pretended all was normal, perhaps he would relax. She certainly wasn't about to rake the whole thing up again – he was upset enough.

It wasn't long before they arrived. The smells wafting from the kitchen told Kate that Sue had been busy.

"Come in, both of you. Leave your wet things in the porch. Goodness, what a downpour." Sue's voice came from the kitchen. "You're just in time. This risotto is nearly ready."

Kate went straight to the kitchen where she found Sue standing by the stove, stirring a large pan. A bowl of prawns sat on the worktop, ready to be added at the last moment.

Kate sniffed the air appreciatively. "This smells lovely, Sue. You've gone to a lot of trouble."

"Well, it's the least I can do after all your help." Sue paused her stirring to add some wine to the pan. "And it's nice to do something a bit different for a change. Most days I just have a sandwich, if it's only Laura and me." She turned her head to Tom, who was standing near the door, arms folded across his chest. "Oh, I forgot to tell you, Tom. Dad is away tonight. He's had to go to a meeting in Birmingham."

"Mmm... I'll stay over if you like, Mum. Keep you company." His eyes flickered over to Kate. "After lunch I'll take you home, Kate, so don't worry. I'll grab a bag and come straight back here."

A puzzled expression crossed Sue's face. "Oh...I thought... Never mind." Sue's cheeks reddened as she glanced from her son back to Kate.

"That's great. Thanks, Tom," Kate didn't wait to hear what Sue was going to say. "I've got a fair bit of work to do, what with the trip to Bath and everything. An evening on the computer will bring me back up to speed."

It was true, she needed to finish her work on the catalogue, and write up her findings on the portraits. She also understood that Tom needed time on his own. It had been a big thing for him to tell her everything, and she guessed that he was feeling vulnerable. But as well as giving him much needed space, she had to reassure him that her feelings for him hadn't altered because of his revelations. Yes, she was shocked, but at the wickedness shown by his fiancée, not by him and the situation he'd found himself in.

"If you're not busy the day after tomorrow, Tom, I thought I could show you what I've been working on." She gave him a bright smile. "Then do you fancy a trip upriver to Truro? I need to check something out at the Record Office and can't afford to put it off for very long. They're closing in September and then it will be months until the new offices are open in Redruth. You might find it interesting." She couldn't have made it any plainer that his disclosures had not put her off.

Sue, Kate noticed, was studiously ignoring this opening salvo, ostensibly engrossed in stirring the risotto.

He moved away from the door and unfolded his arms. That looked promising.

"Er…yes, that should be ok." There was still a hint of uncertainty in his eyes and a slight frown furrowing his brow.

"That's settled then." She deliberately took his hesitant answer as a definite agreement and grinned back at him. "I'll even pack a picnic. If this weather clears, I thought we could go up on the boat. It's been years since I did that." It would take a good hour on the boat upriver… An hour in which they could talk and he wouldn't be able to escape.

Tom grunted. "Well, here's hoping it brightens up. This bad weather might be here for a while."

"Oh, a bit of rain will just add to the fun." And it would probably mean fewer passengers, so less chance of being overheard, she thought.

Kate Wilson, you are a devious woman.

Later that afternoon, Tom slowed the car to turn up the drive to The Beeches, and Kate heard his sharp intake of breath. She looked up from her phone, where she'd been checking her emails, and peered through the rain lashed windscreen.

"What's a police car doing parked on your drive, Tom?" There were two uniformed officers, one in the car speaking into his radio, the other peering through the window of the cottage and getting thoroughly soaked for his trouble.

"No idea." His face had the dark, glowering expression that made him appear bad-tempered and moody. "Though I bet it's something to do with Eve." He turned a troubled face to Kate. "One of the guys where I used to work emailed me to say she'd been asking around, trying to find out where I was. She enjoys causing trouble. Once she finds out where I am, she won't leave me alone." He pulled to a stop behind the police car, jammed the handbrake on, and got out, disregarding the rain. The car door slammed behind him.

Kate, curious and thinking he might need some moral support, got out too. Pulling her brolly from her bag, she struggled to put it up. By the time she'd finished, the two police officers were walking towards Tom.

Kate had a bad feeling.

"Mr Tom Pellow?" It was the older looking of the two police officers who spoke. His gaunt features were definitely not smiling and Kate guessed it was not just because he was getting wet.

Tom nodded. "Yes, that's me. Though I use the name Tom Carbis now…for…erm, business purposes. What's this about, officer? Would you like to come inside?"

Kate was impressed with his *sangfroid*. If two police officers unexpectedly turned up on her doorstep, she would have been panicking, not inviting them in.

"We would like you to accompany us to the station, Mr Pellow. We need to ask you a few questions."

"Yes, yes, but in connection with what, officer?" Tom stood his ground.

"About a Miss Eve Wright." The policeman eyed Kate before adding. "I understand the pair of you were engaged to be married until quite recently?"

Kate's eyes swept to Tom. His face had drained of colour and the telltale nerve in his cheek twitched. She moved quickly to his side and took his arm as he started to reply.

"Yes, we were. But I ended it over a year ago… I don't understand. Why do you need to speak to me? What has she been saying?" His tried to sweep away the water running down his face with a shaky hand.

"Miss Wright is dead, Mr Pellow. There were several emails on her computer mentioning your name. We'd like to eliminate you from our inquiries."

Kate gasped. It sounded like Eve's death wasn't from natural causes. Amid the conflicting thoughts in her head she heard a dazed-sounding Tom reply.

"What? She's dead? My God." He'd gone rigid beside her,

and she heard him take a sharp breath. "I still don't understand why you need to speak to me. I haven't seen her in over a year."

The police officer's younger colleague stepped forward, and looked at Tom with hard, narrowed eyes. "So...there was no love lost between you and Miss Wright?"

Kate could almost see the man's mind working. They thought Tom had something to do with Eve's death. She looked sideways at Tom. Two spots of colour had appeared in his cheeks and his jaw was clenched.

His words came pouring out. "You're damned right about that, officer. Eve Wright was a calculating, manipulative woman. She was the worst thing that ever happened to me, and I'm only glad that I managed to see through her before we got married. I never wanted to see her again."

"Well, Mr Pellow, it appears your wish has been granted."

"But I still don't understand. What has this got to do with me? How did she die? Drugs?" Tom shrugged, there was a bitter edge to his voice. "I know she enjoyed coke occasionally, but she was never really into anything stronger. She enjoyed being in control too much."

"Not drugs, Mr Pellow. Eve Wright was murdered."

The policeman's words came like a punch to Kate's gut. They thought Tom had killed Eve. She knew Tom hated his ex, but murder? No, she didn't believe he was capable of that. He shrugged off her arm and stepped forward, anger blazing in his face.

"You think I did it? My God, if you only knew..."

"Knew what, Mr Pellow?" The older officer, a calculating look in his eye, grasped Tom by the arm. "I think you need to come with us now." He started to lead Tom towards the police car.

Tom's head turned to Kate. "Don't tell Mum, Kate. Get hold of Dad."

She nodded, unable to speak; she was still too much in shock.

Kate couldn't settle to anything. She paced up and down her study, a mass of thoughts and emotions streaming through her brain. She'd eventually managed to get hold of Tom's father, having remembered the firm he worked for, and persuading his secretary to call him and request that he contact her. Twenty minutes later, he'd called her back and she explained what had happened. There'd been silence at the other end of the phone for several seconds, then he told her not to worry.

"I'll drop everything here and get back to Sue. I should be home by seven. Don't say anything to her, will you? I don't want her to find out while she's on her own." Kate assured him she would say nothing. Martin's voice was steady, giving her confidence that he could sort things out. "I'm sure Tom has nothing to do with all this, but I'll arrange for a lawyer in any case. Tom's friend, Rob, is in the police force. I might give him a call too. See if he can tell me anything." She heard him take a breath. "Anyway, how are you? This must have been a shock...to witness, I mean?"

"I'm all right, Martin. I'm worried of course. Not that I think Tom did anything...but...well, he did admit to hating her, so the police could make a big thing out of that."

"Tom would never do anything like that." There was silence, then a long sigh. "Look, it will all be cleared up soon, I'm sure. I'd better be on my way." He hung up.

Kate twisted her hands. Should she go down to the police station? Was Tom even in Falmouth or had they taken him somewhere else? She didn't have a clue. Why hadn't she thought to ask at the time? Too shocked and taken by surprise, that's why. She sat down at her desk and looked up the number of Falmouth police station. It wouldn't hurt to ring up and find out what was going on. At worst, they'd just tell her to mind her own business. She wasn't a relative after all.

Ten minutes later, she put the phone down. All she'd been told was that Tom was helping with inquiries, so at least she knew he was not under arrest. She'd presented herself as his girlfriend – well, she was female and they were friends, but whether Tom would appreciate her calling herself as such, she didn't care. The officer she was speaking to got interested when she explained that she lived at The Beeches.

"So, you can see Mr Pellow's cottage from your house?" he'd asked.

What an odd question. "Erm, yes. Not that I'm always looking, you understand. Why?"

The officer had gone on to make an appointment to call on her the following day, to ask some follow-up questions. He'd refused to say when Tom might be returning home, airily assuring her that sometimes it took time to get to the bottom of things and not to worry.

Bloody Hell! Tom's ex had been murdered, he was in for questioning, and she was not to worry?

She decided she couldn't settle to any work, so she switched off the computer and went into the kitchen to make a drink. Opening the fridge, she remembered she'd used up the last of her milk that morning, meaning to go shopping later that day. She groaned and glanced out the window. It was still raining. *Bugger it*! The weather was turning out to be as miserable as she was feeling. She grabbed her jacket, keys, and her bag, and stepped out onto the puddled drive, shielding her face from the driving rain.

Going round the supermarket – half-empty and unusually quiet with only a worn-out looking checkout assistant to speak to on the way out – brought a welcome feeling of normality. People were still going about their business. The world hadn't stopped because Tom was a murder suspect.

You're worrying too much. It will all get sorted. Tom said he'd never raised a finger to Eve. And you believe him.

Chapter Twenty-Three

After a troubled night – the rain pounding on the windows and the recurring nightmare hadn't aided a restful sleep – Kate got up early. Yawning and blinking, and dressed in her pyjamas, she went downstairs. Perhaps some coffee would help her think. She groaned at the sight that greeted her. The dishes from the night before, still piled up in the sink, were a reminder of how disorganised she'd become.

Kate filled the kettle and flopped down at the table, trying to ignore the chaos around her. Coffee first, then tidy up, she decided. Ten minutes later, mug in hand, she ambled into the dining room and pulled back the curtains. Kate watched as the dust mites hovered and swirled in the beams of sunlight now streaming through the window – a welcome distraction from the nagging thought that it really was time to get dressed and make a start on her day. But it was no good, the mental energy she needed to concentrate on her research refused to make an appearance. Instead, all her thoughts were of Tom.

Resigning herself to a morning of inaction, Kate flicked on the TV and curled up on the sofa, telling herself that there was plenty of time to get ready. The newsreader's face flashed up. After a headline story about the Prime Minister and another Government scandal, came the item she'd been dreading: Eve Wright's murder. Her mug halted halfway to her mouth at the words, "A man is helping police with their inquiries and an arrest is expected imminently."

Kate grabbed the remote and the screen went blank.

The police called at ten thirty. There were two of them, a man and a woman, both in plain clothes. Kate led them into the drawing room where they politely refused her offer of a tea or coffee.

"We won't take up too much of your time, Miss Wilson," said the officer who had introduced herself as Detective Sergeant Hollins.

"It's Dr Wilson, actually." Would she be taken more seriously if they knew that, she wondered?

"Oh, you're a doctor?" DS Hollins looked up from her notebook.

"Not a medical doctor, no, but I have a doctorate."

"Really?" sniffed DS Hollins, tapping the end of her pencil against her mouth. "And how long have you lived here, *Dr* Wilson?" She emphasised the title.

Before she could answer, Kate became distracted by the second officer, who'd stood up to look out the window.

"Erm…only a few weeks. My godmother left me the house when she died."

"Ah, yes. That would be Mrs Saunton." The police officer's eyes looked thoughtful. "She died in mysterious circumstances, didn't she? Found in her nightgown some way into the woods, if I remember rightly."

"Yes. But the police decided there was no foul play involved, didn't they?" Kate's stomach was churning. What was going on? She didn't like the turn the conversation was taking. Was she under suspicion for something?

DS Hollins gave a smile that didn't reach her eyes. "That's right, of course. And now you own the house? That must have been a nice surprise."

"I'm sorry. I don't like what you're implying." Kate glared at DS Hollins. "Win was a much loved friend and mentor. I was devastated by her death and certainly hadn't expected her to leave me the house. Now, I thought this was about Tom Carbis." What on earth did they think had been going on?

"No need to take offence, Dr Wilson." DS Hollins' tone was now all affability. "How long have you known Tom Pellow, or Tom Carbis, as he calls himself?"

"I only met him when I relocated here." Kate paused. "Sorry… I should say I bumped into him the day before I moved in, when I was in Falmouth, but I didn't know who he was, or that we would be neighbours. He came over the first evening and introduced himself, said he'd seen lights on in the house and was concerned in case it was burglars."

"I see. So you're saying you never met him previously?"

"That's correct. But I've subsequently met his parents and his sister. In fact, I'm doing some work for Sue Pellow, his mother. I met her through a mutual friend, before I knew she was Tom's mum. Ruth Morris, the librarian in Falmouth sort of introduced us." Kate knew she was gabbling. Why did all this matter? Surely all they needed to know was whether Tom was here when Eve Wright had been killed. Didn't they?

DS Hollins was writing furiously in her notebook and her colleague had abandoned the window and was now examining the photos on the sideboard. Kate wondered what was so fascinating about the views of the coastline and the shots of her as a child. Or maybe it was the dust that held the officer's attention. Kate's eyes swivelled back to DS Hollins.

"So, did Mr Pellow know your godmother, Dr Wilson? I understand he moved into his cottage about twelve months ago. It's not unlikely that they met?"

A prickle of unease slithered down Kate's spine. Now what were they hinting at? Tom being involved in Win's death? Her heart missed a beat. She swallowed, her mouth had suddenly gone dry. That thought had never occurred to her... Why would it? This was getting ridiculous.

"Win never mentioned him to me. I saw her at Christmas – she stayed at my parents' house in Oxfordshire for the holidays. She'd been a bit upset about some weird things that had been happening."

DS Hollins eyes became alert, pencil poised over her notebook. Her colleague turned round from his perusal of the photos. "What sort of weird things."

Kate wracked her brain to recall the exact conversation. "She'd begun to think the house was haunted. Items had moved, drops in temperature, a strange smell. I put it down to her being under stress. She mentioned an attempted burglary. Someone broke in, but nothing was taken. A couple of months previously she'd had some paintings valued and had been pestered to sell by the people who had done the valuation." Kate knew she had no choice. Now it was all going to come out about Smith and Jevson. Rupert Gormley-Smith would not be happy.

"Do you know who did the valuation?" DS Hollins looked up briefly from her writing.

"Yes, a firm called Smith and Jevson. But…"

"What, Dr Wilson?"

"They were responsible for a more recent attempted break-in here a few days ago. Tom spotted them and I called the police. I was having dinner with him at the time in his cottage. They managed to get away before the police arrived."

"So, Mr Pellow got a good look at them, did he, and was able to identify them?"

Kate squirmed uncomfortably. "Erm, no."

It took about half an hour to explain everything to DS Hollins. Half an hour of embarrassment for Kate, and growing looks of disbelief from the two police officers.

"May I suggest that, next time you are chased down the street, or suspect that you are being followed, you report it to the police, Dr Wilson. You were very foolish to tackle the perpetrator on your own. If things had got nasty…" DS Hollins let her words trail off, their meaning clear.

"I know. But he was such a pathetic individual. I honestly don't think he had anything to do with Win's death…and I'm pretty sure Tom only knew her sufficiently to say good day to, nothing more. Anyway, this is about Eve Wright, isn't it?"

"We are just trying to build a complete picture here, Dr Wilson. Even you must think it odd that two recent deaths have the common denominator of Tom Pellow. Can you verify that Mr Pellow was at his cottage the weekend before last? That would be the fourth and fifth of August?"

DS Hollins's unblinking stare made Kate uneasy. Yes, now the police officer mentioned it, Tom's connection with two fairly recent deaths was unlucky. Coincidence. Win hadn't been murdered. That was just an unfortunate accident, surely? Eve's death? She tried to cast her mind back to the weekend in question.

"Hang on a minute. Let me just check my diary." Kate looked at her phone. That was the weekend before she met Ruth. She'd been on her own mostly. She thought back. Tom had been in the café on Saturday morning, when he'd tried to ignore her. But his car hadn't been outside the cottage when she'd returned home. She couldn't remember seeing it when she'd gone for a swim on the Sunday, and it hadn't been there on the Monday when she'd gone to meet Ruth. In fact, the next time she'd seen him was on the Wednesday, when he'd tried to throw her out of Sue's.

Kate cleared her throat. Now she knew what people meant when they said they'd got a lump there. "I can't confirm Tom was here that weekend, I'm afraid. I saw him in Falmouth on Saturday morning, but after that I didn't see him again until the following Wednesday."

"Did you notice his car parked outside the cottage over the weekend?"

Kate shook her head. "No." Things weren't looking good for Tom, but not for one moment did she believe he was involved in his fiancée's death. Where had he been? If only she knew. Perhaps his parents would be able to vouch for him. "When was Eve Wright murdered?" she asked.

"We think the evening of the fourth, but that is yet to be confirmed by the pathologist."

"It said on the news that she was in London, at her flat. Surely he couldn't have driven from here to London in that time? Like I said, he was here in Falmouth at about ten in the morning."

DS Hollins' eyes bored into Kate. "We know about his other car, Dr Wilson…the rather fast sports job in his garage." Kate closed her mouth. She really didn't know what to say.

DS Hollins started to put her notebook and pencil away. "Thank you for your help, Dr Wilson. We'll see ourselves out. If there's anything else you can think of, get in touch. I'll leave my card here on the table."

Kate watched through the window as the police car pulled

away, its wheels sending up spray as it rolled through the puddles on the drive. It was still wet underfoot, but at least the rain had stopped. She felt numb… Too shocked to think clearly. She sank down on the sofa and grabbed a cushion, clutching it to her stomach.

"Bloody hell."

Chapter Twenty-Four

The rest of Kate's morning was spent in a bit of a haze. After an hour or so trying to work on her book, she gave up and wandered into the kitchen. Restless and depressed, she couldn't stay in the house. She decided to drive into Falmouth and have a wander round. Maybe stop for a coffee at the Ubiquitous Bean.

She parked in her usual place outside her parents' apartment and headed up the road towards the coffee shop, dodging the puddles as she went. The streets were busy, despite the wet weather, but not uncomfortably so, and the Friday rush hadn't quite started.

Someone called her name. She turned round to see Ruth Morris, laden down with shopping, waving frantically. "Hi, Kate. I thought it was you. How are you? Have you done any more work on that journal?"

Word about Tom being under suspicion had obviously not reached her ears. "Hi, Ruth. Good to see you. Yeah, I've done a bit." Kate tried to instil her words with enthusiasm she did not feel.

Ruth's eyes sparkled as she rushed up. "That's great. Are you free later? You could come round to mine and tell me all about it." Then seeing Kate's frown, she added, "Don't worry if you can't, another time perhaps?" Ruth smiled sympathetically. "You look a bit down in the mouth, Kate. Is anything the matter? You look as if you have the weight of the world on your shoulders. Tell me to mind my own business if you don't want to talk."

It was all too much. "Oh, Ruth. I feel dreadful," Kate blurted.

Ruth dropped her shopping bags and put her arms round

Kate's shoulders. "There, there. It can't be that bad, surely? Come home with me, and you can tell me all about it. Win would never forgive me if I left you in a state."

Before she knew it, Kate was being hustled down the road towards Ruth's house. Despite her tears, Kate had almost chuckled at the thought of Win, coming back from the grave, to remonstrate with her best friend.

Fifteen minutes later, Kate was curled up on the sofa in Ruth's front room, a mug of tea in her hand.

Ruth settled into an armchair and placed a plate of custard creams on the arm. "Now, what's it all about, Kate. Not man trouble, is it?" Kate, despite her troubles, noted with a wry smile that the armchair was strategically placed to give its occupant not only a decent view of the TV, but also an equally good view out the bay window onto the street.

"Sort of…but not what you think." Kate took a gulp of her tea, trying to get her thoughts in order. At last, she began to tell Ruth all that had happened. Ruth's easy and sympathetic presence made it almost like talking to Win. As she was speaking, it occurred to Kate that this was the second time since leaving Oxford that she'd been so overcome with emotion that she'd had to share with someone. Last time it had been Sue.

Ruth's verdict was eminently sensible and to the point. "Well, the best thing you can do is just wait and see what happens. No point getting yourself worked up about something that might not happen. You don't believe he's responsible, do you?"

"Of course he isn't."

Ruth dunked a biscuit into her mug and gave Kate a knowing look. "Sounds like you and this Tom are quite close? Bit quick, wasn't it?" She popped the biscuit into her mouth.

"Yeah, well… We do get on, but we're not as involved as you think. That is…we are involved but… Well, Tom only told me about his past a couple of days ago. He's been badly hurt and didn't want to start a new relationship. His fiancée was a complete horror, by all accounts."

"And she's the one who was murdered?" cut in Ruth. "That doesn't look good, does it?"

"But everything I know about him tells me he's not capable of murder. Did Win mention him at all?"

Ruth paused in the act of dunking her biscuit, looking thoughtful. The end of her custard cream dropped with a plop into her mug, and her mouth made a moue of distaste. "No... not really. She told me a young man had moved in when he bought the cottage, and later she did say he kept himself to himself." Kate started to relax, this was sounding better. "She was pleased, because she'd been worried that there might be wild parties and noise." Ruth shook her head and picked up another custard cream. "Apart from that, no, I don't think they had much contact." Ruth glanced out the window, her face screwed in concentration. "Glad that rain's cleared, wasn't it awful? Oh, I remember... She did say he'd cleared the drive of snow, when we had that bad spell last year. I thought that was kind of him."

Kate smiled. That sounded more like the sort of thing he'd do.

The pair sat in companionable silence for a minute or two, Ruth crunching through her biscuits and Kate sipping her tea. The peace was broken by the sound of Kate's phone. She set her mug down and fumbled about in her bag to locate it. At last her fingers closed round it and she pulled it out to see Sue's name on the screen. She sent Ruth an apologetic smile.

"I'd better take this."

"Hi, Sue." Kate tried to sound normal.

Sue's voice was jumpy and breathless. "Oh, Kate. I'm sorry I haven't called you sooner. I...I've been in a bit of a state...but I expect you have too. Martin told me that you were there when it happened... I mean, when the police called."

"Yes, Sue. Sorry I didn't let you know straight away, but Tom told me not to. He didn't want you to worry." Kate paused. "Is there any news? Have the police let him go yet?"

"No, they're applying to keep him for another twelve

hours. They haven't tracked down the friend he says can give him an alibi."

Kate felt vindicated. She hadn't been mistaken in her trust. "He has an alibi? That's great. Who is it?"

"Jack French. Tom was at school with him. The solicitor told Martin this morning, but it seems no one can get hold of him." Kate heard Sue take a gulp of air. "He's in the navy, you see, on a nuclear sub. He and Tom met up before he went off for his next deployment. The problem is, there's no way of contacting him at the moment. It could be weeks before he's able to corroborate Tom's alibi." Sue ended with a sob.

Kate's initial relief at hearing Tom had an alibi dissolved. How long would it be before this friend could be contacted? Would the police insist on keeping Tom in custody until he could prove he was not in London? Her heart went out to Sue, who was now sobbing unashamedly on the other end of the phone.

She tried to sound calmer than she felt. "Sue, don't worry. I'm sure it'll all be sorted. It's not as if Tom doesn't have an alibi at all, is it? As soon as this guy is traced he'll be able to tell the police, and they'll have to release him." Kate knew what she had to do. Sue was ill–equipped to deal with yet another problem and needed her support. "I'll come round to see you this evening, if you like?"

"Oh, Kate. Thank you. I'd appreciate that. Martin had to go back to Birmingham. There was nothing else he could do here, and he needs to keep his job, so he didn't really have an option. And I haven't told anyone else, so I've got no one I can talk to."

"How's Laura?" Kate wondered if Sue and Martin had shared the bad news with her.

"Not good. She had a bit of a relapse yesterday, so we've not been able to talk. I'm sure Tom must have told you how ill she gets. She knows nothing about this. I daren't tell her, even if she does improve."

"OK, sorry to hear that, Sue. Look, I'd better go for now. I'll see you later, I promise." Kate ended the call and looked over at Ruth, who'd been listening to the exchange and shaking her head sympathetically. "Poor Sue. She sounded dreadful."

Ruth leaned across and patted Kate's knee. "You go and keep her company then. From what I picked up, it sounds like her son has an alibi, so that's good, isn't it?" Ruth smiled. "She'll be glad of your support. I gather her daughter is not too well either, poor woman. As if that wasn't enough to contend with."

Kate nodded. "Yes, Laura's had a bit of a relapse." She cocked her head to one side. "Thanks, Ruth. I don't know what I'd have done if I hadn't bumped into you. Thanks for taking me in and listening to me moan."

Ruth held her hands up. "Get away with you! It's nothing. I'm glad you think of me as a friend." Her mouth twisted. "I miss Win, I do, so getting to know you has been a real pleasure. Now give me a call if you need to chat." She leaned over and clutched Kate's arm. "And don't worry, I'm not one for gossip, so I won't tell anyone what you've told me." She rolled her eyes. "Though I daresay the papers will soon be full of it, if the police release his name."

A jolt of shock shot through Kate. What if Tom's name had already been released? Would she get home to find his cottage and her drive besieged by reporters? She grabbed her bag and gave Ruth a hug.

"Oh, Lord, you're right. I'd better get going. Thanks for everything, Ruth. You're a star."

Chapter Twenty-Five

All was quiet when Kate passed Tom's cottage and went up the drive. She breathed a sigh of relief. The police had not released his name to the papers. Opening the front door, she checked the time. It was nearly five o'clock. Time enough to get changed, reply to any outstanding emails, and then go and see Sue.

As soon as she opened the study door, the heady scent of rosemary filled her nostrils, making her skin tingle, and sending goosebumps up her arms. The very air seemed charged.

"Who's there?" she whispered, almost to herself. Somehow, she knew there was a presence there... Someone... Or something. A rustle of papers sent her eyes to the desk. The journal lay on top. That wasn't where she'd left it – it had been safely locked in the drawer. "What do you want? I don't understand." Her throat had dried, making her voice hoarse.

She forced herself to walk over to the desk. The pages of the journal were open at the last entry, and she read again the faded words that Annabelle had written all those years ago. If only she could discover what had happened that night. Where was the lovers' secret meeting place in the woods? Perhaps if she found that, it might give a clue as to what had happened to Annabelle and why she was not at rest. Kate realised with a jolt that she'd accepted that all the strange occurrences were down to Annabelle's restless spirit. She did believe in ghosts after all.

"I'll help, Annabelle. I'll find out what happened." Her voice echoed in the empty room. There was a sigh, or was it just her imagination? She closed the journal and placed it back in the drawer. The air in the room settled. Whatever presence she'd felt had now departed.

She switched on the computer and the screen flickered into life. All thoughts of the past abandoned, she focussed on the present, and started to pull up all the reports concerning Eve Wright's death. There must be something she could do to gather information that would help Tom and reassure Sue.

The newspaper accounts were typically vague and full of speculation, but the thing that cheered her most was that Tom's name did not appear in any of them. Something else that struck her was the fact that Eve apparently had no friends. Her neighbours described her as the sort who kept herself to herself.

"Sounds like your archetypal serial killer," muttered Kate to herself. Her pulse quickened as she saw a mention of a mysterious boyfriend in one of the reports. One of Eve's neighbours, an elderly occupant of an apartment in the same building, described seeing Eve with an unknown man on several occasions. The police were asking for him to come forward, but so far no one had.

Kate chewed her lip. This chap sounded a more likely candidate. If Eve had tried to do to him what she'd done to Tom…well. He might not have been as nice as Tom. She wriggled uncomfortably, ashamed at her feelings. Nothing justified murder, no one deserved that, not even the despicable Eve. However, the glimmer of hope that Tom could be exonerated before his friend surfaced from his submarine manoeuvres flared into a full blown flame. She switched the computer off, and feeling better than she had for a while, headed upstairs to get changed.

The evening turned out better than she'd expected. Sue had been remarkably upbeat, quite a change from the sobbing woman Kate had spoken to earlier that day. Sue explained how she coped, when they sat together, drinks in hand.

"I don't normally let things get to me, Kate, so sorry for being such a misery guts on the phone. You must have thought me a right wuss." Sue's eyes were still red rimmed, but now there was a spark in them and a tone of determination in her voice. "I had a good cry earlier, got it all out of my system." She slanted a wry smile at Kate. "Martin always says not to waste time worrying about things we can't change, and he's right. We've just got to get on with it." Sue sucked in a breath. "Tom will come out of this ok, I know. He didn't do it, and the police will soon realise that."

Kate nodded but remained silent. Any words she added would be completely superfluous.

On the drive back, Kate reflected that perhaps the years of adversity looking after Laura, must have imbued Sue with inner strength. "What doesn't kill me makes me stronger," she muttered to herself as she switched the engine off. In Sue's case it was definitely true.

It was now dark; dark and miserable, and beginning to rain again. Kate shook the drops from her hair, locked and bolted the front door, and headed straight upstairs to bed. It had been a long day and she was too tired to do anything else. With any luck, the morning would bring the news that she wanted to hear, that Tom was no longer under suspicion.

Kate checked her phone – it was three in the morning. She let out a groan. What had woken her this time? Not a nightmare. She hadn't had any dreams. But her skin was tingling and her senses were alert. Something had broken through the barrier of her sleep. She strained her ears, but apart from the occasional gusting of the wind in the trees outside, all was silence. A shadow moved in the corner of the room, catching her attention. Her eyes latched on to it and she watched, breathless and shivering, as the shadow grew, becoming more solid. It formed the shape of a woman, wrapped in a cloak. Kate's heart pounded in her ears, threatening to deafen her. Her throat was constricted, she couldn't scream. She stretched out a hand for the bedside light.

"Don't." The reedy female voice made her gasp, breaking the spell.

Kate swallowed. "Who are you?" Her voice came out as a

croak. She didn't need to ask… She knew.

"Find me…in the woods. Why didn't Father tell someone? You must let John know. Rosemary for remembrance, he said. I've not forgotten…" The last word faded into silence. The shadow shimmered and vanished.

Kate found she could move again. She flicked the light on, but the room was empty, and she was alone. A faint scent of rosemary lingered in the air. She shivered and pulled the duvet round her shoulders, too awake now to think of going back to sleep. Was this what had happened to Win? Had she been persuaded to go outside in the dead of night by this apparition? Kate frowned. If Annabelle was somewhere in the woods she could just as easily be found in daylight. There was no way she was going out on her own in the dark.

"Annabelle. I promise I'll find you." She spoke the words aloud. Wasn't it a sign of madness to talk to oneself, or was she dreaming? Kate gave her arm a sharp pinch. Yes, she was certainly awake – and unconvinced that she was mad. But she'd meant what she said – her search of the woods behind the house would commence in the daytime. On checking, her watch indicated that it was only three fifteen, far too early to get up. Reluctant to plunge the room back into darkness, Kate left the light on and closed her eyes, practicing the breathing technique she'd learnt at yoga. It must have worked, for when she next opened her eyes it was daylight.

The day was wet and overcast. Rain pattered relentlessly against the windows and the atmosphere in the house felt damp and unwelcoming, matching Kate's mood. She'd risen early and by ten o'clock, when there was still no sign of the bad weather abating, she decided to stay put. There was no sense in catching pneumonia traipsing around the woods.

She also decided it would not be too extravagant to turn the central heating on. "Just for an hour or two," she promised herself. Keeping herself busy, she was determined to stop her thoughts drifting to Tom. She succeeded for almost thirty minutes of every hour that crept by.

By lunchtime, the sky was clearing and the sun was

making a tentative appearance. Kate's head shot up from the keyboard at the sound of her phone's ringtone. Would this be the call telling her Tom had been released? Her heart skipped a beat as she read Sue's name on the screen.

"Hi, Sue. Any news?"

"Kate, I'm so glad you're in," Sue gasped at the other end of the line. "It's good news. They've managed to contact Tom's friend, Jack, who has corroborated his story. He'll be free to go shortly."

Kate felt a weight lift from her shoulders. "That's wonderful news, Sue. How did they get hold of his friend so quickly? You said he was away at sea and it could be a while."

Sue giggled, a sound that Kate had not often heard. "Such a stroke of luck... Well, for Tom, not the Royal Navy. Jack's submarine developed a fault in manoeuvres. They had to dock in Faslane." Sue sighed. "Oh, Kate, I'm so relieved it's over. I knew he hadn't done it, he's not capable, but other people might have thought he was guilty."

"Don't worry about that now, Sue. It's over." The sounds of a muffled conversation reached Kate's ears then Sue came back on the line.

"I'll have to go now, Kate. That's Laura calling me. I'll be in touch. Bye."

Kate smiled with relief as she put the phone down. Sue sounded much better than she had done the other day, and with good reason. Now all Kate had to worry about was whether Tom still wanted a relationship with her – it had all gone rather pear-shaped once he'd made his confession. Would he still feel he'd made a mistake in sharing with her? How could she convince him that it didn't matter? She shrugged. Time enough for that when he got back home.

A glance out the window told her that the sun had finally made an appearance. Kate turned back to her cluttered desk and her shoulders slumped in despair. There was so much she needed to write up. Her jaw clenched. *Blow it!* She deserved some time off for all the angst she'd been through. Putting the computer into sleep mode, she headed for the kitchen to grab a bite to eat before an exploration of the woods while the weather was good.

The sun was still shining half an hour later and a rainbow arched over the trees when she stepped outside. She breathed in the evocative smell that always came after the rain. But the sight of the sun didn't fool her into complacency – dressed in wellingtons and her cagoule, she was ready if the weather turned again. She clutched the walking stick, an old one of Frank's still in the umbrella stand by the front door. It would come in useful for moving brambles out of the way. Kate knew to her cost, when blackberrying, that there was nothing worse than getting hooked up on a vicious bramble. Plodding down the drive, she veered off halfway and entered the woods, following the path she and Tom had taken when in pursuit of the ghostly apparition. That seemed like months ago.

Birds called in the trees above, alerting their companions to the presence of a human intruding into their domain. The sound was comforting.

Twenty minutes later, sweating and uncomfortable, she stopped to take her bearings. It felt like she was going round in circles. The undergrowth was so thick, it was impossible to make out where she was in relation to the house. She took a deep breath. It had been hard work to beat a path through the overgrown vegetation, nobody had been there for years. At one point she'd been certain she'd discerned the remnants of a path, but then it had disappeared. How on earth would Annabelle have got this far for an assignation with John in a long dress and cloak? There must have been a path at some point.

She listened. All was silence, apart from the drip, drip, drip of raindrops falling from the overhanging leaves. No birdsong now. Kate turned in a circle where she stood, surrounded by trees and overgrown bushes all tangled up with brambles and ivy. She could just about make out the way she'd come. A shiver ran through her. It was getting cooler. The sun had sunk below the tops of the trees and was no longer visible. Her skin prickled and there was a strong sensation of not being alone. "Who's there?" she called.

There was a rustling in the undergrowth to her right. Her head whipped round. A squirrel shot up the tree trunk and she let out her breath. *Bloody squirrel*!

Her nerves were on edge and soon it would be getting dark. She looked beyond the tree where the squirrel had scampered – disappointingly, there appeared to be only more trees and undergrowth. Then her eyes adjusted... Was that the vaguest hint of a path? And what was that further on? Some sort of mound? Spurred on, convinced she was on to something, Kate forced a way through, slashing at the shrubs and undergrowth with the walking stick. Swiping away the brambles that clawed at her arms and face, and the twining ivy that tangled her feet, she inched forward.

All her senses told Kate that she was on the right path. The ground rose in front of her – definitely a mound. She got on her hands and knees to drag herself up the side, not caring about the effect it would have on her clothes, which were already filthy from the mud and brambles.

Adrenaline pumped through her. She was on to something, she knew it. Almost at the top, she tried to to stand upright, but it was difficult to steady herself as underfoot it was slippery. There was a loud crack and the ground beneath her gave way. She was falling. Her head caught on something hard and everything went black.

Chapter Twenty-Six

Kate wasn't sure how long she'd been lying there. It was dark, and the smell of decaying vegetation told her that she was underground. She moved her right arm and winced with pain. Her cry echoed in the blackness. She struggled into a sitting position, wiping away the debris from her eyes and face. It didn't make much difference, she still couldn't see. The dark enveloped her, solid and smothering. Her pulse started to race. She was panicking, she couldn't breathe. All her nightmares about being trapped now an awful reality. She screamed, a long, piercing noise that emptied her lungs and filled her ears. Then she passed out again.

When she regained consciousness, it finally registered that she was not suffocating; it was still possible to breathe. Kate inhaled slowly and tried to order her thoughts, tried to suppress the panic rising inside her. It couldn't be allowed to take control. She needed to stay calm. This wasn't a wardrobe or a lift, and she was no longer a child. By sheer force of will, her breathing slowed. It was time to work out what to do.

What had she fallen into? Some sort of cave? She felt round with her good arm for her phone, scrabbling with her fingers in the loose earth and rocks. Nothing. It must have been lost when she fell. Her insides curled in terror, but she maintained her slow breathing. Panicking would achieve nothing, and there might be a chance to get out if she didn't lose her nerve and thought things through.

I will get out. I will get out.

How long would it take for someone to notice she was missing? She'd not made any plans to meet up with Sue or Ruth. Mum and Dad were still away, and if they telephoned, they'd assume she was busy. It might be days before they tried again. And Tom? If he came straight home, would he even bother to call her? He was still upset and confused, and this latest disaster with the police and Eve would not have helped. She had to get out on her own.

A hand to her forehead told her it was a sticky mess, with her hair tangled in what she guessed was a mixture of blood and dirt. It hurt like hell. A groan escaped her lips, breaking the cold silence of her prison. Turning her head from right to left she could discern no differentiation in light. Everything was as black as pitch. As far as she could tell, whatever hole she'd fallen through had closed up after her, sealing her in the darkness. Conscious of her pulse quickening, she dug her finger nails into her hand.

Stop panicking. Stop panicking.

Kate remembered something. Her scream had sounded echoey, as if she was in quite a large space. She gave another yell.

"Help!"

There it was, a definite echo. Encouraged, she stretched her arms in front of her and met only emptiness. The same at her left side. She turned and used her left hand to stretch to the right. It smacked painfully into something solid. It took several seconds for the shock to subside and for her to restart her exploration. Surprisingly, it wasn't soil or earth against her fingers, but something that felt very like a course of bricks. Regular lines, curving away from her. The logical part of Kate's brain whirred. This must be the ice house. It made sense – that was the mound she'd clambered up. It had to be. The recent torrential rain, together with years of neglect, had loosened some of the brickwork, causing it to cave in, but the remaining overgrown network of roots above had closed up too, sealing her in.

She snarled to herself. It was all very well and good knowing where she was, but how to get out? She scrambled to her knees and crawled a short distance forward. Her fingers found something. Something flat with rounded corners. Excitement coursed through her. Her missing phone!

At her touch, it flared into life, its glow illuminating her face and telling her it was two in the morning. The screen was cracked but it worked. Hope faded when the display indicated there was no signal.

Bloody, bloody hell!

Having some light gave her courage to stand and take stock of her surroundings. There was still a chance she could get out on her own. On shaking legs, she inched round, following the curved wall. The whole structure had been built as a circle, at a guess, about twenty feet across. It could only be the forgotten ice house. A circle of railings stood in the centre of the structure, enclosing what looked like a bottomless hole. Kate aimed the beam of the flashlight down into the darkness and saw a deep empty pit. She stepped back. Things were bad enough, she wasn't going to risk falling down another hole. Continuing her exploration round the perimeter, her foot struck something. She pointed the flashlight beam downwards and gasped.

A skull grinned up at her.

She stifled a scream and looked away. *Stay calm. It can't hurt you.*

With an effort of will, Kate mastered her breathing and turned her head to look again at the skull. A closer examination of the ground revealed the rest of the skeleton curled up in an attitude of sleep, as if whoever it had been had merely stopped to rest. Nerves now forgotten, and thoroughly curious, Kate played the flashlight over the area adjacent to the bones and spotted something else – what looked like the remains of a bag. Shreds of fibre and something very like leather. An old fashioned valise.

Kate's suspicions turned to conviction. This skeleton must be Annabelle. The girl had been running away to join her sweetheart. She'd have had a bag with her, but what was she doing here? How had she become imprisoned? It didn't make sense.

Kate had become so engrossed in trying to work things out that she'd forgotten her fear. A further inspection of the perimeter revealed iron bars and a gate overgrown with roots and branches – at some point in time, the original entrance to the ice house, she surmised. But now it rested well below the natural ground level. Perhaps if she could poke something through the top of the bars she might be able to access the outside world? Her spirits momentarily lifted then plummeted again. *Who on earth would be wandering around in the woods at any time, never mind at night?*

There was nothing for it. She should rest and then in the morning plan on making a more concentrated effort to escape. Determined not to be defeated and clinging on to the hope that a few hours rest would bring inspiration, Kate sat down, cradling her injured arm to wait for sleep to come.

A breeze whispered in the trees as Kate made her way along the moonlit path through the woods. What was she doing here? And why was she carrying a valise and looking over her shoulder in such a furtive manner? Was she being followed?

She looked down to see she was enveloped in a long, dark woollen cloak covering a flimsy muslin dress. Her thin shoes did not do much to protect her feet from the stones and pebbles. She winced as yet another sharp pain shot through her sole. It felt like a dream but everything seemed real. She could see her breath curling in the air in front of her face, feel the weight of the bag she clutched in her right hand, and the salty breeze caressing her face. A dream had never been this vivid before. Something told her she had to hurry or she would miss the tide, and John would leave without her.

John! The name sent a tingle down her spine. She was Annabelle, going to meet John. He'd arranged everything. She just needed to be there on time, only having packed the barest essentials, as much as she could carry. She'd even left her journal and beloved portrait of John behind. She'd have no need of them soon – she'd see her beloved's face every day. But she'd hidden them carefully, and not even her maid knew about the space behind the panelling or the loose floorboard.

The time that evening had dragged. She'd waited as long as she dared, praying that her father would not return from his meeting in Falmouth until the early hours. From what her mother had told her, sometimes he did not return until dawn was almost breaking. How she'd hoped tonight would be one of those nights! The stairs had creaked loudly on the way down, but no one had stirred. Finding the key to the kitchen door had been easy, it was in its usual spot, hung on a hook in the scullery. It turned smoothly in the lock and soon she'd been on her way, with only the moon to guide her.

A noise made her stop and a shaft of fear went down her spine. A shadow moved out of the trees and stood squarely on the path, blocking her way. In the light of the moon, she recognised her father by his familiar belligerent stance, legs apart and hands on hips.

"Where do you think you're going, my girl? Thought to bamboozle me, did you?" Anger swelled in his voice. Despite being unable to see clearly, she knew his face would be flushed, eyes bulging, and teeth bared in his customary snarl.

"Father, you can't stop me. I love him." She heard herself answer. The sound of her voice was different – higher pitched, younger…and tinged with anxiety.

"We'll see about that." His large hand caught her arm in a cruel grip and he started to drag her along. Her strength was no match for his, as he continued to pull her until the domed shape of the abandoned ice house came into view, menacing and black, silhouetted against the night sky. His breath had become ragged and uneven, but still he managed to force her inside, throwing her onto the ground. His chest heaved with the effort and for a moment she thought he would collapse.

"Father, are you all right?" Despite his bad temper and intransigent opinions, she still held him in regard; he was her father after all. He did not seem well, leaning forward, hands braced on his thighs, and his breath laboured.

At last he pulled himself upright. "Stay there. I'll sort out that blackguard, send him to the rightabouts. A second son marrying my daughter? I've got better prospects for you, Miss." She watched as he spun on his heels, the doors closed with a clang and a key turned in the lock.

"Father! Father, no…" All was darkness.

Chapter Twenty-Seven

Kate slowly became aware of her surroundings. Her jeans were damp and she was cold. What was she doing lying on the ground? Then it came back to her – she was trapped in the ice house. Panic rose up in her chest. How was she going to get out? It hurt to move her legs, they were stiff and sore, and that pain in her arm... She must have caused some damage when she fell. She concentrated hard on her breathing.

Slow down; deep breaths.

How had she managed to fall asleep? And that dream, so vivid? She trawled her mind to recall every detail. Annabelle had been locked in the ice house by her father. Why had he not come back for her? Or sent someone else to release her, at least? Was that what had happened? Who else could the skeleton belong to but Annabelle?

Well, if she didn't get out, there'd be another skeleton joining her, Kate thought grimly.

Kate scanned the darkness. Far above her head, thin beams of light broke through the tangle of roots and mud. And was it her imagination or was that a glimmer just beyond where she'd surmised the gate to be? Cautiously standing up, she flicked on the flashlight. Thank goodness she'd charged her phone before setting off the previous afternoon.

"Sorry, Annabelle," Kate whispered, gritting her teeth as she gingerly stepped over the fragile remnants of what had once been a person. Between the vegetation clinging to the bars it was just possible to make out another barrier. The door. Chinks of daylight peeped through cracks in the timber. They'd not been evident last night because it had been dark. Kate congratulated herself on being right, though what good it would do her she didn't know. And who on earth was likely to be wandering through the woods, in any case? No one had been past here in years, that much was very obvious. A glance at her phone told her it was seven o'clock, but there was still no signal.

Kate crouched down, letting her feelings of despair roll over her. If only she'd made an arrangement to meet with Sue, or Ruth. How long could she last without water or food?

Stop it. Get a grip.

Kate heaved herself up and tore at the roots twining round the bars with her good hand. There had to be something she could do. There was no point just sitting there waiting for death to come. At that moment, a large piece of woody root came away in her hand, jerking her backwards onto her bad arm. Her scream rent the air sending eerie echoes round the chamber. Anger and frustration engulfed her. Why was life so unfair?

Just when everything was working out, it was all going to be taken away from her. She'd been so excited to move back down to Cornwall, and now everything was turning to dust. Her burgeoning relationship with Tom... Her solution to the mystery of Annabelle and John... None of it would matter if she died. Giving in to despair, hot tears coursed down her cheeks.

Then, above the noise of her own sobs, something else could be heard. Kate gulped and held her breath, straining her ears. A faint whining...and scratching. Kate froze. Was it rats? Swallowing hard, she listened again. More whines and scratching, then...a bark. It was a dog!

"Help! Help me, please! I'm in here!"

Fired with renewed hope, Kate summoned all her strength and yelled at the top of her voice.

The barking outside got louder, moving from what seemed to be above her head to where the door was located. The scratching was frantic, the barking more insistent. Kate added to the cacophony with her own yells, believing this might be her only chance at rescue. Finding the hardened root that had caused her fall, she stretched her arm through the railings and thudded it against the door.

A man's muffled voice could be heard. Someone was there! Kate screamed and waited, holding her breath. There was a moment of silence, then...

"Kate? Kate, is that you?" Muted as it was, she recognised Tom's voice.

"Yes, I'm trapped. The ground gave way and I fell in. Thank God you're here."

"Hang on, I'll get you out. Are you hurt?" Despite the muffled sound, the anxiety in his voice was evident.

"Think I did something to my arm when I fell, but that's all." No need to tell him it hurt like blazes.

"Look, I'll call the emergency services. I don't like the look of what's above you."

Kate heard Sal bark again and Tom's admonishment before he added, "If I start bashing at this door or whatever, it might bring more stuff down on you. Do you think you can hold out for a bit longer?"

"Yes, I'll be fine." Of course she would, Tom was here now. She could manage being in the dark with a skeleton for as long as it took, knowing Tom was going to rescue her.

The doctor smiled at Kate as she lay on the trolley.

"It's as I thought. A clean break. We'll get you plastered up, and then you'll be able to go home." He paused before leaving the cubicle. "From what I understand you had a very lucky escape...and all thanks to a dog?"

Kate nodded. The painkillers she'd been given were beginning to take effect, and her head was feeling quite fuzzy. She felt Tom's hand squeeze hers as he answered for her.

"That's right. I was taking Sal for a walk after we found Kate wasn't at home, and Sal just took off. It was as if she knew Kate was in trouble." Tom smiled at her. "Mum said when I dropped Sal off before coming here that she's going to get extra treats for being such a clever mutt. And I'm definitely going to buy her a new collar and lead, something befitting her Superdog status."

Kate chuckled. It was something she thought she might never do again. How quickly things changed.

Tom stood up. "Look, I'm just going outside to give Mum a call, and let her know they'll be discharging you soon. Can't get a signal in here."

"I know that feeling." Kate grinned, struggling to get her tongue round the words.

Ten minutes later he returned, a wary look on his face. "Mum is insisting that I bring you back to hers when you're finished here." He paused, and Kate sent him a questioning look.

"I sense a 'but' coming," she said.

"Err…yes. I told her that I was going to look after you this evening. Don't worry. I've got everything sorted, a meal, comfortable chair, somewhere to put your feet up… You can sleep in my spare bedroom if you want." That familiar twitch appeared in his cheek. "I think we need to talk, or rather, I need to talk to you, Kate. I need to tell you something." The intense look in his eyes left her in no doubt – he had something important to say. Her heart flipped and she knew it wasn't down to the medication. Had he finally sorted his feelings?

Kate looked round the comfortable sitting room. It felt strange to be back. The last time she'd been here was the night Tom had invited her for a meal and they'd disturbed Rupert and his uncle trying to break in at The Beeches. Such a lot had happened since then. Her relationship with Tom had undergone several changes in such a short space of time. Another change seemed to be on the cards, if her senses were correct.

Tom had barely left her side since she'd been released from the ice house, apart from the short time when he'd taken Sal to his parents' house. He'd insisted on remaining with her throughout the long hours at the hospital. After the taxi brought them back to his cottage, he'd settled her on the sofa with a stern admonition not to move, while he sorted things in the kitchen.

Kate took him at his word and lay back against the welcoming folds of the cushions. Her arm ached beneath its cumbersome plaster cast, but at least her head was clearing from the drug-induced mist that had hampered clear thought.

The sounds coming from the kitchen told her that Tom was busy preparing something, then the kitchen door opened and he appeared, bearing a tray laden with a cafetière, milk jug, and cups.

"Thought we might as well have a cup of coffee until dinner is ready, as it will be a while," he said, putting the tray down on a side table table and pulling it over to where Kate could easily reach it. "I'm doing a beef bourguignon, so that will take a couple of hours, won't it?"

"Not sure, offhand, but you're probably right." Kate frowned. "Have you got a recipe? All the ingredients?" It seemed like a complicated meal for him, a self-acknowledged novice in the kitchen, to want to produce at short notice.

His face took on a guilty expression. "Yes, I'd got everything planned, you see. That's what I was coming to see you about this morning." He sat down beside her. "Sat in that police cell…well, it gave me time to think…about me… about us."

Her stomach did a somersault. What was he going to tell her? That he'd decided they'd be better off as just neighbours and friends? "Go on," she replied, then held her breath.

"Well… Oh God, this is really difficult." He turned to face her and she saw all the uncertainty in his eyes. "I've been an idiot. Freezing you out, I mean. I just couldn't handle you knowing what Eve had done to me. I was convinced you wouldn't want anything to do with me. Told myself I shouldn't trust another woman again. I couldn't bear the thought of you telling your mates and everyone else, and becoming a laughing stock."

"Oh Tom!" Relief flooded through her. She leaned towards him and grasped his hand. "You know I'd never do that. And I don't think you're weak or stupid. People like Eve are evil, anyone can fall into a toxic relationship. You managed to get

200

out, that says something about you."

"Well, anyway." He smiled. "I'm sorry for the way I treated you. Can you forgive me? Is there a chance for us?"

"Oh, yes," she whispered, "of course there is. Now come here and kiss me."

The coffee went cold.

Chapter Twenty-Eight

Kate opened her eyes and for a moment she couldn't remember where she was. Then it came to her, and she gave a satisfied sigh. She turned her head and Tom tightened his grasp, pulling her closer to him, nestling against her. Her movement must have awakened him.

The stubble of his chin grazed her bare shoulder. She smiled to herself. In spite of the impediment of a bulky plaster cast, she and Tom had made love at last, and it had been wonderful...every time.

"Mmmm...it feels nice waking up next to you." His breath tickled her ear. "Tell me I can do this every morning." He nibbled at her shoulder and she wriggled round.

"Blast." She groaned. "Forgot about this damned cast. Yes, I'd like to do this every morning too. I'm sure it will be even better when I get rid of this."

"Well, I thought it was pretty fantastic, actually." He gave her a naughty grin. "Now you've got me thinking about what it will be like when you're fully mobile, and I've got a very vivid imagination."

"You have, have you?"

"Oh, yes," he murmured, moving on to nibble her ear. Some twenty minutes later, he finally drew away and sat up. "I'll make us some coffee, and we'll try and drink it while it's hot this time. Can you manage to shower by yourself, or do you think you'll need a hand?"

Kate swung her legs over the side of the bed. "Hot coffee sounds wonderful, and yes, I think I can manage." If she and Tom didn't stop getting distracted with each other, they'd never get over to Sue's as they'd promised to do later that day. Kate didn't mind betting that Sue might just bowl up and interrupt them. Now that would be embarrassing.

A flash of disappointment crossed Tom's face as he tugged on a pair of jogging bottoms. "Oh well, it was worth a try." He grinned. "If you're a good girl, I'll even make breakfast."

"Oh yes, please, I'm starving. We didn't get round to eating that beef bourguignon, did we?" Yes, they had been rather swept away in the moment. Tom had only remembered to switch off the oven before pulling her upstairs the night before.

"We'll have it tonight instead." Tom blew her a kiss as he disappeared out the door. "Give me a shout if you need anything. See you downstairs."

It was well after noon before they arrived at Sue's. His mum must have heard Tom's car coming up the drive, because she rushed down the steps before Kate had a chance to open her door.

"How are you? It must have been awful in that hole, and with a skeleton too! I was so worried when Tom phoned me. Come in, come in." She didn't give Kate a chance to answer. "Oh dear, is your arm very painful? Tom told me it was broken."

"Mum, stop fussing," cut in Tom. "Give Kate a break."

"I'm fine, Sue, honestly. Just this," Kate indicated her injured arm, "and a few cuts and bruises, that's all."

Poor Sue, she had enough on her plate worrying about Laura, she didn't need the stress of worrying about somebody else.

Sue bit her lip and blushed. She whispered in Kate's ear as she ushered her into the house. "Sorry, love. I'm just so relieved to see you. What with Tom and the police business, and then you getting trapped... Well, it's all been a bit frantic. Thank goodness the real culprit has been caught. Now we can put everything behind us."

Tom had told Kate the previous night that the police had arrested someone for Eve's murder. The man had been identified by Eve's elderly neighbour, and, under interrogation, he had confessed.

Kate reassured Sue as they headed for the conservatory and received a surprise of her own when she saw Ruth sitting next to Laura on the sofa.

"Hello, Ruth. I didn't expect to see you today. This is a nice surprise." She smiled at Laura. "Hi, Laura, good to see you up."

Laura returned her smile and Ruth got up and gave Kate a cautious hug, being careful not to jar her bad arm. "It's good to see you, Kate. When Sue rang me up yesterday and told me the emergency services were trying to dig you out, well, I was beside myself. Good job Tom found you when he did."

Tom came up and put his hands on Kate's shoulders. "It's Sal you can thank for that. She was off like a rocket into that wood. If it hadn't been for her I don't think I'd have thought of looking there. Not straight away, anyway." He gave her a squeeze. "But she's found now, aren't you, love? And not the only one either."

Kate's heart had skipped when he called her love and a warm glow spread through her. She almost missed Ruth and Sue's expressions of surprise and puzzlement.

"What? Who else has been found?"

Kate found her voice. "That skeleton… I'm pretty sure I know who it is." She paused for effect, delighted to see their excitement. "It can only be Annabelle."

Gasps came from both ladies.

"Good grief, I wonder what happened?" said Ruth. "But that would certainly explain why I couldn't find any records for her."

Tom manoeuvred Kate towards the other sofa, helped her down, and sat next to her. "The police forensics team have taken the remains away for identification, but they are reasonably sure they are not of a recent date," he said, holding Kate's hand. "But you already know it's her, don't you, Kate?"

She had confided her weird dream to him when they were in the ambulance.

"Yes. I'm certain." Kate gave her open-mouthed audience of three a full account of her dream.

"Well, I never!" exclaimed Ruth, once Kate had finished. "And from your description of Annabelle's father, it fits in with the accounts of his illness. Seems to me he had a stroke before he got very far. He couldn't tell anyone he'd locked Annabelle up, and then the family moved away."

"But did anyone else who lived in the house subsequently not know about the ice house?" asked Laura. "I don't understand. Surely they would have found her then?"

Ruth shook her head. "I think, because it was early in the year, the ice house wasn't being used. According to the estate papers, Annabelle's father had closed it off and planned to build a new one nearer the property. A keen huntsman, he wanted to keep the woods free of disturbance, so that he could shoot game there."

"So he had a ready-made prison for Annabelle," muttered Laura.

A look of horror crossed Sue's face. "It doesn't bear thinking about."

Ruth continued. "The Tracys moved away before anything was done about it, then the house was left empty for some years. Another family had it before Win's lot bought it in the late nineteenth century... The seventies, I think. By that time there was no mention of an ice house in the deeds, just woodland."

Kate suddenly recalled something. "I remember Win telling me that her parents discovered some sort of structure. They never had the funds to do anything with it, and as a child she was told to steer clear because it might collapse." She chuckled. "When I was little, she always told me there was a witch in the woods instead. I suppose she thought that was more likely to make me stay away from possible danger. It worked. Now, if she'd told me there was a spooky building to stay away from, I'd have been there exploring."

Tom leaned close and whispered in her ear, "I'm glad you stayed away when you were little. We might never have met."

"I know you probably think I'm mad, but I'm sure it was Annabelle reaching out to me that gave me the idea that she was somewhere in the woods. It also explains why Win went out in the cold and dark." Kate didn't want to come out and say she'd actually seen and heard Annabelle – something she'd only shared with Tom.

"You really think she saw something?" asked Sue, disbelief in her voice.

"Stranger things…stranger things," Ruth replied.

Sue grunted and remained silent.

After all the explanations and speculation were over, Sue bustled out to the kitchen to sort out some refreshments. Kate followed her.

"Tom tells me that you want to give him Annabelle's portrait."

Sue turned, a smile on her face. "Yes, I thought he should have it. It will look nice in his cottage." Her smile became enigmatic. "She brought you two together, so…"

"Sue, you really are a terrible woman!" Kate gave her friend an affectionate slap on the back. "I don't know what you think you're going to achieve."

Sue took Kate's hand, her face now serious. "Oh, I know I'm an interfering busybody, but I do want to see him with someone nice. I'm glad you're his friend, Kate. He's been so much more relaxed since he's met you, even if you did both get off to a horrid start. But he's beginning to trust again, and that's down to you."

"I like him a lot, Sue, but it's early days yet." Kate looked into Sue's eyes and saw the concern hidden behind her lighthearted tone. "Let Tom and I sort things between us. There's no need for you to try and push us together. We'll find our own way." She gave Sue's shoulder a final squeeze.

"Come on, you two, what are you doing?" Tom was standing in the doorway and Kate wondered how much he'd heard.

Sue led the way carrying a tray full of tea things, and Kate followed, a jug of milk in one hand. As she passed Tom he took the jug off her, and leaned in to murmur, "You're right, Mum doesn't need to push us together. We'll find our path. But Kate…" She looked up at him, wondering what he was going to say, hoping it was what she was thinking. "I very much hope you and I share the same path. It's been lonely on my own."

"Me too," she answered and saw his eyes crinkle into a smile.

Chapter Twenty-Nine

Six months later, at a gathering beside the family crypt of the Earls of Batheaston, Kate and Tom watched as a small coffin was placed inside.

"I'm glad they're together now, even though they couldn't be together in life."

The pressure from Tom's hand told her he felt the same.

"The earl was really keen for Annabelle to be laid to rest next to John," he replied. "Said the puzzle of who John had loved, and the legend that he'd died of a broken heart, had been a mainstay of the family's history. He was delighted when the mystery of the portrait was solved." Tom grinned and holding his hand over his mouth added, "He's planning on doing an exhibition and using it as a publicity feature… Thinks it might push the visitor numbers up."

The vicar stepped forward to lead the prayers as the crypt doors were closed, and finally the small group of participants in the simple but moving ceremony trooped back to the main house.

Tom's parents were there, and Charles Lanyon, the Earl of Batheaston, and his wife Daphne, the Countess, Freddie and his brothers and sister, plus Ruth and her gentleman friend, who she'd introduced as Bill. They gathered in the main salon, where wine and nibbles had been laid on. The earl, a tall gentleman in his late fifties who reminded Kate of her old headmaster with his old-school air, thanked them all for coming, and singled Kate out for a special mention.

"Well, this day wouldn't have been possible without the marvellous investigative skills of Dr Kate Wilson, who risked her life to get to the bottom of things." He grinned at Kate, who blushed and giggled.

"Well, I don't know about that," she answered. "I certainly didn't think I was about to risk my life when I set off into the woods, I thought I was just going for a walk."

Everyone laughed and then the earl proposed a toast. "To John and Annabelle, who are together at last."

A short time later, Kate and Tom headed back to Falmouth in Tom's car. His parents were staying over at Lanyon Court, Sue happy to be renewing her acquaintance with her cousin and his family. Kate had gleaned from Sue that the earl was offering to lend his weight to a campaign Sue was involved in, to fight for more research into Laura's condition.

"With his connections, we might be able to make progress," Sue had excitedly confided to Kate. Laura herself, though continuing to improve, was still not well enough to attend and was being looked after by a friend for the couple of days Sue and Martin were to be away. Kate was pleased that her friend was having a much needed respite break. She'd been through a lot with her daughter's illness, and the worry of Tom being suspected of murder.

Not to mention looking after me when I had a wobbly.

Before long they arrived at The Beeches. Tom pulled the bags out of the boot as Kate unlocked the door. He hadn't actually moved in, but more often than not they spent their nights together. Kate smiled as she watched him dump the bags in the hallway. The worry lines round his eyes had become less apparent, and he was certainly not the grumpy man he'd been when she had first met him.

"What are you smirking at?" he asked as she stood leaning against the doorpost.

"Oh, just thinking you've changed quite a bit from the bad tempered oik you were when I first met you."

His eyes widened in mock surprise, "Don't know what you mean. Me, bad tempered?" He moved towards her and pulled her into his arms. "I've got you to thank for that, Kate darling." He nuzzled her hair. "I was in a bad place then. Don't know where I'd have ended up if I hadn't met you – you, and your crazy haunted house."

Kate had her arms round his neck and pulled him down to kiss. After they broke off she tipped her head to look up into his eyes. "Well, it can't be haunted anymore, not after today, surely? Annabelle is finally with John."

"Hmmm, hope so. I don't fancy having to race off into the woods just when I'm about to kiss you again." He laughed.

"Is it me, or is it getting cold in here?" Tom rubbed at his arms as Kate looked up from her book. They were in the drawing room, Kate reading while Tom worked on his laptop.

"Now you come to mention it, it is a bit chilly. You don't think—?"

Tom turned to see what had caught her attention outside the window behind him.

"Oh my goodness, look." Kate, mouth open, stood up and moved towards it. It was almost dark outside, but she could clearly see what was on the drive. Tom's hand gripped hers, and they both watched in awed silence as two figures stepped from the shadows into the light shed from the drawing room. A gentleman dressed in a many-caped overcoat, the toes of his gleaming boots shining, and wearing a curly beaver hat on his head. Kate drew in a breath as he looked directly at her. There was no doubt, it was the man from her portrait – John. The diminutive figure next to him, shrouded in a cloak, raised her arms and removed her hood. The face which bore that enigmatic smile had to be Annabelle.

The pressure from Tom's hand became stronger. Kate heard his gasp. "Bloody hell. It's them."

"Shhh," was all she could reply.

They watched as John tipped his hat and bowed, while Annabelle blew a kiss, wafting it towards them with a translucent, elegant hand. The couple turned, linked arms, and strolled off down the drive, disappearing into nothingness.

"Did that really happen?" It was Tom who broke the silence.

"I think so…or we are both sharing the same hallucination," whispered Kate. "Now we know for sure that they are both at peace. It was lovely of them to come and thank us."

"What were you saying before, that I'm a changed man? Well, you've convinced me to believe in ghosts and…you've convinced me that true love does exist. Do you remember me saying I like things absolutely right?" The look in his eyes told her he was not making some flippant remark.

She nodded her head. "Yes, I remember."

His lips curved up into a smile. "Well, I think the time is absolutely right for us, Kate."

She held her breath, mesmerised by the look of intense longing in his eyes. "Will you be my happy-ever-after, Kate, as they say in all those old fashioned stories?"

Kate knew her happy ever after could only be with him. "Oh yes, Tom," she murmured just before their lips met.

THE END

Fantastic Books
Great Authors

darkstroke is
an imprint of
Crooked Cat Books

- Gripping Thrillers
- Cosy Mysteries
- Amazing Horrors
- Fascinating Historicals
- Exciting Fantasy
- Young Adult
- Non-Fiction

Discover us online
www.darkstroke.com

Find us on instagram:
www.instagram.com/darkstrokebooks

Printed in Great Britain
by Amazon

83684163R00130